A LOTUS PALACE MYSTERY

Red
Blossom
in SNOW

USA TODAY BESTSELLING AUTHOR
JEANNIE LIN

Red Blossom in Snow: A Lotus Palace Mystery. Copyright © 2022 by Jeannie Lin

ISBN: 978-1-957952-00-0

This is a work of fiction. Names, characters, places and incidents are the product of the author's imagination or are used fictitiously. Any resemblance to actual events, locales, or persons, living or dead, is purely coincidental.

Cover design © Deranged Doctor Design (www.derangeddoctordesign.com)

Cover photograph ©

Pingkang li map image © Jeannie Lin

Print Edition 1.0

Pingkang Ward (li)

East Gate

North Gate

South Gate

West Gate

100 meters

House of Heavenly Peaches

Lotus Palace

Spring Blossom Teahouse

MAP INFO

The Pingkang ward or Pingkang li is arguably one of the most well-documented sections of the Tang Dynasty capital. There was also extensive documentation on the capital city of Chang'an overall during the Tang era including census information, building permits, and petitions.

The buildings and layout of the ward were re-created using information in this article:

Heng Chye Kiang. (2014). Visualizing Everyday Life in the City: A Categorization System for Residential Wards in Tang Changâan. *Journal of the Society of Architectural Historians, 73*(1), 91-117. doi:10.1525/jsah.2014.73.1.91

This map was designed and created by Jeannie Lin using the Dungeon Scrawl online dungeon builder.

CAST OF CHARACTERS

Note: The family name comes first for characters who have both given and family names listed. I.e. Bai Huang has a given name of Huang and a family name of Bai.

- **Song Yi** - A courtesan of moderate fame in the pleasure quarter. A member of the House of Heavenly Peaches. She first appears in *The Hidden Moon*.
- **Li Chen** - An accomplished scholar and official, he first appears in *The Lotus Palace* as the newly appointed magistrate and has overseen all of the investigations in the series.

SECONDARY CHARACTERS

- **Bai Wei-ling** - Known as Wei-wei. The only daughter of the Bai family. Protagonist of *The Liar's Dice* and *The Hidden Moon*.
- **Gao** - A street-smart informer who was appointed constable after saving Li Chen's life. First appeared in *The Lotus Palace*. Protagonist of *The Hidden Moon*.
- **Yue-ying** - Former servant in the Lotus Palace pleasure house. Bai Huang's wife and Mingyu's sister. Protagonist of *The Lotus Palace*.
- **Bai Huang** - Wealthy and handsome aristocrat, known for being a playboy. Yue-ying's husband and Wei-wei's elder brother. Protagonist of *The Lotus Palace*.
- **Mingyu** - Former courtesan in the Lotus Palace

pleasure house. Married to Wu Kaifeng. Yue-ying's older sister. Protagonist of *The Jade Temptress*.

- **Wu Kaifeng** - Former head constable of Chang'an known for his exacting and intimidating demeanor. Mingyu's husband. Protagonist of *The Jade Temptress*.

CHAPTER 1

Tang Dynasty China, 850 A.D.

Song Yi wasn't the most beautiful woman in the Pingkang li. She wasn't the most musically gifted, nor known for being the most captivating hostess. One didn't have to be famous to make a living in the pleasure quarter. In fact, being so well-known, so infamous could be a great disadvantage.

Such had happened to clever Li Jilan who composed poetry that received great praise until one set of lines was deemed subversive. She was sent to the executioner for treason. Captivating Mingyu had a circle of powerful admirers who ended up dragging her into their dangerous schemes.

To survive in Pingkang, one didn't have to be most or best. One simply had to have a compelling narrative. A story that was intriguing enough. Alluring enough. Provocative enough. And possess just enough ability to not slip into obscurity.

Song Yi had never wanted to attract a crowd of admirers. She had no need for dashing young men to fight over her, to die for her, to declare their never-ending love for her. She just needed a few steady and dependable patrons who liked her enough.

Steady and dependable was what they called Magistrate Li Chen. For a time, Song Yi had fancied that he liked her enough. But then he had disappeared, his favor collapsing like the waves, as they say.

She hadn't seen or heard from Li Chen for months until this very night at Director Guan's banquet, when she learned that an undemanding patron carried his own kind of curse.

The banquet was in its second hour and the half-moon had hidden behind a blanket of clouds. The only trace of it was a ghostly light behind the gray. With no moon visible to gaze upon, it should have been acceptable to close the doors so the three of them weren't freezing, but no one paid musicians so much thought. They were merely hired entertainers. Not bonded or enslaved, but not much higher in status.

Song Yi's fingers were stiff from the cold, but she plucked out a dancing melody on the strings of the guzheng nevertheless. Her courtesan-sister Pearl accompanied her with a softly penetrating counter-melody on the flute while Little Sparrow struggled to keep up on the erhu. Every time the girl tried to draw her bow smoothly over the strings, her shivering would interrupt the flow of the sound, creating a warble that Song Yi hoped the scholars in attendance would overlook.

The fashionable silk robes they wore to perform only made matters worse. The bureaucrats gathered warmly beside lit braziers and glowing lanterns within the banquet room while Song Yi felt the evening breeze through every thin layer of her robe.

Their three melodies wove around one another in a final

circling dance before fading at the song's end. A voice cut into the silence. Their host, the illustrious Director Guan, was making a formal welcome and announcement.

"Oh good, poetry recitation," Pearl whispered with glee. "We can get a break."

Little Sparrow sprang to her feet. "I'm going to see if we can get tea!"

"Make it wine instead," Pearl suggested, grabbing the discarded erhu out of the way so Sparrow's robe wouldn't become entangled in it. The girl had already flitted off.

"Try not to make a face every time she plays a wrong note," Song Yi said gently. "Sparrow is trying to practice."

"Not nearly enough," Pearl said beneath her breath.

As the big sister of their courtesan house, it was Song Yi's responsibility to keep the peace as well as make sure Sparrow kept up with her training. Unfortunately the girl was easily distracted. She had pulled one of the director's retainers aside to speak to him with eyes wide and hands fluttering.

They were between the mid-autumn and winter festivals, but the cold weather seemed to be coming in early to Changan that year. Song Yi attempted to rub some feeling back into her hands. Warmed wine sounded wonderful.

"Oh look," Pearl whispered, excited. "It's your noble gentleman."

Song Yi's pulse skipped. Her heart pounded erratically, but she did not look. Instead, she fiddled with the wooden bridges that held the strings of her instrument. She knew exactly who the *noble gentleman* was.

She'd suspected Li Chen would be here tonight. Director Guan was well-known as the magistrate's benefactor.

"He's in uniform. So disciplined and *authoritative*," Pearl cooed.

Song Yi twisted at a tuning peg, which really shouldn't do in the middle of a performance. So she twisted it back, tightening and untightening aimlessly. She was a fool for not preparing a better way to occupy herself.

The gathering wasn't large enough to hide. And why should she hide? Li Chen was just someone she'd poured wine for over polite conversation. He wasn't even that highly ranked of an official. He hadn't so much as touched her hand.

Miraculously, she was no longer shivering. She was actually burning up. Or rather, her cheeks were burning. If she asked Pearl whether Li Chen was looking her way, Pearl would tease her mercilessly. Instead, Song Yi risked just a single glance, lifting her gaze then lowering it.

There was the dark-eyed and serious look she was so familiar with. Jaw squared, brow furrowed, shoulders straight. Li Chen's uniform, a forest green robe, draped over him in crisp, orderly lines. His hair was hidden beneath a black cap that tied beneath his chin.

He was not looking at her. Just as she was not looking at him. Their gazes slid just past one another.

Director Guan snatched Li Chen up and hovered over his protege with a protective air. As Guan made introductions, Chen nodded from one man to the next.

Li Chen wasn't unsmiling. He was merely focused. Song Yi had said as much to the others to defend him when they'd complained he was stiff.

She had seen what Li Chen looked like when that rigid expression softened and those eyes warmed. It had taken some time to get past his well-mannered reserve, but then he had stopped coming by. All of her efforts were wasted.

Song Yi returned her attention to her instrument, but not fast enough.

"Why so cold, Elder Sister?" Pearl asked.

Pearl only called Song Yi that when she wanted to taunt her.

"The magistrate will think you indifferent," her younger courtesan-sister went on.

"I *am* indifferent," Song Yi replied, running her fingertip lightly over a taut string. It hummed beneath her touch.

Pearl snorted.

"It looks like we'll have no tea or wine," Song Yi mused, looking to Sparrow who had become lost in a conversation with the young man. He was dressed in blue and gray scholar's robes. Sparrow was only sixteen and showed the boldness if not the refinement of a courtesan ten years her senior. Her quarry looked as if he were searching for a means of escape.

Song Yi used the excuse to spy on Li Chen again who was most certainly not acknowledging her. Furtive and meaningful glances were an entire language at gatherings like these. As were sweeping glances. Searching glances. Li Chen employed none of those. It was impossible not to look her way. The viewing portal which framed the uncooperative moon was right behind her.

So that was the way of it.

Some courtesans could play the abandoned lover to great effect, but Song Yi was never one for such scenes, and neither was Li Chen. They'd had only a short string of late-night conversations. He'd finally relaxed enough to recline on the seat in her parlor. They'd laughed together with heads bowed close, but never, ever touching.

She was pulling her strings too tight again. Pearl's all-knowing look faded.

"What a know-nothing bureaucrat," Pearl huffed with disdain as if that had been her intention all along.

"Maybe you should go rescue that poor scholar from Sparrow," Song Yi suggested.

Pearl immediately set her flute down to obey. Song Yi

didn't have any sisters by blood, but she loved the two fate had given her.

After a few poems had been recited, they would be expected to play again. She stood as well to stretch out her legs and wander over to one of the braziers for warmth. Li Chen wandered to the opposite side of the room. Could she get him to do that all evening? Swim about the chamber in circles like a carp to avoid her.

Such games were unbecoming of her. She was Song Yi of the House of Heavenly Peaches. Subtle, graceful, uncomplicated.

She had first met Li Chen at another banquet thrown by Director Guan He a year ago. Before that, she had only known the magistrate by reputation. He'd been appointed to the capital several years earlier. He was young for the post. Talented. Honest.

Song Yi had been playing another stringed instrument, the pipa, that night. It was simpler and required less focus than the guzheng. She had glanced up mid-song to find him watching, but not with the serious, penetrating gaze which he employed presently. His gaze had seemed far away, as if he were daydreaming. His eyes had widened with surprise when they met hers, and she'd smiled without meaning to.

She'd looked quickly away. The smile wasn't meant to be an invitation. It wasn't meant to be anything other than a smile, unrehearsed. Li Chen was supposed to be an exacting and relentless lawman, but in that moment, he had looked so...guileless. Like someone who hadn't seen enough of the world rather than too much of it.

He showed up at their doorstep two weeks later, asking about her. It turned out he was from Yu prefecture and had heard she was from there also. That first night they had spoken for hours until dawn. The sitting fees had cost him a month's wages. Even Mother had felt bad for him.

Old Auntie had cackled. "Radish boy! Probably thought he was going to get something if he just stayed longer."

Li Chen admitted later he hadn't meant to linger so long. He limited his next visits to exactly one hour. Pearl thought him uptight. Song Yi had thought Li Chen sweet. He was homesick.

Yet now he couldn't meet her eyes. Perhaps he was embarrassed by how much undue attention he'd paid her. He was the county magistrate with responsibilities and duties to attend to. Or he might have simply lost interest. Some scholars came to Pingkang to spend every last coin, while for others, the pleasures of the district were just a novelty that quickly faded.

Pearl returned to where they had left their instruments with a subdued Sparrow following behind her, eyes cast downward. Apparently, Pearl had scolded the younger Sparrow for something. Song Yi left the warmth of the inner chamber to go to them. It would be time to play again soon.

Li Chen was directly in her path now, deep in conversation with Director Guan. Song Yi didn't veer as far away as she could have. She passed by, close enough to detect the minute tightening of his jaw before she drew away.

His avoidance could also be fueled by shame, Song Yi realized with a pang in her chest. Visits to a courtesan house were a frivolous indulgence to someone like him. It didn't matter the reason, truly. She was experienced enough to know how to smooth over such cracks to allow him to save face. She didn't need for admirers to declare their undying love or to remember her in poems and laments.

If Song Yi had to describe her approach, she would say that it was practical. Her patrons served a purpose for the moment. Li Chen's evening visits, lovely as they were, had kept their house running and her sisters fed.

Song Yi had managed to hold a talented and honorable

7

magistrate's interest for a brief period of time. It had to be enough.

It was probably better for Li Chen and for her that they didn't have to maintain the illusion for too long.

FOG SETTLED thick over the streets of Changan. It wove through the falling darkness of the evening, transforming the lanes and alleyways of the capital city into a maze of spectral shapes. It hid Li Chen as he waited outside the courtesan house, gathering his courage.

The more he thought of it, the more he was convinced he had managed the banquet last night poorly. He knew how he was meant to conduct himself in the tribunal court and his administrative offices. He knew how he was supposed to conduct himself in courtesan houses like the House of Heavenly Peaches. Banquets where he was to mingle with bureaucrats and ranking officials on one side and interact with courtesans on the other created an undefined area of contention. Unfortunately, the code books didn't have any guidance on this.

He was saved from having to go up to the door when the person he'd come to meet appeared at the front of the house.

"Miss Song Yi."

She turned abruptly, searching through the fog.

"I didn't mean to startle you," he said, drawing closer.

"Magistrate Li," she greeted, letting out a breath.

They stood before one another, edges blurred by the surrounding mist. She wore a pale robe that made her seem to blend into the fog. Blue, he thought, or maybe gray.

Song Yi usually avoided the butterfly-bright colors favored by the other entertainers in Pingkang. The night before, she'd been clothed in the deepening blue of an evening sky, of twilight fading into dusk.

She had immediately drawn his attention. Song Yi didn't need flashy colors or flirtatious glances to do so. It was always her presence that pulled at him. She had a calming, soothing aura about her with darkly luminous eyes that were searching and thoughtful.

Chen's gaze strayed to the heavy cloak lined with fox fur about her shoulders. "You're going somewhere."

She pulled at the edges the garment. "I have an engagement tonight."

"Of course." He hadn't thought of that.

"It's good to see the magistrate…after so long."

Song Yi was looking up at him, her expression inquisitive. She was being kind. They'd spent several hours the night before in a banquet hall while he painfully tried to figure out the proper way to engage with her.

In many ways, the last months had been plagued by the same indecision.

They stared at one another, the silence stretching long between them.

Li Chen broke the silence first. "I could escort you. To wherever you're going."

She hesitated. "It's far away. Outside of Pingkang."

"I'll hail a carriage."

He turned to the street and raised his arm to wave down a passing transport, grateful to at least be of use. It wasn't long before a carriage came to a stop before them. Li Chen turned and offered his arm to help her up. She took hold of him only briefly as she stepped past him. The time apart had made them awkward around one another.

Song Yi turned once she was seated to look down at him. This wasn't going at all to plan—most likely because he hadn't made a plan.

"It was good to see you last night," he said, at last admitting it.

"Out of the corner of your eye?" she asked with a tilt of her head that wrecked him.

"Yes." The little laugh he gave was meant for himself.

"Even the most stuffy of bureaucrats could at least manage a sly glance," she chided.

He drew closer, his chest warming. "You looked well."

It wasn't what he'd meant to say. *Pretty* seemed too terse. *You looked like the only thing I ever wanted to see*, was inappropriate after their last parting had ended abruptly, without farewell.

"Where to?" the carriage driver asked impatiently.

"Chongren li," she replied.

"May I ride with you for a bit?" he asked in a rush.

The carriage had started forward before lurching to a halt.

Song Yi hesitated, her teeth worrying over her bottom lip, before she replied, "Of course, Magistrate."

She moved aside to allow him room on the seat. As the carriage started forward, they fell into silence once more. The fog hung all around them.

"I didn't forget you," he said, going immediately to the heart of the matter.

"Admirers come and go," she replied lightly.

"I know exactly how long it has been since we last spoke."

Her expression softened. When she looked at him like that, he couldn't remember why he'd ever tried to stay away.

He had been investigating the Incident at the Yanxi Gate, a high-profile assassination that led to threats to public officials and a series of murders in the city. Song Yi herself had received a warning that he was certain was meant for him. The danger was so imminent he'd used his authority as county magistrate to lock down the wards and put the city on curfew.

"I feared being seen with me would put you in danger," he explained.

But the danger was long settled by now. The Yanxi Gate conspiracy had been adjudicated months ago.

"I thought it was because you were about to be married," she replied.

Song Yi turned away to watch the buildings pass by. Lanterns formed dots of light that marked their path through the streets.

The carriage passed through the ward gates with nothing more than a few respectful nods from the city guards.

He had mentioned his potential betrothal to Song Yi, hadn't he?

"My family wishes for me to be married soon," he'd complained sullenly one night. It was late and he'd had more than a few cups of wine in Song Yi's sitting room.

The reveal had given her a moment's pause before she'd lifted the flask to pour him another cup. The movement caused her sleeve to pull back, exposing her bare and elegant wrist.

"It's a wonder you're not long married already, Magistrate," she'd said, in that soft silk voice that warmed his skin.

Marriage didn't necessarily prevent officials from visiting the courtesan houses, from courting song girls, from taking lovers, but Li Chen couldn't imagine dividing his intentions so. It would be courting disaster, not to mention disrespectful to his future wife. And to Song Yi.

But that business had also concluded long ago.

"The arrangement never came to be," he confessed.

"I know," Song Yi replied. "I heard."

When she looked back to him, the fading daylight cast her face in shadow. He could see the glint of lantern light in her eyes. Shapely, inviting, peach blossom eyes which were slender in shape, tapering toward the corners. Those lovely eyes watched for his reaction and he could see the questions gathered behind them. He hadn't known there was gossip about his failed betrothal. Then again, people tended to be careful what they said in passing around a magistrate.

"The heavy fog always reminds me of Yu prefecture," he said, looking into the swirl of gray around them. In terms of changing the conversation, it was an inelegant attempt. He was better at asking questions than answering them.

"The signal of the coming winter," Song Yi agreed. "When my family first arrived in Yuzhou, I thought we were at the edge of the world. The fog surrounded us, erasing the shoreline so there was no telling where heaven or earth began."

He loved listening to how she described the world.

"Like gray ghosts rising from the water," he remarked.

Song Yi fell silent. Why had he said that? Talk of his home sometimes made him melancholy, but he'd always been careful not to let their conversations drift that way.

"My mother sometimes said that," she revealed quietly. *"This is a place of ghosts."*

They had come from the same place. It was a part of their past they shared, and why he'd formed an immediate bond with her.

"I have a memory," he began. Song Yi leaned in to listen closely and he could smell her faint perfume. The creak of the wheels beneath them threatened to drown out his words. "A memory of a thick blanket of fog that covered everything one morning. Everything disappeared beneath it, the streets, the buildings, the people. I was studying in a library when I saw someone emerge from the mist. It was a girl."

"She was beautiful, of course," Song Yi teased, but only half-heartedly. He'd brought up bad memories with his talk of ghosts.

"She was," he paused, remembering. "She was searching for something. I've never forgotten the look on her face. Sometimes I wonder if the girl was real, or did I dream her?"

Song Yi shifted in the carriage seat. She'd probably heard many versions of this same story. *I saw you in a dream once. I dreamt of you before we ever met.*

Li Chen had thought of that strange memory the first time he'd seen Song Yi appear through a silk curtain, but he thought it best not to mention that now. He didn't want her to think of him as just another vapid admirer.

They had reached the gates of Chongren ward. Song Yi tensed beside him and he asked her if there was something wrong.

"Nothing's wrong," she said, followed by a deep breath. When she faced him again, she was smiling, but it was accompanied by a slight narrowing at the corners of her eyes.

"The Yanxi Gate assassination, it was brilliant how you solved that so quickly, Magistrate."

"It wasn't just me. In fact, it was hardly me at all."

"We all followed the stories in Pingkang, especially in the House of Heavenly Peaches."

Her smile had faded. The corners of her mouth tugged downward and her pretty eyes had become clouded, a dark sky in turmoil.

"Your constables arrested one of our patrons, General Lin Shidao's son. He was charged with treason."

"We were mistaken in that," he said quickly. "Lin Yijin was exonerated."

"Yes, of course. I wouldn't dare to criticize your office, Magistrate Li."

His heart pounded. "No, it's...I don't mind if you criticize me. I don't mind anything you say to me. I make mistakes all the time."

Song Yi appeared genuinely troubled. He asked her again if anything was wrong.

She bowed her head for a moment, then looked back at him. "I am really glad to speak to you again, Magistrate, but I really should have found a way to refuse when you asked to accompany me here."

Her smile this time was a mixture of joy and sadness. He realized she hadn't brought any instrument with her. She was dressed in a simple robe that, though pretty, wasn't meant to entertain.

She leaned forward to give instructions to the driver and they headed down a residential lane toward a gated house. The carriage slowed and it was obvious there were no banquet halls or drinking houses here.

The housekeeper came out to light the lanterns outside the gates. The posts were painted red as a sign of good fortune. The servant held the door open when he saw their approach.

"Lin Yijin was our best customer," Song Yi told him. "When he was charged with treason, no one wanted to come by anymore lest their own reputations be tainted. News of exoneration rarely spreads as quickly as news of scandal and ruin."

He started to tell her about all his office had done to make amends, but he held back. Nothing Song Yi said was untrue.

"Young Lord Lin has remained shut away since the ordeal and our house...hasn't seemed to recover either. We still are hired for engagements and our regular patrons still come by here and there and we have a few long-time friends—"

Chen nodded, hoping she would take that to mean she could stop explaining. He understood well enough now.

Soon the drums that signaled the closing of the ward gates would sound. As magistrate, he had authority to move freely through the city in the evenings, but Song Yi wouldn't be able to leave the ward to return to Pingkang until morning. Just after the sun came up.

It was that sort of engagement.

"This is the place," she said unnecessarily. The house inside the gate wasn't opulent, but it was a spacious residence with an inner courtyard encased in a surrounding wall. Not unlike the Li family manor in Yuzhou, but this was the capital. A house like this in the city either belonged to a family with a respected name or an official of modest rank.

"Thank you accompanying me, Magistrate Li," she said.

"It was—" He exhaled and met her eyes, unable to finish the sentiment.

Song Yi gave him a look that was not unkind.

If he hadn't stayed away for six months. If he had come to her immediately after his arranged marriage had fallen apart, would things be different?

They wouldn't have been. He knew that. He knew she had other patrons and admirers and that courtesan houses were expensive to run. The magistrate's office had access to every tax record, deed, and contract in the county.

Li Chen watched as Song Yi climbed down from the carriage to turn to the open gate.

"Will you be needing a carriage when you return?" he asked.

She shook her head, granting him one final, faint smile. He really should go now. Someone was waiting inside for her.

Li Chen directed the carriage driver to take him back to the administrative compound where he resided. Before they turned the corner, he glanced back to see Song Yi still at the gate, watching him as the carriage pulled away. Then she disappeared into the darkness of the evening, behind the clinging fog.

CHAPTER 2

*L*i Chen didn't dream of Song Yi. To dream, he would have needed to fall asleep. Instead he'd lain awake with the bitter taste of regret in his mouth, waiting in the empty hours for dawn.

They said envy was like the torment of sand in one's eye. An apt metaphor.

He rose before daylight with a final admonishment that he'd indulged himself enough in base emotions. He had duties to fulfill.

The house attendant was accustomed to Chen's early morning routine. There was a wash basin set out for him along with his magistrate's robe, brushed clean and pressed.

The first splash of cold water on his face did wonders for clearing his head, as did his daily ritual.

The magistrate's residence was situated in a corner of the administrative yamen, a walled compound that occupied two blocks in the center of the ward.

It was customary for a magistrate to live within the walls of the yamen. Chen was a mere stone's throw away from the tribunal court as well as the offices where he would receive petitions, render judgment, and coordinate all the tasks large and small that went with administering the eastern half of the capital.

The last magistrate had lived in the residence with his family. There was ample room to house a wife and children as well as any household servants a magistrate chose to bring with him.

In Chen's case, his needs were simple, which left him largely in solitude once the yamen gates were pulled shut at the end of the day.

His rooms looked out into a viewing garden embraced by clusters of tall bamboo and pruned shrubbery. Magnolia trees grew beside the rounded moon gate which led to the administrative section of the compound, but within the courtyard there was the illusion of privacy and seclusion. The controlled wildness of the greenery and carefully placed stones pushed back against the sprawling city beyond.

His rooms and the tidy garden provided what little separation he was allowed between his daily life and his work. The residence he lived in didn't belong to him. It was issued by the state to be vacated when he was reassigned to another jurisdiction. A magistrate stood on the lowest rung of the bureaucracy, one that interacted directly with the populace. The position carried more responsibility than power.

Li Chen took tea in the pavilion each morning, seated on the stone bench. The house servant would set the tray upon the table and leave him to his daily contemplation. In these final weeks of autumn, the mornings grew colder. With the sun rising later, Chen stood from the stone bench while the sky was still dark. He passed through the moon gate, away from seclusion and tranquility and into the county offices.

In that pattern lay another routine. His daily practice of waking, taking tea in the garden, and crossing over to begin his duties as magistrate typically ended every year when he made the journey back to his family home. The trip to Yuzhou and back took nearly a month. When he returned, winter would be upon them and the weather too cold to sit comfortably among the bamboo drinking tea.

It was several weeks before he was due to make the trip. Plenty to keep him busy putting the affairs of the office in order before he handed the duties temporarily to deputy staff and clerks.

A string of lanterns lighted the path. He entered the long courtyard surrounded on either side by the various offices of the yamen. His was the one at the very end, situated to the side of the main hall where tribunal court was held.

The offices would soon fill with clerks and functionaries with their own set of daily tasks. Shortly after that, the front gates would open to admit petitioners bringing their claims and disputes. The place quickly became a hive of ants with a flurry of activity flowing through the halls between officials and clerks and runners. Chen wanted to be settled and prepared before it all stirred into motion.

He was the first to open the doors of the offices. There, he made his way to his desk where the same towering pile of notices that had bid him farewell the night before remained in place to greet him this morning. Chen opened the east window and spent a moment inspecting the gray morning light. The fog from the previous night had thinned, leaving only wisps in the morning air that would soon burn away.

Li Chen returned to the desk and sat. Ceremoniously, he rolled back the sleeves of his robe, one first and then the other, and reached for the notice at the top of the pile of papers. Two neighbors in dispute over a strip of land. He consulted property lines and wrote out a judgment, placing it methodically onto the left-hand corner of his desk to be picked up by a runner.

His hands paused on the residential map. Every dwelling

and resident was accounted for in the city, with few exceptions. Li Chen was certain he could find out who Song Yi's patron was without so much effort. The one she'd obviously gone to spend the evening with.

What a worthless, pig-headed fool.

Chen closed his eyes and rubbed a hand over his temples. He had no business knowing. He had no business wanting to know. Even though it wasn't prohibited for him to look, he was certain such behavior constituted, on some grounds, a breach of etiquette. It was at least petty. The best way to get rid of the sand in his eye was certainly not to rub in more sand.

Chen grabbed the next petition from the stack and started reading.

It had been three years since he'd been assigned to Changan. Before that, he had spent time in smaller districts. Remote circuits reaching out to villages where he couldn't understand the dialect, forcing him to work through interpreters and crooked enforcers. Local customs intertwined with written law in what was often a tenuous balance.

It had been an honor to be assigned to the imperial capital. He'd been twenty-six years of age at the time, twenty-nine now. They said it was his connection to Director Guan He that had brought him to such an elevated position so quickly.

There was no shame in that. Every man of rank had his share of contacts, but Chen hadn't bribed or charmed Director Guan. The official had served as prefect in the Yu region where Li Chen had grown up. As a long-time friend of the family, Guan had acted as his mentor and had seen to Chen's education ever since the loss of his father.

He became aware of the drone of beating drums in the distance. The ward gates were opening. Within the next

hour, the magistrate's office would be open to receive suppli-
cants. He'd wanted to be farther along through the petitions.

Gradually, the yamen came to life around him. Chen
finished another judgment and dipped his official jade chop
into a dish of cinnabar ink to stamp onto the decision. The
next petition was a matter of property damage. A shipment
of goods left in the care of a broker. Chen consulted the code
books, rendered his judgment. The jade block made a solid
clap as it sealed the decision. The small stack of papers to the
left grew steadily. Progress.

A messenger came in, bowed, and took the stack of
papers from him to sort and distribute.

In a city the size of Changan, the magistrate's office was
responsible for juggling a myriad of responsibilities. The
petitions brought to him contained tax liens, trade notices,
reports on road repairs. Enough to keep his mind churning.
He enjoyed it. The ever-changing set of problems prevented
tedium from setting in. There was little time for his mind to
wander, yet inevitably it did wander.

He'd wanted to come calling on Song Yi to see how she
was, and he'd done that. But would it be such an imposition
to visit once more for a cup of wine and for conversation?
Just a friendly visit...between friends.

The ink brush hung suspended from his hand and a drop
of ink splashed onto the paper below. Just then, a dark presence outside his door drew his attention.

Constable Gao. It wasn't every day that the head
constable came into the administrative compound, but
whenever he did, his presence was immediately felt. He
moved through the corridor like a silent shark through still
water. Awareness rippled in his wake. His rhythm, the very
energy of his presence was so different to the rest of them.
Gao's place was in the streets, not in these halls.

Even after nearly a year in the position, the constable's

uniform still appeared ill-suited and stiff. Gao's reputation of being a street enforcer clung to him.

At first, Chen had feared Gao's past would interfere with his work on this side of the law, but if anything, the constable's shady reputation was an advantage. No one dared to cross Gao. Li Chen wasn't entirely comforted by the observation, but illegal activity in the alleyways and gambling dens had become more subdued with Gao patrolling the streets.

Li Chen had a sense now, from the sight of Gao's dark look, that the peace was about to be broken.

"Li," Gao called, dispensing with his title or any honorific at all.

"Constable."

The constable's eyes narrowed and the lines of his face grew sharp. "There's something you should know."

Chen set his brush down.

"A body has been found," Gao began ominously. "In Pingkang li."

The pleasure quarter, the same place he'd been just the day before. The ward was notorious for courtesan houses as well as brothels and gambling dens. People moved in and out of the gates with various passes and privileges during all hours of the night, making the ward difficult to regulate.

"It was reported in the alleyway outside of the House of Heavenly Peaches."

Chen started to rise to his feet but stopped himself. His first thought was of Song Yi and whether something had happened to her, but she hadn't been there last night.

"Does this require my immediate attention?" Chen asked with forced calm.

Gao raised an eyebrow. "I thought you might have an interest."

He was concerned with all crimes and unusual occurrences in the eastern section of the capital. A magistrate was responsible for any case of wrongdoing in his jurisdiction. A crime that went unpunished was his own failing.

He could have said all those words. Gao would have listened without argument—and believed none of it.

"We should go see," Chen said grimly.

He rose to head to the street. Gao followed closely behind, providing what details he knew. A local informant had happened upon the body early that morning, before the drums had opened the ward gates. The informant had immediately sent a messenger to the magistrate's yamen.

Chen hated to admit it, but crime wasn't uncommon in a city the size of Changan with its many residential wards and steady influx of merchants and travelers. A constant stream of petitions and grievances came to his desk every day. A certain level of lawlessness had to be tolerated. Chen couldn't chase down every illicit gambling operation and crooked merchant in the market, but murder was another matter. Murder could not be dismissed.

Li Chen called for the wagon to be readied. As an official of the sixth rank, he was authorized to travel by palanquin or by horseback, but he preferred to move through the streets with less fanfare. His presence tended to put people on guard as it was, which was counter-productive to getting witnesses to provide information.

Gao joined him in the wagon. They started off through the streets and Chen was reminded of his visit to the Pingkang li just the day before. The one that hadn't ended so well.

The streets of the pleasure quarter were quiet in the morning hours. It was a place where lanterns burned late into the night and shuttered down to sleep during the day.

The House of Heavenly Peaches was a moderately sized house despite its lofty name. Li Chen had been a regular visitor for a brief time and was accustomed to the flutter of rose-colored curtains and soft music that came from the house. This morning, the lanterns were extinguished and the building silent.

One of his constables stood at the entrance to the alleyway in the austere black uniforms that differentiated them from the citizenry.

"Magistrate. Head Constable," the man greeted them with a bow before relaying the details.

The body had been found by a passerby that morning. No one in the surrounding buildings could identify the victim.

The first glimpse of the body lying in the dirt made Chen pause. He wasn't completely inured to the sight of death even after facing it throughout his career. Gao, however, appeared unperturbed. The constable moved ahead to inspect the body while Chen lingered a step behind.

From the silk clothing, the victim was a person of means. Chen would investigate regardless of who was involved, but a crime against the upper class meant more scrutiny and pressure from outside.

He stood beside Constable Gao to stare down at the unfortunate victim. He was bearded with gray streaked through his hair. His skin had taken on a chalky pallor and his face was frozen in a grim mask with mouth open as if in a last gasp.

"Was he found lying like this?" Chen asked.

"Exactly like that," the younger constable affirmed. "No purse on him."

The common explanation would be the man was out late drinking and had met his misfortune at the hands of a thief.

"No visible wounds," Chen remarked.

"Strangulation," Gao surmised.

He wasn't yet ready to come to that conclusion. They would need to do a closer examination of the body. Ligature marks around the neck and throat could take time to show.

"He was dragged out here," Gao continued.

Chen could see the marks in the dirt as well, more visible now that the sun had risen higher. He backtracked toward the entrance of the alleyway to follow the trail, holding a lantern overhead. The faint marks in the dirt made it difficult to discern where they had begun.

"He was lying still as he was being moved. No kicking or fighting," Constable Gao said from behind him. "He was unconscious or already dead by the time he was brought here."

"Ambushed in the street and then dragged out of sight to strip the body," the other constable offered.

"Choking the life out of someone takes time," Gao replied with a casualness that sent a shiver down Chen's spine. "There are easier ways to overpower and rob someone. However, these things aren't always neatly done."

Chen straightened. "Could this be retribution? For debts unpaid?"

Gao shrugged. "I can find out."

This was one of those times when Li Chen had to stand back. Gao knew people who knew things. People who would never talk to a magistrate. "Employ a thief to catch a thief" was the phrase they liked to use in bureaucratic circles, except the people Gao associated with were worse than common thieves.

There was a door partway down the passage. The neighboring buildings also had openings into the alleyway, but Chen knew where this particular door led.

He instructed the constables to move the victim out of the streets and onto the wagon. The body would be transported to the coffin house for the formal inspection of the corpse. Then he stepped away to leave the constables to the menial task of handling the body.

Gao remained beside him as the others were dispatched.

Together they wound around to the main street. The House of Heavenly Peaches was the most prominent building of the intersection. It was a modest fixture, two stories high, tucked into the corner of the square. The doors remained closed and the windows shuttered.

Li Chen took the lead up the steps to rap on the door. It opened a crack to reveal a young girl with a thin face and a pair of large, shining eyes.

"Miss Sparrow," he greeted.

"Magistrate Li!" she exclaimed too brightly. "Miss Song Yi isn't here."

"I am not here for a social visit," he replied sternly. "You must be well aware of what has happened by now."

Her expressive eyes widened farther. "I can't believe it. Right there in the street—"

The girl was suddenly swept aside to be replaced at the door by a calmer, more refined presence. Madame Shi, the proprietress and den mother of the Heavenly Peaches looked coolly out at him. Despite the early hour, her hair was coiled and pinned, her complexion powdered and smooth.

"Your man woke us this morning to inform us. It is tragic what has happened." The look on her face was one of concern, though her voice remained steady.

"Forgive the intrusion, Madame Shi, but I must ask, was he one of your patrons?" Chen asked.

"We've never seen him before. As I told the constable."

Chen went through the questions again, ignoring the tight press of Madame Shi's lips as she grew more and more impatient. None of them saw or heard anything last night. Nothing unusual had taken place.

"I would speak to the rest of your house, Madame Shi. To make certain that everyone is safe."

He worded the command as the politest of requests.

Madame Shi blinked at him, hedging for a moment before taking control of herself.

"Of course. We are so happy to see the magistrate, as always." She stood aside to beckon him inside.

Sparrow and Old Auntie, the elderly caretaker, were assembled in the main parlor, just beyond the painted screen at the entrance. It had been a while since Chen had been inside, but everything was as he remembered.

A garish landscape painting spanned the far wall, depicting a majestic tree with twisting branches from which hung the legendary peaches of immortality. The furnishings were similarly overstated. Lacquered cherrywood and embroidered pillows. Pink curtains hung between the rooms through which hostesses could appear and disappear, floating as if on clouds. Everything appeared faded in the daylight.

"Bring tea for the magistrate," Madame Shi entreated and Sparrow started for the kitchen.

"There's no need." He wasn't here for niceties. "If you could bring everyone down here."

Sparrow looked uncertainly at Madame Shi who spoke up quickly. "Song Yi is not here. She had an engagement last night—"

He didn't need the reminder. "There's another girl. Miss Pearl."

"Also away," Madame Shi replied smoothly. "Visiting a friend."

He looked to Sparrow. The girl worked the hem of her sleeve with nervous fingertips while the Old Auntie pinned him with a steely look. He was told Auntie had been a courtesan of some renown in her day, but now no longer felt the need to be pleasing to anyone.

"Were there any callers here last night?" he inquired.

"No one," both Sparrow and Madame Shi said at once. Auntie remained silent.

"It was a quiet night," Madame Shi said, speaking alone. "Business has been slow lately."

Song Yi had said as much, but he had assumed there would still be a few patrons coming by. "The parlors were completely empty?"

"Lin Yijin was our best customer," Old Auntie croaked. "Until you chased him away."

Her black eyes narrowed with accusation. The Yanxi Gate incident. Arresting the general's son had been his sworn duty.

Madame Shi moved smoothly between them. "Festival season is past," she explained. "Without the exams this year, our sitting rooms have been woefully empty."

A woman didn't come to run a pleasure house within the bustling capital without being exceedingly clever. Madame Shi was quick-witted as well as silver-tongued. Chen suspected his constables had been easily swayed by her. Elite courtesans in Pingkang were skilled at adopting the words and manners of the noble class.

Chen turned to address Sparrow. "Have you seen the man who was found in the alley, Miss Sparrow?"

"I don't see why that is necessary," Madame Shi cut in before Sparrow could answer.

"It is possible one of the other ladies of the house might recognize the stranger."

"I can speak for every patron who walks through our doors," Madame Shi insisted. "And Sparrow is frightened enough as it is. Don't give the poor girl nightmares."

"What about you, Old Auntie?" he pressed, ignoring Madame Shi to address the elder woman directly.

Auntie sniffed. "Busybody."

"I'm a magistrate, Auntie. Duty dictates that I'm a busybody." He graced his response with a faint smile, but Auntie shook a bony finger at him.

"Don't you try to charm this old woman, Li Chen. I'm too old and you're not that charming. I did go out into the alleyway and all I saw is some stupid egg who drank too much and got himself killed. All those fools look alike to me."

Between Madame Shi's pretty courtesies and Old Auntie's sharp tongue, it was easy to decide the women weren't worth the effort, but there was trouble and it was at their door. It was his responsibility to find who had done this.

"We will need to speak to Pearl and Song Yi once the ladies return," he insisted. "They may recognize the victim's face."

"Of course," Madame Shi said easily. "As soon as they return. If you have nothing else—"

Chen did have more, but Gao interrupted his questioning when he peered around the painted screen.

"Where is your man?" Constable Gao asked.

All eyes turned to him.

"The fellow who guards the door. To keep unwelcome guests from entering," Gao continued pointedly.

"That fool Bao abandoned us days ago," Madame Shi replied. "Took our hidden stash of money."

The constable's blunt manner had its usefulness. Li Chen had come to drink at the Heavenly Peaches on several occasions and he'd never noticed a manservant guarding the door. He supposed it was this Bao's role to remain unnoticed unless there was trouble.

To another point, Li Chen was the magistrate. There were many in these lanes who preferred to stay beneath his notice.

"Why wasn't that theft reported, Madame?" Chen asked.

She sighed at him with forced patience. "Such small matters are better handled amongst ourselves, Magistrate."

Chen exchanged a look with the head constable who was

far from satisfied with the answer. He meant to delve into the issue when the air in the room suddenly changed. Li Chen felt it before he turned. Song Yi stood behind him.

She met his eyes first before looking to the others. He could sense from their reactions that they had not been expecting her this morning. The entire room grew warmer in Song Yi's presence, at least to him.

"Magistrate," she said with a frown. "What has happened here?"

CHAPTER 3

he evening had gone as Song Yi had anticipated. She had watched Li Chen's carriage until it had disappeared into the mist. The house servants had expected her. She glided past them through the tidy garden and into the house. Scholar Zhao was busy writing a letter when she came into his room with tea.

Zhao was a long-time patron of hers. One of her first admirers. His hair was gray at the temples and his eyes were kind. It was an ideal arrangement. He was often gone from the capital so his demands were few.

She'd rubbed at the knots in his shoulders as she inquired about his time away. Told him she had missed him. Teased him that he worked too much.

In her head, she went over every word Li Chen had spoken to her and everything she hadn't said. There had been a hollow, haunted look in his eyes before he rode away. She should have spared him that. She could have deflected, made a vague apology with a promise to meet with him at another time so Li Chen could have remained blissfully ignorant.

"You seem distracted," Scholar Zhao remarked.

Her hands had stilled against his neck. She hadn't caught anything Zhao had said before that.

"I must be picking up your bad habits," she said lightly, her hands resuming their work.

He permitted the jest, though he didn't smile.

Song Yi forced herself to remain focused for the rest of the evening. Zhao was generous. They had history. She had been young when they first started their acquaintance. Young, but not entirely inexperienced. He'd had a wife then and two sons, no desire for more heirs or a concubine. Song Yi only filled the role of an occasional companion, but on those occasions it was unacceptable to split her attention.

Zhao wasn't lavishly wealthy and not prone to extravagant gifts, but he was reliable and unchanging, even after nearly eight years. Because of their steady, uncomplicated arrangement she was able to keep herself clothed and fed.

Zhao took her to his bed a little while later and made love to her quietly in a well-worn path that had become easy to walk. He fell asleep soon after, breathing heavily, while she lay with her eyes open, trying not to think of Li Chen.

Li Chen, the dark-eyed prodigy from Yu prefecture. Song Yi should have been worried that someone in the capital had roots so close to her own. Close enough to have heard the whispers and rumors. But the past was so long ago and so far away that it no longer felt real to her. She no longer feared ruin from it. What reputation did Song Yi have left to be ruined?

She should have refused the carriage and Li Chen's company, but it was best they be honest with one another. Patrons came calling at the drinking house, pretending they were the only ones, while knowing very well that they weren't.

Courtesans were entertainers. The House of Heavenly Peaches was a business that protected and fed all the girls

JEANNIE LIN

within it. Song Yi played at romance and courtship, but hers was a practical profession and she knew Li Chen wasn't the best of prospects.

"Wasted time," Old Auntie had complained when Li Chen had abandoned her.

He wasn't the sort to take her as his mistress and become a benefactor. Magistrates were frequently transferred and, even more importantly, Li Chen was Li Chen. He was reserved by nature.

Long looks couldn't buy anything. They were emptier than promises and the house needed more than flirtation and idle banter to keep their doors open. Winter was coming and they had lost their wealthiest banquet guests in the last year.

"Politics!" Madame Shi had lamented.

Song Yi woke alone the next morning and dressed. She'd left Scholar Zhao the night before to retire to the guest chamber. Sleeping side by side wasn't something they'd ever done.

Scholar Zhao gad expected her visit to last the week. It was the same routine they'd kept for his previous stays in the capital.

Song Yi was making an absolutely poor decision. She knew this as she'd brought Scholar Zhao his morning tea along with her apologies and the excuses she had rehearsed all night. She was full of regret. Sad with remorse to have to leave him so suddenly.

The bureaucrat was not happy to have their visit cut short. His mouth was set in a hard line as she apologized and departed.

Zhao might never inquire after her again, Song Yi realized as she rode back to the Pingkang li. The game of courtship went both ways. She was telling him, not so subtly, that she was no longer suited to be the moon in his night sky.

That's what Zhao had said once, wasn't it? A long, long

32

time ago. It hadn't wooed her then but she'd tolerated it. Zhao had always been kind. His affections had been sincere, but, as poetry went, it was pretty uninspired.

Alone in the carriage, her time once again her own, Song Yi could think of Li Chen again and curse him for the hot and cold nature of his attention. She was thinking exactly of that, and exactly of him when she entered the house. Which is why it was such as shock to find him there.

"Miss Song Yi." Li Chen's eyes widened at the sight of her. There was a catch in his breath.

"Magistrate Li."

"I didn't realize you would return so soon," he began haltingly.

She glanced at the others in the room. He'd brought his head constable and, if she wasn't mistaken, there was another man hovering in the alleyway.

"What has happened here?" Song Yi repeated, lowering her voice to address Li Chen directly.

A moment earlier, she had caught him mid-interrogation, demanding answers from Mother and the others in a commanding tone. Now the magistrate became more subdued, courteously matching his tone to hers. "There's been an unfortunate incident."

"Someone was found in the alleyway outside," Madame Shi chimed in.

"Dead," Constable Gao made a point to add. "He was killed and then dragged into the alley out back."

Li Chen's gaze raked over the room to watch for any reaction. At the same time, Song Yi realized Pearl wasn't there. Madame Shi flashed her a sharp look and she remained silent.

"We should check the rooms," Li Chen went on. "To ensure nothing is out of order."

"Of course, Magistrate."

Song Yi took his side. Li Chen paused, but then relented, allowing her presence as he started through the house. Song Yi didn't know what had happened here last night, but she did know that whenever there was a negotiation, their house always sent whoever was most suited for the task to the front.

Song Yi was big sister. This was Li Chen. She was most suited.

Madame Shi fell into step behind them while Constable Gao trailed at the rear, conducting his own inspection of the premises.

Li Chen seemed to remember the layout quite well. He started upstairs, looking through the windows down into the alleyway and making a cursory inspection of the banquet area. His face was a mask.

"So tragic," Song Yi remarked, following as Li Chen traveled down the stairs with his spine straight and shoulders rigid. "And so frightening. Was it street thieves?"

"We cannot yet say."

"Not likely."

Both the magistrate and his constable answered at once with Constable Gao being the more forthright of the two. Meanwhile, the look of distress on Mother's face was louder than a signal drum.

Li Chen walked back toward the kitchen and opened the rear door. Outside lay the fateful alleyway, currently empty.

The search of the rest of the bottom floor led them to Song Yi's chamber. Li Chen stood aside so that she could go through the motions of allowing him inside. Always such manners.

Mother's eyes darted to her as she moved to open the door. She sensed the magistrate's presence close behind her, sending a prickle of awareness down the back of her neck.

She knew his moods and there was nothing light or companionable about his manner at the moment.

"Magistrate." She gestured toward the sitting area, palm up.

How many times had she invited him in this way? Magistrate Li, please come in. So happy to see you. Her pulse skipped as he brushed past. Mother took the opportunity to grab onto her sleeve. Song Yi shook her free. Constable Gao was right behind them. Not many men unnerved her, but the constable did. He had a dangerous reputation.

Li Chen stood over the sitting area. There was a low narrow table used for serving drinks with a long, padded seat beside it. They'd reclined on that seat together a lifetime ago. Song Yi had recited a poem by Li Bai. Chen had corrected her. She'd made the mistake on purpose just so he could.

The magistrate turned in a slow circle while Song Yi held her breath. Something had happened here and he knew it. The furniture had been shifted around and one of the stools was missing. Chen paused, gaze fixed onto the arrangement, before turning to face her.

"Many things have changed since you were last here," she said, heading off his line of questioning.

He nodded, but she knew it wasn't acceptance. She could see the questions lingering in his eyes. She had her own questions.

Mother wanted Li Chen distracted. Mother wanted him gone, but pushing him out the door would only make him more suspicious. Song Yi moved into the sitting area to draw his attention. It worked, not because she was pretty but because Li Chen was courteous.

"I wanted to remove old memories," she said softly, glancing around. "This arrangement feels more balanced."

Chen's gaze lingered on her face and Song Yi considered that maybe she had underestimated herself.

"There are things I wish had been done differently," he told her.

She had succeeded in distracting him, but only for a moment. The clear-eyed magistrate returned before she could draw her next breath.

"If everyone would come outside," he instructed.

The entire house was brought out to the street where a wagon awaited them. A shrouded form had been laid out in the back, covered with a heavy canvas.

Constable Gao stepped forward and took hold of the covering. A feeling of dread gripped her. She held her breath as the canvas was lifted away to reveal the lifeless face, gray in pallor. Sparrow gasped and turned away. Auntie shook her head slowly while Mother stood absolutely still.

"Do you recognize this man?" Chen directed his question at all of them.

Sparrow answered immediately, no. Song Yi took a moment longer to consider, looking over the frozen features. The man's face was narrow and bearded. There was gray threaded in his hair. His skin had become sallow and ashen. His eyes were thankfully shut, but the final expression on his face was far from restful.

It wasn't the first time Song Yi had seen death. This time was easier. She was older now and this man, thankfully, wasn't anyone she knew or cared for.

"No," she replied finally. "I've never seen him before."

This last, grisly exchange had at least served the purpose of getting Li Chen and the head constable away from the house. Chen apologized for the intrusion and took his leave.

Madame Shi waited until the wagon had rolled clear of the square before pulling Song Yi back inside.

"What are you doing back here?" Mother demanded. "Scholar Zhao was expecting you for the week."

"His interest has been fading," Song Yi said dismissively.

"I know you," Mother snapped. "A man's interest in you only fades when you want it to fade."

"Zhao hasn't been devoted for a long time," she said, exhausted. "You should be more concerned about what's happening here, Mother. Where is Pearl? And Bao would never steal from us. Gone for days? He was here just yesterday."

Song Yi had overheard Madame Shi making her excuses to Li Chen before rushing in to stop her. Why had Mother lied about Pearl and the manservant Bao to the magistrate?

Mother ushered Song Yi back into her chamber and waved Sparrow and Auntie away, shutting the door behind her.

"That man from the alleyway *was* here last night," Madame Shi confessed in a harsh whisper, her eyes wide with dread. "He came here asking for you."

SONG YI TRIED to calm her den mother down, but Madame Shi had kept quiet for so long that the words poured out of her.

"He asked for you," Mother said, her voice shaking. "He told me he was a merchant traveling through and had heard of your fame."

Song Yi frowned. "That's rubbish."

How had Mother fallen for such drivel? Madame Shi had a keen eye for sorting out swindlers and con men.

"He was well-spoken. A gentleman," Mother insisted. "He said he wanted to meet you."

"Did he give a name?"

"Just that he was a merchant from Hebei."

Nothing sounded right. "Did you tell him I wasn't here?"

Mother started pacing. "He seemed so well-mannered

and easy to please. You know our business has been poor lately."

Of course, Song Yi knew. She was the elder sister of the house. Its woes were her woes.

The Heavenly Peaches had lost its best patron. Lin Yijin was wealthy and careless with money. He was the sort who attracted an entourage of cronies around him, many of who were similarly wealthy and careless with money.

Their house had been Lin Yijin's favorite drinking spot. The rooms he had filled several nights a week now stood empty and his misfortune had dragged their house down as well.

"The stranger asked for me by name?" Song Yi pressed. "What did he want?"

A tiny knot formed in her stomach. Song Yi used to hope for news of her past, from the places and people she had left behind.

Mother suddenly looked much older. The worry lines deepened around her eyes and mouth. "I asked him if he was an old acquaintance, perhaps he'd come by before. Just an admirer, he said. Just passing through. He was only here for the night."

Song Yi had an idea of what this man had wanted. Travelers came to the capital wanting to experience the glittering pleasure quarter for themselves. Wine and music and beautiful women. They weren't there for a drawn-out courtship.

"You sent Pearl—"

"I told her to pretend to be you," Mother said miserably. "He was impressed by your reputation. Pearl is clever enough. What harm could there be?"

"Then what happened?"

Mother wrung her hands. "I presented her to the gentleman. He seemed to like her well enough, and asked to continue the conversation privately."

"You left Pearl alone? With a stranger?"

How had Mother gotten so reckless? They knew the scholars and bureaucrats who frequented their parlors. Those men had reputations to uphold and could be held to the rules and customs of the pleasure quarter. Travelers didn't know the difference between the courtesan houses and the brothels of the north end.

"What about Old Auntie?"

"Auntie was resting in her room. She was complaining of a headache."

The realization came to her. Sparrow wasn't told to stay. Bao wasn't nearby. Mother and Auntie had stood down and closed their eyes and their ears.

"Mother!" Song Yi scolded brokenly.

"Our house has been empty," Mother said defensively, her lips trembling. "Not just tonight, but every night this week. This man had silver and asked to speak to you privately. It might not have come to...to that."

But it might have. Pearl would have known what she was being asked to do, but she didn't have the experience to navigate those waters alone. That was the true art of being a courtesan. It was flattery and deflection, the delicate management of emotions. It was not getting cornered.

Song Yi pressed her hand over her eyes. If she had been there, none of this would have happened.

"You brought him to this chamber and presented Pearl as me. And then you left. When you came back—"

"Sparrow was the one who found him. An hour had passed, perhaps longer."

Song Yi didn't want to imagine what had happened next. Pearl was quick-witted, but she was young and less experienced. Even with all the experience in the world, it was impossible to predict how a man would behave once he got her alone. Had he become possessive? Angry? Had he threatened Pearl?

"Sparrow screamed and I rushed in. Everything had been tossed about. The man was just lying there, on the floor. I tried to wake him, but he was already gone."

Dead in her chamber. Song Yi shuddered.

Mother went on. "We searched everywhere for Pearl. I even sent Bao into the streets to look for her."

"This had to be an accident," Song Yi reasoned. "Pearl was trying to defend herself."

Her den mother shook her head. "He looked like he had been choked to death. Little Pearl is so thin. She's smaller than you are. The man wasn't an ox, but he was much larger and stronger than she was. Someone else had to have done this."

"And then they took Pearl?" Song Yi couldn't believe it.

"Or she went with them. I've thought of this all night. I haven't been able to think of anything else. Pearl must have had a lover. He came and saw her and became jealous."

"Pearl didn't have anyone. She would have told me."

"Then it was one of her favorites. After he killed the man, they became frightened and took his money and fled."

"His purse was missing when you came in?"

"Of course it was. I wouldn't steal from the dead."

It had only been a few nights ago when Song Yi and Pearl had laughed together at the director's banquet. Theirs was a small house, just Pearl and Sparrow and herself. Other girls had come and gone, but the three of them who remained were like sisters. Still, sisters kept secrets from one another. Song Yi knew this from personal experience.

She looked about the sitting area again. It had been swept clean, but there was a stain on the rug from what she hoped was merely spilt tea. The furniture had been quickly rearranged and not entirely straight. And yet she had prattled on about balance and removing the past.

She had been so nervous. Li Chen would have seen right through her.

"I didn't know who this man was and now Pearl was gone, and he was lying there, dead. If anyone found him here, we would be ruined. Our reputation is in pieces as it is. So I told Bao to drag him out into the street. It was late, the house was empty. No one saw him."

"But Magistrate Li and his constable were already here. They already suspect something."

"They can suspect all they want," Mother snapped, irritated. "We can deny everything. Bao was worried they would put the blame on him, so I gave him what little cash we had and told him to run and hide."

Which gave Mother someone to blame for the killing if Li Chen started questioning her story. Would Madame Shi sacrifice a servant like Bao to protect them? A chill went down Song Yi's spine.

"What else happened? Did you see or hear anything else?"

"Auntie said she had heard footsteps while she was resting. Someone moving at the back of the house. And a man's voice."

All of that could be made up. Auntie was as fierce about protecting their house as Mother was. Song Yi noticed a pale shard near her foot. When she bent to inspect it, she saw it was a sliver of porcelain. There was another, much larger piece behind the leg of the chaise. Carefully she reached out to slide it toward her.

Song Yi froze then, her heart stopping.

"What is it?" Mother asked.

"There's something on here." She pulled the shard out from beneath the seat. It was nearly the size of her palm with wickedly sharp edges. A thin red stain smeared over her hand and she dropped the porcelain as if she'd been stung.

Blood.

Song Yi wiped her hand over the rug, horrified. Mother crouched down beside her. "We have to get rid of that."

Song Yi stared at the shard. It was curved like a claw. Likely broken off a tea bowl. The sight of it brought home what had happened here in her very own chamber.

She drew a silk handkerchief from her sleeve and picked up the shard with it, wrapping it carefully inside.

"We're not getting rid of it, Mother," she said firmly. Slowly, she rose to her feet. Her knees were shaking. "I'm taking this to the magistrate."

"But he'll think we did this! No one will believe us. Not after we moved the body. Not with Pearl missing."

"Mother, Magistrate Li already doesn't believe you."

Li Chen had been in charge of the capital for three years now. During that time, his office had built a reputation for solving difficult cases. It was said his new head constable could get anyone to talk. The thought of what that could mean made her blood run cold.

Song Yi's heart pounded. She didn't know if this was the right thing to do, but she knew trying to cover up the killing wouldn't work. There wasn't enough guile in her to keep Li Chen distracted for long.

"We have to find Pearl," Song Yi resolved, trying to calm the twisting feeling in her stomach. The stranger had come asking for her and then something awful had happened to Pearl who was now missing.

"I need to go tell Li Chen the truth about what happened here." She looked around at Mother and Auntie's clumsy efforts to hide the evidence. "We won't be able to charm our way out of this."

$\mathcal{L}$i Chen tied a scarf over his nose before entering the coffin house. Beside him, Gao forged on with his face uncovered. The air had cooled with the coming of autumn, but that wasn't enough to tamp down the smell. Some of the bodies inside had been there for over a week.

A soul was tied to where it was born. For many families, it was destiny to live and grow and die all on the same plot of earth under the same swath of sky. Even though Li Chen had traveled through the provinces, appointed to one county seat after another, and now to the capital of Changan, he expected to be laid to rest in Yuzhou alongside his ancestors. It was there where descendants, the generations to come, would know to light incense and keep the tombs swept.

The business of attending to the spirits was a part of life. He himself was supposed to journey home in a week's time to observe *jìchén*, the anniversary of his father's passing. It was a journey Li Chen took every year. A son's primary duty was to honor his father and, as only son, his responsibility was even more pronounced.

The coffin house was where the dead whose homes were

far away were laid out. Inside the wooden structure were the bodies of migrant laborers or travelers who had died during a journey. The remaining bodies were those who were unidentified. In the coffin house, their families had one final chance to claim them.

Incense burned from the altar erected inside, both as an offering for the spirits as well as to offset the smell. Most of the deceased were already encased in coffins or bundled into heavy wrapping to await the corpse-walkers who would transport the bodies on their final journey home.

The victim Li Chen was here to inspect was laid out on the wooden table at the back. Chen had waited for the better part of the day before proceeding with the examination. A corpse became rigid immediately after death, but would loosen after time had passed, making the examination process easier.

With the weather cooling, it wasn't as noxious in the coffin house as it would become in the heated summer months, but it still wasn't a place one could breathe freely. Because of the taboo nature of contact with the dead, the coffin house had to remain shuttered, no matter how stifling the smell was.

Chen had summoned the handler, an aging servant who moved among the bodies as if they were nothing more than cords of bamboo. Bone-thin with probing eyes that resembled a mantis', the man had held the position for the prior magistrate as well.

The handler had already set to work laying out the body and arranging the limbs. Oil lamps flickered around the examination table and a lantern had been lit and set beside the corpse for closer inspection.

As magistrate, it was Li Chen's responsibility to head up the inquest. He would identify the cause of death and then seek out the killer if it was indeed a wrongful death. At the present, that certainly appeared to be the case. He held his lantern over the corpse to highlight the area around the throat.

The skin's gray pallor had darkened. Beneath his chin, the neck which had been unblemished hours before was now mottled with bruises. Ligature marks or bruising sometimes took a day or more to show after death.

"You were right," he told Gao. "Strangulation."

Gao said nothing. Chen imagined the constable was trying not to breathe more than he had to.

Constable Gao had searched the victim for anything that might identify him. The stranger's purse had been removed, presumably by thieves. In the alleyway, Gao had performed the service of closing the man's eyes while the other constables had gone to search the local inns and taverns. If the stranger had come from outside Changan, he must have paid for lodgings nearby.

Chen asked for the clothes to be cut away, and the handler set to work, his knife tearing through the expensive cloth of the man's robe.

"I thought you had examiners to do this," Gao said as they watched the layers of cloth being pulled aside.

"This is a special case."

A magistrate wasn't permitted to directly touch or search a corpse. It was mean work relegated to servants, runners, and constables.

Chen paused to write in his journal, using a charcoal stick to scratch out the characters. He made a note of the bruises and the pallor of the skin before inspecting the scalp for any lacerations or injuries. He'd encountered a case at his first post where a man had been killed with a blow to the head, then hanged to mask the death as a suicide. There was no such wound here.

"Is this a special case because this man was obviously rich

or because it happened at the House of Heavenly Peaches?" Gao posed.

"He is not obviously rich and it did not necessarily happen in the Heavenly Peaches," Chen corrected mildly. He asked for the handler to raise the eyelids for him then close them again. More notes.

"He was rich." Gao lifted a belt ornament inlaid with jade from the pile of clothing. "Yet the thieves didn't bother to take this?"

Chen didn't comment. He had hired Gao as head constable after the previous constable had been killed. At the time, none of the other constables had been willing to step up into the post. Li Chen recognized the value of a head constable who knew things he didn't and thought in ways he wasn't accustomed to. Gao certainly fulfilled that role.

"This is a special case because the circumstances of the death are not clear," Chen replied in response to Gao's earlier question.

The handler gripped the corpse's chin with his thin fingers. It took some effort to pry the mouth open. No discoloration there. Or injury. Some victims might bite their tongue during a seizure or struggle, or it could become swollen in cases of poisoning. Chen used a wooden instrument to lift and push aside the organ to inspect the sides of it.

These were the types of observations not written in the Tang code which laid out his responsibilities. This was also the sort of menial work that put magistrates at the lower ranks of the bureaucracy.

When Li Chen had first come to his appointment in the imperial capital, he'd had a head constable he could trust to perform these examinations. Unfortunately, Constable Wu Kaifeng had resigned his post to run a teahouse. Now Chen was left with a head constable who was a former street thug. At least Gao would be able to keep himself alive.

With the inspection of the head complete, Chen moved on to the throat. The handler ran his fingertips carefully along the sides of the windpipe, feeling for any indentation or depression.

"The windpipe hasn't been crushed," he reported.

The bruising on the sides of the neck pointed to the grip of hands. Someone had grabbed the victim face-to-face and held on. The cold and numbing certainty ran through him. It was murder.

"How long would you say it takes to choke a man to death?" Chen asked Gao.

"Haven't ever done it."

Chen was grateful for that.

"It takes a while to render a man unconscious though," Gao continued. "A minute or more."

Constable Gao had been quite informative on the way to the coffin house of quicker ways to execute robbery. There was knifing. Clubbing. Simply shoving or holding a man down and grabbing his purse was easy enough.

"Killing is another matter. Killing will get you executed. Thieving might earn you only a few lashes if they recover the money," Gao had informed him, as if Li Chen wasn't the magistrate who handed down such punishments. "If a lot of money is stolen or it's a repeat offense, they'll brand you with an iron, then march you off to a work camp."

This was most definitely a killing and not just an unfortunate robbery attempt. Whoever had done this had deliberately overpowered the victim and squeezed the life from him.

What would it take for one person to take another's life? The thought still sent a cold chill down his spine every time.

Chen moved downward to inspect the torso and

47

abdomen. The victim was well-fed. Rich, as Gao had already pointed out. Chen paused during the inspection of the victim's arms.

"There's a stab wound here."

The body had been stabbed halfway between the shoulder and elbow of his left arm.

Li Chen hadn't detected it in the alleyway because of the dark color of the man's clothes. The handler dutifully cleaned away the blood around the wound and Chen held the lantern over it.

Gao moved around to look. "Strange place for it. And that wasn't done by any knife worth having."

It was a puncture wound in the man's arm with ragged edges where the flesh had torn. Not being able to search the body directly was a constant hindrance. Li Chen directed Gao to the sleeve to search for where the weapon had entered the body. He hoped the handler hadn't inadvertently cut through it.

Fortunately, Gao was able to locate a gash torn into the cloth.

"A messy affair," Gao concluded. "He was struggling against someone when they likely stabbed him."

There were no other discernible wounds.

"Could someone smaller and lighter than him have done this?" Chen asked.

"A woman?" Gao asked archly.

Chen eyed him. "Yes, a woman."

It was easy to lay blame on the courtesans of the pleasure quarter for the crime, but Li Chen had a duty to all of the wards in the eastern circuit. He had a duty to keep the rumors under control and to protect the courtesans of the House of Heavenly Peaches until he knew more.

"Three women against one," Gao pointed out.

"One of them an old woman, another a young girl."

"With one unaccounted for and a missing manservant as well."

Gao had a point. They hadn't been able to find out where Pearl had disappeared to or where Bao, the man who attended to the door, had gone. At least Song Yi wasn't a part of this mess. Chen had accompanied her away from Pingkang li earlier that same night.

"None of the courtesans showed any signs of guilt when they saw the body," Chen offered in their defense.

"Those women could convince any man of anything," Gao said with a smirk. "They're lucky to have the county magistrate as their protector."

"I am not anyone's protector—" Chen had to stop himself. "I am just considering every angle."

They had gotten waylaid. He bent to continue the examination and discovered a ring on the victim's left hand. It appeared to be carved out of ivory—or was it mutton fat jade, called so because of its pale, milky color? The corpse handler tugged at the ring, but it wouldn't budge.

Gao brandished his knife. "I can cut it free."

Li Chen grimaced. "I don't believe that will be necessary."

The handler tried twisting and tugging some more, but to no avail.

"A clean cut, right at the knuckle," Gao urged just as someone peered in through the door.

"Magistrate Li." It was a runner from the yamen. "We've been searching for you."

Li Chen tried to look beyond the runner to the daylight outside. He'd spent most of the day away from his offices. The petitions would be piling up on his desk by now.

"Someone came to see you. The lady said it was important," the runner reported.

"Lady?" Chen asked.

Behind him, the handler let the corpse's arm drop with a thud. Chen tried not to wince at the impropriety of it all.

"From the House of Heavenly Peaches," the runner reported.

The runner didn't have her name. Had Song Yi come looking for him in his office? Was she waiting for him now?

Li Chen looked to the handler and then to Gao. The examination wasn't complete and the coffin house was an hour away.

"Have her leave a request with the clerk," Li Chen directed.

This was now a murder investigation. Whatever Song Yi, if it was indeed Song Yi, needed from him would have to wait.

Even if he wanted to fly to her.

IT TOOK Chen longer than he'd planned to return to the Pingkang ward. There was the matter of washing up. Paperwork. The day's petitions.

A murder in the pleasure quarter certainly needed to be addressed, but other disputes and complaints also needed attention. The line of petitioners alone kept him occupied through the afternoon.

With his long list of duties, Li Chen couldn't be seen rushing to the courtesan house. He had to act responsibly, deploying constables to Pingkang to search out witnesses and informants that Chen could then follow up on later.

By the time Li Chen arrived in the ward, the sun was setting. The streets were illuminated with lanterns in preparation for the evening activities. Nighttime was when the drinking houses of Pingkang came alive.

The House of Heavenly Peaches was located just outside

of the center of the ward, where the most prominent courtesan houses were located. Opposite the house was a collection of street vendors and small shops. The teahouse across the way could be seen as competition, though it didn't offer anything in the way of entertainment the way the Heavenly Peaches did. Chen had become quite familiar with the area lately, something he didn't like to admit.

That evening, the doors and windows of the Heavenly Peaches remained shuttered, which was to be expected given the circumstances. Chen went up to the door to knock and it was Old Auntie who answered. With a scowl, she pointed him down the street.

Chen found Song Yi in the pawn shop, placing an armful of silk onto the counter. She was dressed plainly in pale blue with her hair pulled back and pinned with a wooden comb. The look softened her features, though her eyes remained sharply expressive.

"How much, Uncle?" she asked the broker. "And don't cheat me."

The pawn shop owner raised his thick eyebrows at her but didn't seem to take offense. "Miss, I'm always fair."

"We have known each other for how many years?"

"I'm always fair to *you*, miss," he amended. And then gently, "Difficult times?"

"Winter is coming, Uncle," she replied with a wave of her hand. "These are summer dresses."

Song Yi's manner changed when she spoke to the pawn broker. The set of her shoulders relaxed and her expressions were unguarded. She became more lively. Animated. Chen hated to consider it, but Song Yi seemed *warmer*. Song Yi would tease and banter when she was with him, but there was always a sheen of refinement to it.

The broker inspected the silk garments and re-folded them carefully before setting them aside. Then he counted out a handful of coins and set them on the counter. Song Yi glanced sideways at them, as if with disinterest, and made no move until the broker added two more coins.

Li Chen knew courtesans who were fiery bright centers of attention, commanding a room by force of will. Song Yi's energy was a more subtle, calming resonance.

He stepped forward only after Song Yi had secured the money into her purse.

She jumped at the sight of him. "Magistrate Li."

"Miss Song Yi. You came to see me today?"

Long lashes fluttered nervously. "Magistrate, you didn't need to come all this way. I told the clerk I would come again tomorrow."

"The matter seemed urgent."

The shop owner's gaze darted back and forth between the two of them before dropping furtively behind the counter.

Chen decided to ignore the broker's suspicious behavior. The man was probably nervous about some petty infraction. In his experience, most people had little knack for subtlety.

"But I see this may not be a good time," Chen amended.

"No, this is—" Song Yi blinked, large eyes fixing on to him, and just like that, the cool mask of refinement was back in place. "I always have time for you."

The silk of her sleeve whispered against him as she left the shop. Instead of returning to the Heavenly Peaches, Song Yi headed toward the nearby teahouse.

"I was hoping to speak privately," she explained over her shoulder.

He halted, staring at the teahouse located directly across from the courtesan house. "We would have more privacy at the Heavenly Peaches."

Song Yi continued down the lane, undeterred. "I would like to avoid the scandal of having the magistrate come by twice in one day."

Despite the cool evening weather, Li Chen could feel heat rising up his neck. There was no hiding from what was about to happen.

The proprietor of the teahouse greeted him as soon as he stepped inside. "Magistrate Li, good to see you again!"

Song Yi slowed to cast him a sideways glance. Chen clamped his mouth shut.

They continued up the stairs with him trailing behind her. Song Yi selected a seat in the corner beside the window. Which also happened to be the table he usually sat at. It had a direct view of the courtesan house. He did his best not to glance that way.

Song Yi sat with her back straight and her hands folded primly in front of her while tea was poured. Steam rose from their cups, forming a thin curtain between them.

"I come here sometimes," he admitted into the silence.

She nodded and took a small sip of her tea. Her lips curved delicately over the rim of the cup before she set it back down, fidgeting as she centered it before her.

They were both accustomed to meeting in her private sitting room where there were accepted rules of conduct and topics of conversation between them. It was unusual for him to see her outside like this, engaged in mundane tasks.

A sudden thought came to him. "Whose clothes were you selling at the pawn shop?"

She frowned at him, confused.

"Has Pearl returned?" he pressed.

Her eyes widened when she realized what he was insinuating.

"Those weren't Pearl's clothes," she explained. "Or rather, they didn't belong to Pearl specifically. We don't own the robes we wear. All of our silk belongs to the house. Our instruments as well. Everything really."

He'd never considered the logistics of the courtesan

53

house before. Silk garments were expensive. A courtesan couldn't afford to own an impressive wardrobe on her own, but an entire house could share a collection of dresses among them for their many outings and engagements.

"Not so glamorous, is it?" she asked quietly, flashing him a half-smile.

Chen considered what he had seen. "If Pearl ran away and needed money, she would have to sell her clothes."

"Pearl hasn't run away—"

"What was she wearing when she left?" he asked, undeterred.

Song Yi blinked at him, pretty eyes narrowed as she considered her answer.

"Indigo blue with white chrysanthemums," she replied finally.

The same dress Song Yi had worn at Director Guan's banquet. It was his turn to take a long drink. He had tried so hard not to pay any attention to Song Yi that night so, of course, he knew every detail about what she'd been wearing.

"I don't believe Pearl ran away," Song Yi told him. "Our servant Bao didn't run away either."

This was new. Li Chen sat back and waited, employing very much the same strategy Song Yi had used on the pawn broker. Silence in the middle of a conversation was an uncomfortable pause. Amazing what some would confess to, just to alleviate that discomfort.

Song Yi swallowed, touching her fingers nervously against the side of her neck. "I wanted to come to you because I think you already know, Magistrate."

"What do I know?"

"Pearl was with the stranger before he was found dead," she confessed.

"So Madame Shi, Old Auntie, and Little Sparrow—they all lied," he posed calmly.

"They didn't kill him," she protested.

"How would you know, Miss Song Yi? You were away."

She fell silent, casting her eyes downward. It had been an uncomfortable endeavor, taking Song Yi to a suitor, but at least Chen knew she wasn't a part of the deception.

"We don't know who the stranger was. Sparrow found him lying in my chamber," she said, speaking softly so only he could hear. "And Pearl was gone."

Li Chen listened carefully to the new version of events. There had been a struggle. Madame Shi had instructed the doorman Bao to drag the body outside before sending him into hiding. Sparrow and Auntie cleaned and straightened the sitting room.

"Is there anything else?" he asked quietly.

"Mother said that the man's purse had already been taken when they found them. Bao ran away after he moved the body, not wanting any more trouble."

Trouble was exactly what they had here. Li Chen could feel his jaw clenching tighter with each new detail. Song Yi hesitated when she saw the look in his eyes.

"There's…there's something else," she continued.

Reaching into the pocket of her sleeve, Song Yi pulled out a small bundle wrapped in cloth and placed it onto the table in front of him.

"It's sharp," she warned as he unwrapped it.

Chen inspected the fragment of porcelain, turning it over within the cloth, before wrapping it again.

The shard was blood-stained along the edges and large enough to be held in someone's palm. That explained the strange wound in the victim's arm. Someone had taken hold of the broken fragment and wielded it like a crude knife, likely slicing his, or her, own hand in the process.

He looked up to see Song Yi watching him with large, anxious eyes. They were known as peach blossom eyes, sweeping elegantly upward at the corners. The slender shape of them gave a hint of both affection and intensity. Those eyes seduced with hardly any effort.

At least he was aware of his weaknesses and fully willing to admit them.

Li Chen picked up the shard of porcelain and tucked it into his belt. Then he slid his teacup aside so there was nothing between them.

"Why are you telling me all of this, Song Yi?" he asked gravely.

She swallowed. "Because it's the truth."

"You weren't even there last night. Why were you the one dispatched to speak to me?"

He locked his gaze onto hers and she flinched. "Everyone is frightened right now."

"Your den mother wasn't so frightened that she couldn't calmly lie to a county official. She wasn't afraid of dragging a dead body through the dirt in the middle of the night. Hiding evidence—"

"We did all of this exactly because we're so frightened," she insisted.

He didn't miss how Song Yi included herself, whether or not she had been present for the crime. The women of the Heavenly Peaches stood together.

"Fear makes people do irrational things, Magistrate. We're a house full of women with no one else to protect us."

A houseful of clever women against one man. He was beginning to see Gao's point.

"Everyone should have been truthful from the start," he told her. "Now things will be more difficult for you. Particularly for Madame Shi."

"She only meant to protect us."

"I can't show you any favoritism," he interrupted. "Any of you. Madame Shi will have to come and tell me all of this

56

directly. She cannot send you to bend my ear. And if I catch her in any more lies, it will not go well for her."

He was breathing hard and Song Yi could no longer meet his eyes. She bowed her head with her hands folded in her lap. "I understand, Magistrate."

He usually didn't mind her calling him by the honorific. At times, he quite liked the sound of it on her lips. He hated it now.

"I came to you with the truth as soon as I could," she said demurely. "For our sake and for Pearl's. You always try to be just. And fair."

Fair. *Heaven and Earth.* Everyone in Pingkang knew he'd taken a liking to Song Yi. Even the proprietor of this teahouse probably knew it. Chen had spent half the night torn that Song Yi had a lover and wishing it was him instead. How was he supposed to be fair and just with that thought cooking inside his head? How could he properly handle this case?

Chen sank back in his seat, sighing sharply. "Is there anything else I need to know?"

Song Yi looked stricken and Chen knew immediately he would regret asking.

"Pearl is gone and it's my fault," Song Yi said miserably. "The man who was killed came to the courtesan house looking for me."

CHAPTER 5

*A*fter Li Chen left, Song Yi hurried back to the Heavenly Peaches where Mother and Old Auntie were waiting for her. They knew she had been talking to the magistrate. All she could tell them was to be prepared. And tell the truth before they were caught in more lies.

The next day came and went while she waited for constables to come storming in to arrest Mother. By that afternoon, no one had come. Instead, they received inquiries from former patrons. Would the House of Heavenly Peaches be open for business that night?

As soon as the doors opened, a horde of guests stepped through the threshold looking forward to wine and gossip. Within an hour, their parlors were full with callers, something the Heavenly Peaches hadn't seen in months.

Wine flowed like spring rain, and Song Yi plucked melody after melody from the strings of her zither. Without Pearl, there was only Song Yi and Sparrow to keep everyone entertained. Madame Shi painted on a smile and played hostess while Auntie kept busy in the kitchen.

Song Yi knew what had brought them in. By now

everyone had heard of the body found out in the alleyway. Scandal made for good drinking conversation. They were there to formulate theories and spin tales.

The dark stain of death hung over the house, even in the rose-gold light of the lanterns. Song Yi played the final notes of a dream-like song. Raindrops on bamboo leaves. As the sound faded, there was a pause where she listened for the sound of footsteps. For the pounding to come at their door. Li Chen had been adamant Mother would need to answer for what had happened.

Perhaps the magistrate wasn't as uncompromising as he appeared. Even something as wrenching as death could come and go unanswered. Much like the tragedy that had brought her to Changan so many years ago.

She began another song. If she continued to play, she wouldn't need to answer any questions. Halfway through the song, she saw Auntie waving urgently from the kitchen. Song Yi gestured toward Sparrow, but Auntie shook her head.

Song Yi let the last notes fade. Sparrow only knew a few songs on the pipa, but the girl would have to do. A party of bureaucrats up front showered Song Yi with praise when she stood. They tried to convince her to sit and drink with them. Song Yi smiled and promised she'd return, knowing they'd likely forget by the next round of drinks.

"The magistrate," Auntie croaked, gesturing toward the back door.

"Alone?"

Auntie nodded, which was some relief. Li Chen wasn't here to drag Mother away in the middle of the evening. She went to the door and took a deep breath before opening it.

Li Chen stood in the alleyway with his back to her, head bowed in thought. He turned to face her, immediately squaring his shoulders.

There was always a pause whenever he saw her. A

moment spared to take her in.

The magistrate's uniform had been replaced with a dark blue robe. Instead of the official headdress, his hair was tied back in a top knot. He looked more scholar than bureaucrat.

The lantern light from the street fell over half his face, casting the other half in shadow. "Am I less frightening this way, Miss Song Yi?"

"I never said I was frightened of you."

Song Yi stepped out into the alleyway, closing the sounds of drinking and laughter away behind her.

As he came closer, she could see the dark circles under his eyes, as if he hadn't slept. She'd barely been able to sleep either. Someone had died in her very own sitting room and then she'd made the decision to throw Mother and the rest of them to Li Chen's mercy.

She should be afraid of Li Chen. He held absolute authority over them. She'd thought in the teahouse, with his eyes burning into her, that he meant to use it. Here, the darkness chiseled away all those hard edges.

"I know you came to me because you trusted me," Chen said.

She tilted her gaze up to him. "They say you're incorruptible."

"Incorruptible," he echoed.

She couldn't tell if it was a question or a statement.

"When we were in your sitting room," he began finally. "You were trying to distract me from something."

Song Yi tensed. "You knew."

Li Chen sighed. "I knew. But it still worked."

Apparently it hadn't. She watched him with her heart pounding.

"I've been thinking over what you told me. Over everything." The line over his brow sharpened. "I consulted the Code."

"The Code?" she asked faintly.

"For legal matters. There are detailed regulations and rules of conduct—" He quieted, his expression growing more serious, if that was even possible. "It's a good thing that you came to me on your own. Before any formal charges were issued."

The blood drained from her face. *Formal charges*. Against Pearl? Against Mother? Against the entire house? She was certain Li Chen could see every emotion flickering across her face.

"Is anyone in the sitting room now?" he asked quietly.

She shook her head. They'd kept the guests out in the common rooms that night.

Chen directed her back inside with a nod and she had no choice but to obey. He followed behind her through the kitchen and then into the corridor toward her chamber. Sounds of music and conversation drifted to them from the main parlor.

She paused at the door. Since the incident, she could no longer bring herself to stay in these quarters. Instead she'd gone upstairs to the room Pearl had shared with Sparrow.

"It would have been easy to slip out unseen and out the back door," Chen remarked.

Her private quarters were indeed set apart from the main parlor. Song Yi entered and took a moment to light the lanterns from an oil lamp she'd retrieved from the kitchen. The room filled with a warm glow, illuminating the sitting area. She jumped at the sound of the door being pulled shut.

Li Chen had closed the door behind him. "Tell me where you found the broken porcelain."

He crouched beside her as she pointed beneath the padded chaise. He leaned in to inspect the area, his shoulder brushing against hers. Li Chen wasn't imposing in the same way his constable was. His presence had a different sort of

61

weight to it. A sort of dignity and solidness she usually found comforting, but these were very different circumstances.

"Mother said the furniture was thrown about when she came in."

"I will need to question Madame Shi directly," he said, and Song Yi fell silent, nodding. He proceeded to run his hands along the carved back of the chaise. "There's a crack."

She saw it as she peered closer. There was a thin line where the frame had split. Chen asked her if the crack was there before and she answered that it wasn't.

"If he was stabbed here," Chen murmured. "Then shoved against the seat. The porcelain piece would be dropped here."

He went through the motions as he recreated the events in his head. She tried to see what he was seeing and it sent a shudder down her spine.

"This is bothering you."

His remark surprised her. Li Chen was still looking at the seat and not at her.

"Not any more than knowing what happened."

He did turn to face her now. "I am relieved that you weren't here when this happened."

Song Yi started to tell him that she wished she had been. Maybe she could have stopped it, but that was foolish of her. She could have been the one who was missing instead of Pearl. Or worse.

"I need your assistance with something," Chen said, sitting on the bench and looking up at her.

How could he be so calm? He was right where the stranger would have been. She did notice a stiffness to his movements as he lowered himself back against the seat.

"Lean over me and put your hands here." He touched his hands to either side of his neck.

She did as he asked, positioning herself above him to place her hands lightly against his throat. Chen's eyes were fixed onto her. She could feel the muscles of his throat move against her fingers as he swallowed. Her heart hammered hard in her chest.

When he reached up to place his hands over hers, she jumped back.

"He was strangled?" she asked, aghast.

"It's a possibility."

He kept his gaze steady on her as he spoke, and she swallowed past the sudden dryness in her throat. This wasn't how she thought it would be. Their first touch.

Did magistrates train to remain calm in situations like this? The same way she trained to make playing an instrument seem effortless?

"I thought—I thought he was stabbed to death."

"The wound was a minor one."

Li Chen watched her closely now, looking as if he were sorting through the thoughts in his head.

"Pearl is the same size as you," he surmised.

"She's smaller."

"I don't know if she would have the strength to do this by herself," he reasoned. "Perhaps if the man was startled by getting stabbed. If he'd hit his head against this seat—I shouldn't alarm you with these details."

Song Yi didn't know if she wanted to know or be kept ignorant.

"You're handling this very well," he assured.

Well? She could feel her skin crawling. "You said it was a good thing that I came to you, Magistrate. What about the others?"

What about Mother?

He rose to his feet. Face-to-face like this he was a head taller than her. They had been in her quarters alone before, but she'd never worried about him making advances. A woman in the pleasure quarter could never be too careful and even the most civil of gentlemen could turn on a smile. Even though she knew this, she still allowed herself to let down her guard around Li Chen.

"If Pearl did do this, she had to have done it to protect herself," she insisted. "That would call for leniency, wouldn't it?"

He hesitated. "I can't be seen showing favor."

"Of course. I wouldn't ask that of you."

It was a softly spoken lie. She was asking it of him with every glance. Li Chen held their fate in his hands. She'd put their house at his mercy because she'd believed he would be merciful. But what he revealed next was a shock.

"I will no longer be overseeing this inquiry," Chen said. "I've asked another magistrate to take the case. Magistrate Yang Yue from the western circuit of the city."

"Why?"

He grew quiet. "You know why."

Her heart pounded. Li Chen was someone she knew and understood, at least in part. This Magistrate Yang Yue was a stranger to her.

"You'll be treated fairly," Chen promised. "I asked for leniency toward Madame Shi and for your house."

"Then I should thank you. Is there anything else?" she asked, looking about the sitting room.

There was more. She could see it in the tightening of his jaw, but Chen nodded. "That is all."

He departed as quietly as he had come. She saw him to the back door and watched him disappear into the darkness of the alleyway before closing the door. Immediately she sensed a presence behind her.

"You should have invited him to stay longer," Mother chided, pinning her with a knowing look.

"It wouldn't be fitting."

There was still an inquiry and a victim without a name. There was still a killer who needed to be brought to justice.

"Am I to be thrown into chains?" Mother asked. The casualness of her tone masked genuine concern.

"No. Not yet, at least."

"Good girl."

She glanced sideways at Mother and caught sight of a calculating look before her expression smoothed over once more. Song Yi had inherited so many of her own mannerisms from Madame Shi.

"He's handed the investigation over to Magistrate Yang Yue from the western section."

Mother snorted. "What kind of fool relinquishes such authority?"

Song Yi should be flattered. Apparently Li Chen didn't think he could remain objective around her. "He believes this is the proper way to seek justice."

"Some wrongs are never set right. You know this as well as I."

Madame Shi had purchased her from the procurer when she was still young and had treated her kindly. She'd taught Song Yi about music and poetry. Not as art forms, but how to use them to feed off of the scholar-gentry of the capital. Song Yi trusted her den mother, but she also knew there was a shrewdness and a hardness about Madame Shi that her birth mother had lacked.

"Perhaps we were wrong about you and the most honorable Li Chen." Mother's gaze narrowed onto the spot where he had stood not so long ago. "A magistrate might be a good friend to have after all."

Mother didn't seem worried at the prospect of facing the new magistrate. Why would she when she had effectively put Bao, then Pearl, and now Song Yi between herself and any threat of danger?

CHAPTER 6

"There have always been such tales of treachery in the pleasure quarter," Magistrate Yang Yue remarked. "A dangerous place, is it not?"

The meeting was held in Li Chen's office that morning. Chen sat across from Yang Yue as the elder official reviewed the case notes. Though they held equal positions, Yang was fifteen years his senior and well-established in Changan long before Chen had been appointed.

"The Heavenly Peaches is a moderately-sized house in the Pingkang ward," the magistrate continued.

"I've found most of the stories to be exaggerated," Chen replied evenly.

Yang frowned with the air of one who had seen it all. "It's to be expected from a place where scholars and courtesans would gather. The ladies of the House of Heavenly Peaches certainly proved to be clever storytellers."

Chen braced himself. "You've questioned them?"

"One after another," Magistrate Yang confirmed. "Not a word out of place."

The imperial city encompassed two separate county seats.

Yang served as county magistrate of the western half of the city, while Li Chen administered the eastern side. It wasn't uncommon for their offices to cross paths. Crimes committed in one half of the capital often involved tracking down perpetrators fleeing to the other side.

"It was quite intriguing, going through the indenture records. Have you seen them?" Magistrate Yang asked.

"Not as of yet."

Apparently, Yang had searched out additional documents. Chen didn't see the relevance, but he had to respect Yang's judgment.

"Each one reads like a tale in and of itself," Yang began, thumbing through the papers. "Madame Shi, formerly known as courtesan Yu Shi. Originally indentured to the House of Heavenly Peaches for three hundred taels of silver. Current owner. The girl they call Sparrow. Name is listed as one Ma Que. Orphan. Indentured at five years of age to Madame Shi for two hundred taels of silver. Currently not registered. Then there's courtesan Song Yi..."

Li Chen straightened. He forced his hands to unclench.

"The daughter of an unnamed noble family is what the records indicate. Claims to be officially registered as *yiji* and trained to play several instruments...indentured for *a thousand silver*," Yang remarked, eyebrows raised. "Impressive."

Li Chen shifted uncomfortably. It seemed inappropriate for Yang to appraise and evaluate Song Yi and her house in such a manner. Yang Yue was only doing his job, but Chen wondered if he was wrong to hand the fate of these women over to someone who would reduce them to numerical sums.

He forced the thought aside. He knew he'd made the right decision.

Yang Yue was demonstrating he was more than capable of objectivity, something Li Chen couldn't practice under the present circumstances.

"The missing one they call Pearl," Yang continued. "Registered as courtesan Zhu Ling. Daughter of a tenant farmer from Suzhou. Orphaned at four years of age and indentured to Madame Shi six years ago for five hundred taels of silver. Madame Shi may be able to file a claim of lost property. Enlisting a bounty hunter may be her best chance of finding the girl. As for the deceased, he remains unnamed."

"He asked for Miss Song Yi before he was killed," Chen said, keeping his tone neutral. "Could he have been someone from her family searching for her?"

Yang shook his head. "I suppose this is an area you're more familiar with, the Pingkang ward being in your county, but it's my understanding that no one ever comes for these lost daughters. The names they're registered under aren't even their real names. Their families have been erased."

Maybe the names were left out of the record books, but Song Yi had spoken to him of her family, hadn't she? They'd lived on the banks of the river. He seemed to recall her mentioning a brother once.

"It's the only thread we have to follow," Chen insisted. "You might be able to identify who this stranger was."

"Your report indicated that none of the women, including Song Yi, recognized him. If we are to believe their word—"

"I do believe it."

Yang paused. The older man regarded him for a moment before speaking. "I will certainly consider Magistrate Li's suggestion, but the courtesan has denied knowing the man and we have no family name to track down."

"If you need me to speak to her—"

Li Chen stopped himself. He was overstepping his bounds. The inquiry had been transitioned to Yang and it was no longer his place to chase down this information.

"I humbly apologize. You must have already considered this very thing."

Yang accepted the apology with grace. "It is possible that he was just an admirer who had heard of her. It happens more than you would think. I was besotted with a courtesan once."

Chen regarded the senior magistrate with surprise.

Yang Yue tapped his fingers lightly together, his expression taking on a faraway look. "I saw her on a barge on the river one evening during the mid-autumn festival. She was playing a song on the guzheng. The notes touched my soul in a way I hadn't felt in a long time." He chuckled, remembering. "It was long past my student days, but I still thought of the courtesan night and day. I sought out the banquets where she would be so I could hover at the edges of her presence. She was young, skin like new-fallen snow, while I was already seeing my first gray hairs. I had no hope of ever catching her attention, but I dreamed of her anyway." He shook his head, a faint glow lingering in his eyes. "She was known as Bright Jade. Such names they have!"

"Mingyu?" Chen asked. He knew of her. "She retired a few years ago and runs a teahouse in the northern section of Pingkang now."

"A teahouse?" Yang echoed curiously. Then the senior official sighed, laughing. "Better to let her memory remain in the clouds. It's good to fall hard like that at least once. So we old fools can dream and remember when we were young fools."

Chen suspected Yang's story was advice from an old fool to a young one indeed.

It was possible their traveler had ventured to the pleasure quarter after hearing some poem or romantic story about Song Yi. There were certainly enough poems from lovesick scholars floating around. He'd written a few himself, back in his academy days.

"What of Pearl?" he asked, steering his thoughts back to

the investigation. "My constables haven't been able to find any trace of her."

"She doesn't want to be found," the senior magistrate concluded.

Chen frowned. "What makes you say that?"

"The girl couldn't have gotten far. None of the gate records indicated anyone left that evening, and the guards have been vigilant about who they let in and out since the death was reported. Your constables haven't found her because she doesn't want to be found. She might still be hiding in Pingkang."

He considered it. "It's the most logical conclusion."

"They say the most likely explanation is usually the correct one. We have a murder. We have one man and one woman missing from among the suspects. The two of them lived under the same roof for a long time, yet were forbidden to be together. One night, the manservant strangles a rich patron and then the two of them run away together."

Li Chen frowned. Pearl and the manservant Bao...On the surface, it seemed obvious, but something didn't fit quite right.

"According to the courtesans, the servant Bao was still at the house when the man was found dead. He was the one who dragged the body outside," Chen recounted.

Yang Yue gave a nod. "A simple explanation, you see?"

How had he *not* seen it? Chen was indeed too close to this case. He knew Song Yi and Pearl and all of the ladies of the House of Heavenly Peaches. He'd already formed his own impressions and biases.

"What you're saying makes perfect sense," Chen murmured. "Yet the story almost fits too well."

"It's likely the girl and the servant will be found together," Yang proposed. "Only then will we know the true story. I wager we will discover the deceased was merely a victim of circumstance."

There was a constant flow of traders in and out of Changan. The dead man easily could be just another traveler who met his misfortune. Still, it bothered Li Chen that the body went unclaimed. In a way, it was even more important they identify the victim than catch the killers. Without a name, without family to claim him, the victim's soul would be left to wander as a ghost. It was the greatest injustice, an injustice to the spirit on top of his wrongful death. It was Li Chen's responsibility to right such wrongs and return the stranger to his family

"You needn't worry about such details any longer," Yang assured, as they concluded the meeting. "I hear you have a journey planned."

"Yes, to observe the anniversary of my father's passing." That had to be why this particular death bothered him so much. Every year, when the cold autumn wind began to blow, his mind would wander toward the past.

Yang bowed in farewell. "Have a good journey then, Magistrate Li."

Chen returned the bow. "Thank you for your assistance in this, Magistrate Yang. I can rest easy with this inquiry in your capable hands."

Chen spent the rest of the morning reviewing tax records from the merchants of the eastern market until he was interrupted by a hand depositing something directly onto his desk. He stared up at Constable Gao and then down at the pale circle of jade.

"Tell me you did not—"

"Goose fat," Gao assured him. "The ring was wedged onto his finger, but I finally managed to pull it off. Whoever killed him certainly wasn't doing it for profit. Between the belt ornament and the ring, there's enough to bribe at least a few judges."

Chen blinked up at the constable humorlessly before reaching to pick up the circle of jade. The carving formed a pattern of interwoven knots. A yellow vein ran through the milky jade.

"You should take this to Magistrate Yang. He's in charge of the inquiry now."

Gao grinned as Chen handed the ring back to him. "Not afraid I'll run off with it?"

"Not particularly. I happen to know you aren't easily swayed by money."

"Only the wealthy can be blinded by greed," Gao concurred. "We peasants wouldn't know what to do with so much money."

As Chen stared at the circle of jade in Gao's hands, a thought occurred to him.

"I almost overlooked that ring," he said aloud.

"This?" Gao held it up. "How can you overlook it? It's worth a fortune."

When Li Chen had first inspected the body in the alleyway, he had failed to notice the ring. It wasn't until he'd examined the body at the coffin house that he discovered it.

"When we brought the ladies of the Heavenly Peaches out to identify the victim, we only revealed his face," Chen recalled.

Gao's smile faded. "That's true. And you looked scandalized for even doing that much."

Because of etiquette and propriety.

"I'll take the ring to the magistrate," Chen volunteered.

After he made one other stop first.

～

THE TRIP through the city from the county seat to Pingkang took over an hour as Chen wove around afternoon crowds.

The root of the problem, he figured, was distance.

After a brief search in the alleyway, Gao and the other constable had taken care of moving the body onto the wagon. It had been promptly covered up so as to not offend any onlookers.

Death was taboo. Touching a corpse was relegated to members of the lower class. Even staring at a corpse for too long was considered ill fortune lest the spirit decide to latch on.

The victim had come looking for Song Yi. When she was asked to identify him, they had only shown her his face. Faces could change with time or appear unrecognizable in the utter stillness of death. *Song Yi had never seen the ring.*

There was a small chance she would recognize it. The white jade ring could be the link they needed to identify the victim.

Li Chen knocked on the door of the courtesan house.

"You again?" Old Auntie rasped as she opened the door.

He'd heard she'd been beautiful in her youth. He could still see traces of comeliness in the sleek shape of her cheekbones. Despite the stoop of her shoulders, Auntie held herself upright with a regal air. Chen imagined she was tired of a life of trivial pleasantries so she no longer cared to bother with them. Either that, or she really didn't like him.

Auntie waved him toward the market area with a bony hand.

The ward market consisted of a cluster of lanes near the center of the ward where sellers gathered with baskets of vegetables and cakes fried in oil. Wares were laid out directly on tattered mats on the ground for barter or purchase. It was a humble gathering place and it was also illegal. Marketplaces in the city were subject to regulation with prescribed hours of operation. Night markets such as this one, ghost markets as they were often called, were prohibited by law.

The milling crowd dispersed like ants fleeing a spill of water at the sight of his magistrate's uniform. Sellers quietly packed up their baskets and drifted every which way, which, if he thought of it, was the same strategy herds used to evade a predator.

The parting of the crowd made it easier for him to find Song Yi. She was dressed in a gray robe with her hair pulled up and swept over one shoulder, exposing the long line of her neck. The sight of her was a punch to his chest.

She was leaning over to talk to a man who squatted on the ground beside a basket. The seller had spotted Li Chen even if she hadn't. The man's eyes darted to him nervously while Song Yi went on, holding up two fingers to indicate something. The man nodded hastily, his eyes growing wide as Chen approached.

Realizing something was amiss, Song Yi looked over her shoulder and finally saw him. She turned back to the seller after no more than a second's glance.

"Miss Song Yi," he greeted.

"You look surprised every time you see me," she replied, not looking at him.

"Surprised?"

"Surprised," she repeated handing the seller a coin and receiving a bundle of charcoal which she stashed in her basket. The seller regarded Li Chen warily, but relaxed when it appeared the magistrate was not there to disband the unauthorized market.

Song Yi started down the lane. "You look startled, as if I'm never supposed to be anywhere but in the parlor pouring wine for you."

"That's—that's not true," he said stiffly. "It's a pleasant surprise. I was going to say you look well."

Song Yi flashed a smile at him that loosened the tight knot in his shoulders.

"Though wine does taste better when you pour it," he amended.

Now she was the one who looked surprised. "Magistrate, that almost has a ring of poetry to it."

He realized she was deliberately leading him away from the lanes of the market. Li Chen didn't care where she was going as long as she didn't mind if he followed. Somewhere, at the back of his mind, he reminded himself there was something he meant to ask her.

"I did write a poem about you once," he admitted instead.

"Oh, is it time for confessions now?"

"I'm a magistrate, confessions are what I'm trained for." He really should have been able to make a better go of that one.

Her easy laughter set everything right, sending him floating through the clouds. It felt good to exchange light banter with Song Yi. As if that in and of itself was a great accomplishment. She was here, listening to him. He'd do anything to keep this feeling alive.

"Here is my confession." She came to a halt and he did as well, ending up closer to her than he'd intended. She turned to him and rose onto her toes. Her voice dropped to a whisper. "I know why you always go to that teahouse."

Her lips brushed against his ear as she spoke, sending a shock of sensation down his spine.

They were back in the lane between the Heavenly Peaches and the aforementioned teahouse. The one where he would linger over a single cup until it grew cold, hoping to catch a glimpse of her across the road.

When he turned his head, she was right there. He wanted to kiss her so much that it hurt. Even though it was daylight and they were out in public.

He moved toward her, but the second's pause cost him. Song Yi took a step back.

"Your turn," she said faintly.

He could think of nothing. Or rather, he could think of no confession that wouldn't reveal everything. "What do you want to know?"

Her expression grew serious. "What happened between you and Lady Bai?"

Who in the heavens was Lady Bai?

Once again, his silence cost him. Song Yi took another step back. "You were certain the two of you would be betrothed. I thought that was why you stopped coming by, upstanding gentleman that you were."

Lady Bai. Bai Wei-ling. Constable Gao's wife. It took him longer to process than it should have.

"She...she preferred someone else," he stammered.

"The stone-broke constable?" Song Yi asked in disbelief.

"She was in love."

He and Lady Bai had decided to dissolve the betrothal before it ever happened.

"I suppose the wealthy can afford to believe in love," Song Yi scoffed.

"I'm not wealthy," he insisted.

She pressed her lips tight, saying nothing.

How could he get the Song Yi of a moment ago back? The one who was laughing and warm and seemed to like him?

"I stayed away because it was the proper thing to do," he tried to explain. "Out of respect for the Bai family."

And then he had stayed away from Song Yi because he had been away for so long he wasn't certain his presence was still welcome. And then he'd stayed away because nothing could ever come of what he felt for her.

"You are under no obligation to stay or to go," Song Yi interrupted while he struggled with his response. "Whenever you wish to return, the pleasure quarter is always here, unchanged regardless. But the proper thing to do is come calling in the evening, Magistrate Li." She took a deep breath and let it out slowly. "I'll play you a song and pour wine for you. I'll wear silk. I'll wear perfume. We'll talk of anything you like."

He had liked what they were talking about just now. Except for this part. The part where he seemed to have lost the entire thread of the conversation.

"I'm not here for any of that right now," he protested.

"Why did you come then?"

The ring. He fished for it in his belt and held it out to her. She stared at the pale circle of jade in confusion.

"This was on the stranger who came to the Heavenly Peaches. The one who asked for you. Do you recognize it?"

Confusion gave way to disbelief. Song Yi narrowed her eyes at him before coming in close to inspect the ring. She stepped away as soon as she was done.

"I don't recognize it."

Disbelief transformed into anger on her face.

"There is a proper place and time for everything, Magistrate. I would have thought you knew that," she said in a tone that reminded him the thinnest of blades were often the sharpest.

"I do." The air had become unseasonably warm. "I know it."

"Then call on me this evening, Li Chen. *Properly*."

She whipped around and disappeared into the courtesan house, dragging the door shut behind her.

CHAPTER 7

*T*he sun was down and the lanterns lit. Song Yi was wearing silk. She was wearing perfume. There was warmed wine on the table.

Mother tried to call her down to the parlor an hour earlier to play a song for some guests but she had refused. Sparrow was there in her stead, plucking out a tune on the pipa. Song Yi tapped out the rhythm with the tip of one finger. A missed note only increased her sense of impatience.

Li Chen finally arrived. Sparrow or Auntie must have known to direct him to her because he came up the stairs unannounced, looking dark-eyed, refined, with a hard set to his jaw that was nearly grim in its seriousness. His robe was the color of night without stars.

If he had arrived that evening in uniform under the guise of official business, she would have done something unspeakable for a courtesan. She would have turned him away and shut the door.

She could feel his eyes lingering on her as she rose from the seat. Layers of silk whispered against her ankles as she moved. She imagined she was water as Mother had taught her when she'd first come to the house. Water from the great river, flowing over rock and parting mountains.

The silk she wore wasn't for him. It was for her.

"You said you wrote a poem about me," she said, doing away with the usual courtesies.

"I did."

She held out her hand, heart pounding. "Where is it?"

His eyes never left hers. "I burned it."

"Then it never existed," she replied.

"It existed."

Li Chen had moved close enough that she could hear every draw of his breath.

They had spent so much of their time together at arm's length. Her pulse jumped to have him so near. He seemed suddenly taller, his features sharper.

When he reached for her, it was to thread a strand of her hair between his fingers. She shivered, despite the warmth gathering in her cheeks.

If nothing was to come of this. If this was just a whim of the moment, then there was no harm if he just forgot all of those manners. Just once. Her heart beat wildly and her lips parted with her next breath.

"Song Yi," he said her name once, perhaps seeking permission, and then he was kissing her. He halted only to breathe in deep, hands circling around her waist to pull her close, and then kissed her again.

She could learn a lot about someone from the large and small ways about them. But all the observation and study in the world could not predict this moment. Li Chen kissed with an intensity that swept her up. His mouth was warm as his lips caressed over hers. When he finally pulled away, they were both breathing hard.

Li Chen cradled her face in his hands to look at her, his pupils dark with wonder.

"Perhaps," he said finally, his chest rising and falling. "I preferred someone else as well."

Something took hold of her heart and squeezed. A wild light shone in his eyes. Here, with her skin flushed, it was easy to believe in impossible things. When she was close enough to feel the heat of his skin and the beating of his heart.

Li Chen was powerful and just and honorable and he wanted her, so maybe she was worthy of all those things. It was so easy to get caught up. An illusion can be seen from both sides of the mirror.

Her next words could gracefully ease him away or entangle them further. She had her kiss. It had been worth everything, every misstep and sacrifice.

"Magistrate," she began, her voice trembling.

He frowned. "It's strange to have you calling me that. Now."

A chorus of voices rose up from the main parlor then, and the voices were not in harmony.

Li Chen broke away and moved to the stairs in long strides. Song Yi hurried to catch up to him. Down in the parlor, Madame Shi could be heard making demands.

"Who are you? I am filing a complaint with the magistrate's office! The *real* magistrate."

Mother stood at the front doors, facing off against a group of men in constable uniforms armed with clubs. The head man held up a paper written in bold black characters. Song Yi spied the first two characters and her stomach sickened.

Injunction.

"What is this?" Chen demanded. His voice carried easily to every corner of the room. Everyone quieted as he stepped forward.

"All business at the House of Heavenly Peaches must

cease immediately, by order of Magistrate Yang of Changan county."

Song Yi went to stand beside Mother, who looked her over with a shrewd eye. She was no innocent maiden for her face to heat the way it did. She threw a dismissive look in answer to the question in Mother's eyes. *It was just a kiss*, she was trying to say.

They watched together as Li Chen read through the injunction with frown lines cutting deep into his brow.

"It's nighttime. The wards are closed," he argued with quiet forcefulness. "The injunction can start in the morning."

"The order is to take effect immediately," the constable declared.

He was a large man, as constables often were. A meaty hand rested against the hilt of his sword. Li Chen eyed him with steely resolve.

She tightened her arm around Mother's shoulders as they watched the standoff.

When Li Chen spoke again, he was loud enough for all to hear, "I will personally take up this matter with Magistrate Yang tomorrow."

Then, to the intruders, "Post your injunction."

Li Chen ordered the stables to saddle a horse for him and set out before the first light of dawn. He would need to travel the span of the imperial city in order to reach the western county seat. The sun had risen high by the time he crossed the county line. By the time he reached the yamen, the gates had just opened.

"Magistrate Li Chen to see Magistrate Yang Yue," he told the clerk who was surprised to see him arriving unannounced and unattended.

He didn't have to wait long. Yang called him into the study where Chen found the senior magistrate at a desk behind a tall stack of petitions very much like the stack that would be waiting for Chen when he returned to his office.

Yang rose to his feet and bowed at a respectable angle. "Magistrate Li," he greeted.

"Magistrate Yang." Li Chen's bow was slight to nonexistent.

"I believe I know why you're here," Yang replied sagely. "I tried to send a message to your office."

"Forgive my impertinence, but my office didn't receive any message. What was your reason for the injunction against the House of Heavenly Peaches?"

"I deemed it necessary," Yang replied calmly. "The inquiry is under my jurisdiction."

His pulse pounded. "There was no coordination with our constables—"

"Are the magistrate's objections due to the method of execution or to the judgment itself?" Yang asked coolly.

Chen was caught flat-footed. Yang Yue was the senior official between them.

"I wouldn't presume to question your judgment."

But that was exactly what he had done last night, what he was doing now. A magistrate's conduct should be scrutinized, but it was Chen who had handed control of the inquiry over to Yang Yue. He dug his nails into his palm in frustration.

"Magistrate Li, my constables reported you were present when they carried out the injunction, is this correct?"

Li Chen took a breath before nodding slowly. Last night, he had been seen first questioning and then ceding to Yang's authority in public.

The senior official bade him sit, which he did. Yang

folded his hands into his sleeves and regarded Chen with a knowing expression.

"At the risk of overstepping my bounds, did you not hand over this inquiry because of your close association with this very establishment?"

He swallowed forcibly. "That is correct."

"You showed great foresight in doing so, Magistrate Li. And great wisdom again last night by following the proper chain of authority."

His anger drained away to be replaced with shame. "I challenged your authority publicly, Magistrate Yang. I was out of line."

Yang dismissed the misstep with a wave. "The judgment was administered appropriately, in the end. For my part, I came to my decision after further review. Regretfully, I was unable to consult your office beforehand; however, the courtesan house transacts most of its business in the evenings. With the inquiry into a wrongful death still open, and given that the inhabitants of that house are under investigation, I deemed it inappropriate that they should be seen to profit off the scandal."

Heat rose up the back of his neck. "The magistrate is absolutely correct," he admitted humbly.

"The ladies of the house should recognize they have been treated with an exceedingly light hand in this case. They are fortunate to not be facing charges of murder as of yet."

The senior magistrate's last words hung ominously. Yang had not ordered Madame Shi imprisoned or issued an arrest warrant for Pearl. Though Yang had not discussed it with him directly, Li Chen knew the other magistrate was showing leniency for his sake.

Li Chen had lost sight of his duties. He'd handed his responsibilities over to Yang, and then had gone rushing into Song Yi's arms as if all the troubles could be swept aside.

"Magistrate Yang, I see that you have been protecting, not only the best interests of this city but my interests as well," Chen admitted.

"It is difficult to remove one's emotions entirely from one's duties, Magistrate Li. I was young once too."

The senior official was showing Chen more magnanimity than he deserved. He'd come here in a temper, expecting to cross swords with this man, but instead, Yang was taking the time to provide guidance and mentorship.

Guilt crashed over him. "Magistrate Yang, I was calling on one of the courtesans of the house last night. She and I... we have conversed several times over the past year."

Song Yi was clear of any suspicion. He'd transferred the case to Yang Yue, but there had to be some impropriety in engaging with someone so close to an investigation.

"Magistrate Li, there is no need to confess anything to me," Yang said kindly, more like an uncle than a colleague. "Though there is an injunction against the establishment, there is nothing to bar the courtesans from their trade. From what I understand, there are numerous banquets and functions within the city that require music and artistry."

Li Chen swallowed. Though that was good news for the courtesans of the Heavenly Peaches, it didn't address his concerns. He most certainly was not visiting Song Yi for her musical talent.

"Magistrate Yang, sir, I feel as if I can benefit greatly from your guidance on this matter." He stopped, clearing his throat anxiously. Maybe he was revealing too much. He certainly couldn't go asking the elder magistrate if he was breaking any laws by kissing Song Yi. Or, if the kissing itself wasn't an infraction—would doing more be allowable?

Yang could see the distress on Chen's face. "You do not have to ask for permission," Yang replied with amusement. "On a personal note, I would say this. A thousand silver is no mean amount. Certainly not on a magistrate's salary. But if you care for the young lady, it would be best to get her far away from Madame Shi and the House of Heavenly Peaches."

～

THROUGHOUT THE TWO-HOUR ride back to his offices and then for the rest of the day, Li Chen kept on hearing the senior magistrate's words.

You do not have to ask for permission.

What was he supposed to do then? Trust his own judgment? His *judgment* and every other part of him knew what it wanted. He desired Song Yi. He wanted whatever they had, this courtship, to go on. But he also knew, deep in his soul, that it was never about what he wanted.

He had duties and responsibilities and the honor of his family name to uphold. He needed to marry a suitable wife one day. He would seek promotion within the imperial bureaucracy. Those principles were not hinged on wants.

As much as Chen wanted to, he didn't go to Song Yi that night. He still ventured to Pingkang after sundown like a stubborn mule following the track of an overturned cart.

He considered going to the teahouse across the way to gaze at the courtesan house from afar, but that hideaway had been exposed. The House of Heavenly Peaches was also dark that night, closed by injunction.

Li Chen found himself sitting at one of the food stands in the unauthorized night market, huddled in his cloak with the hood pulled up, and a cold bowl of noodles in front of him. From there, he had a view of the glaring yellow injunction pasted over the doors.

Director Guan, who had been a mentor to Chen in his youth, had told him no one who wanted a brilliant career wanted to remain a magistrate. It was all responsibility with little power.

Li Chen sensed that truth keenly as he shivered there on the splintered bench.

The cold was coming in quickly this year. A sharp chill hung in the air. He was there for an hour before the doors of the shuttered house opened silently. Song Yi emerged carrying a bundle that must have contained her instrument. Little Sparrow trailed behind with her thin arms wrapped around a pipa.

Song Yi turned to say something to the girl. Her breath was visible in the air and the gossamer layers of silk draped around her, so alluring when she glided through banquet halls and parlors, suddenly appeared paper-thin. Chen was brought back to his academy days when he'd only dared to watch her from afar. He was no braver now despite his degrees and accolades and appointments.

He watched until the two ladies disappeared into the streets, moving on foot to whatever engagement they'd managed to secure. Had he given up his ability to protect them by recusing himself from the murder inquiry? It had been the proper thing to do, but did that make it the *right* decision?

Leaving the noodles uneaten, Li Chen rose to go. A cold breeze whipped through the lane like a slap across the face. He couldn't remove the injunction, but he could do something for Song Yi and the House of Heavenly Peaches. The inability to resolve the murder was his failing, not theirs.

CHAPTER 8

With their doors closed, Song Yi had become the sole earner for the house. Sparrow could provide accompaniment, but the girl wasn't yet registered as *yiji*, qualified to entertain on her own at official functions held by bureaucrats and government officials.

The week had been full of late night engagements playing autumn songs, love songs, battle songs, drinking songs. Sometimes Song Yi was half-asleep while her hands moved over the silk strings.

It seemed at least a little good fortune had come to her, because the engagements kept coming.

Their meals had shrunken to a bowl of thin rice porridge each. They ate the leaves for nourishment after drinking their tea. Sparrow would help carry her instruments to banquets and functions. While Song Yi played, the girl would sneak nuts and sweet meats from the tables for them to share. Some days, Song Yi would try to sleep in to get by with only one bowl of rice to tide her over for the evening, but Auntie and Mother insisted on spooning extra portions into her bowl.

"Scholars won't find you pretty if you get too skinny," Auntie said gruffly.

Song Yi also went out whenever they needed oil or rice or charcoal because she was able to get better prices. The sellers all liked her. Everyone liked her. She was so exhausted.

And Li Chen? He supposedly liked her too, yet was nowhere to be seen. *Typical.*

Song Yi hated to admit it, but she was too busy to think about him. Much.

She barely thought of Pearl either. They still didn't know where her courtesan-sister had gone. The prevailing theory was some illicit lover had done the deed. Fingers pointed at Bao, though Song Yi still couldn't believe it. Bao was fearsome looking, but docile in spirit. Auntie had taken him in from the streets years earlier.

Other theories surmised the killer was a nobleman and the county magistrates were covering it up. There was also the lone madman theory. Or ghosts. Or Constable Gao, though probably not Gao as he would have used a knife instead of strangling the man.

Moving around as much as she did, Song Yi tried to search for any news, but no one had seen Pearl. Song Yi hoped her little sister was safe. If she could ever spare a coin, she would remember to light incense in the temple and pray for Pearl's well-being.

The ugly yellow injunction was still pasted over their door eight days later when Mother called her into the parlor. She sat primly as Madame Shi straightened her shoulders dramatically and smoothed out her robe. Mother had decided to make a formal event of whatever this was.

"Song Yi, tell me. Are you besotted with Magistrate Li Chen?"

This again. "I have no illusions when it comes to the magistrate. You've taught me the danger of having unrealistic expectations, and I'm perfectly able to handle myself with him without getting too close."

Mother frowned. "Well, that's disappointing. You're going to have to work at being a little warmer when speaking to the magistrate. It's in his profession to weed out liars and false witnesses."

She stared at her den mother in confusion.

"Song Yi." Mother sighed. "My dear girl. You're going to have to convince him that you feel all the things you're certain you don't feel. It will make him more amenable to helping us."

"Li Chen won't remove the injunction, Mother. I know him."

Li Chen had started to defend them, only to bow down to official words written on paper. He was who he was. A man of rules and regulations. One kiss hardly changed that.

"This has only just begun. If this injunction remains, we'll need all the support we can get. Magistrate Li is our best chance right now."

"You and Auntie have always said that a magistrate was a poor choice of patron."

"We said that *this* magistrate was a poor choice. And most of that was because Magistrate Li was so reticent and cold in his affection toward you."

"He isn't cold—"

"You did kiss him the other night, didn't you?"

There was a flutter in her stomach. "Actually, he kissed me."

Mother's eyes sparkled. "Even better."

Song Yi wasn't nearly as thrilled as Mother. A suitor who kissed her senseless then disappeared like the morning fog was hardly a catch.

"I would do anything for you, Mother, but Li Chen hasn't called on us since he practically pasted that cursed banner on our door himself. I don't think he wants anything to do with us anymore. It wouldn't be good for his reputation."

"I thought the same, until this arrived."

Mother reached beneath her seat and brought up a basket. She set it on the table between them and lifted the silk cover to reveal four plump and golden persimmons.

Fruit? Song Yi raised her eyebrows at her den mother.

"Oh, and it also came with this," Mother added dramatically, producing a thin leaf of paper from her sleeve.

Song Yi unfolded the note and inspected the various seals and stamps affixed upon it. Flying money.

"An *insulting* amount," Madame Shi scoffed.

It wasn't an insult and they both knew it. Li Chen had sent a gift to their house without asking for any arrangement between them. Song Yi could see the thoughts weaving together in Madame Shi's head.

"No, Mother," Song Yi warned.

"We could use the money," Mother admitted. "The weather is getting colder and the silk and grain taxes will come due soon. I could have exchanged the note for silver, and we could have spent it to nothing within days."

Song Yi's heart broke as she watched the emotions flicker over Mother's face. She knew Madame Shi better than she had ever known her real mother. When her family had suffered tragedy, her birth mother had closed up and folded into herself. Madame Shi would never shut down like that. She always tried to appear poised and fearless, but Song Yi knew how much Madame Shi worried and fretted over the girls in the Heavenly Peaches.

"When did this arrive?" Song Yi asked quietly.

"Two days ago. I would have told you then, but I didn't know what we should do. This is a generous gift from the magistrate, but that's all it is, a single gift, when it could be transformed into something more."

Song Yi closed her eyes.

They weren't without options. If things got worse when winter came, they could go to their various patrons and suitors to ask for money, but then word would get out that they were begging. That would break the illusion of elegance and refinement. The scholar-gentry wanted to believe that the exchange between courtesan and suitor was one of genuine admiration. Their callers were utterly devoted, but only as long as the illusion held.

There were other possibilities. The parlors were sitting empty so the furniture could go. They could all sleep in the same room to conserve charcoal. There were more robes in the wardrobe that could be sold off, though Song Yi imagined many of those would go to the silk tax.

But once those things were gone. When they had no more lavish costumes to wear to engagements and the instruments were pawned, they'd have no livelihood left. They would have nothing left to trade but their bodies.

Then there was Li Chen, whom Mother wanted to hook like a fish. There were admirers Song Yi had felt something for in the past. A sense of warmth, a racing of her pulse. Once, when she was younger, she'd even allowed herself to hope. A courtesan could leave this life through marriage, but more often she left to become a concubine or a servant. Or she remained in the quarter like Old Auntie and Mother to bring in new girls.

With Li Chen, she wasn't so wide-eyed and innocent. But she had still hoped for some feeling to grow between them. He was reserved and earnest and tried so hard to only say things he truly meant. Li Chen was intelligent enough to understand the game but pure-hearted enough to forget. Their moments would have been selfish ones for her to hold close.

She opened her eyes to find Madame Shi watching her.

Mother had decided that Li Chen was someone they needed. It was a very different game, trying to use a patron's influence for their own benefit.

"I don't know if I can do this," Song Yi admitted, heart sinking. "But I will try."

"You're always such a good girl," Mother choked out.

Song Yi would do anything for their house. For Mother and Auntie and Sparrow. And Pearl too, if she would ever come home.

"Now, let's put all this away and prepare ourselves. No ugly sad faces." Mother brushed her fingers gently over Song Yi's cheek. "I would think you'd be happy to have some purpose after pining about all week."

"I'm not pining."

Maybe she had been pining over Li Chen. Why throw yourself into inadvisable love affairs if not for the oblivion of being mindlessly wretched over it?

At least Song Yi now knew she would see him again soon. Mother would make sure of that.

A wave of sadness overtook her as she looked at the paper money. It was too much to hope for a few passionate embraces, the warm touch of skin against naked skin, a string of sweet words to carry in her memories after everything was done.

Money shaped things into a form that was more predictable and far less pleasing. Money complicated matters, adding layer upon layer of unspoken need and meaning. Song Yi had been hoping, perhaps too innocently, that she and Li Chen wouldn't have to do that to each other.

CHAPTER 9

*T*he dreaded reply from Madame Shi came three days after Li Chen had sent the money. He tried to do it as discreetly and as quietly as possible. No need for thanks or any mention at all. Wasn't that the way things were supposed to be done? Everyone saves face. He was a firm supporter of unspoken rules as well as spoken ones.

He'd even stayed away from Song Yi so the money would be seen as a gift and not some form of payment, but now he was being formally invited to dinner.

"Constable, what does one do in this situation?" he asked Gao, hoping the constable's worldly knowledge of the routines of common men would be of use.

"I never get invited anywhere," was Gao's reply.

"What does your wife say?" Chen asked, grasping at the last fish in the pot.

The reply came back a day later. "She says to bring a gift of tea," Gao reported.

That wasn't the sort of advice he was looking for, but it wasn't bad advice.

The fog rolled in thick that night. The invitation had

directed him to a room at another courtesan house, the illustrious Lotus Palace rather than the House of Heavenly Peaches. The House of Heavenly Peaches was still shut down by official decree.

Li Chen entered the towering pagoda beneath the glow of what must have been a hundred lanterns swaying overhead. A line of ladies greeted him at the door.

"Magistrate. Honorable Magistrate Li," they sang. "Welcome!"

A quiet meeting in a closed and private room would be more preferable, now that he thought of it.

The sitting room was off to the side of the main parlor. The moment the door was opened, he saw Song Yi inside and his heart leapt.

Her sleeves were a subtle violet, her robe ivory. Amidst the clash of color in the Lotus Palace, the sight of her was a much-needed breath. Space and silence from the surrounding noise.

Song Yi smiled when she saw him. It was only a half-smile, uncertain and anxious, but still happy. Her smile conveyed so much of what he was feeling that he had to keep from rushing to her.

He should have thought more on what to say. Li Chen was usually more skilled with words, but those were words that had to do with procedures and judgments. If he could write a structured essay for the occasion, he'd fare much better.

Chen surged forward, deciding on something between an apology and a declaration of how difficult it had been to keep himself away from her. He stopped short when another voice rang out.

"Magistrate Li, we're so glad you've come!"

He turned haltingly, like a cart with a bad wheel.

"Madame Shi, I brought you tea." He bowed, presenting

the parcel with both hands. And then, "Miss Song Yi. Always a pleasure."

It was decidedly less grand than what he'd wanted to say.

Was that a spark of amusement in Song Yi's eyes?

The servants of the Lotus Palace took his cloak and guided him to his seat. He was positioned opposite Madame Shi and Song Yi at a square banquet table that was entirely too large for just the three of them. The servants of the Lotus Palace brought small dishes of cold pickles and bowls of clear soup with melon and greens.

It was clear that Madame Shi was to do most of the talking. She inquired about his health, the daily operations in the yamen, how the citizens of Pingkang praised the work he was doing, so much more aligned with the populace than the dear and dusty bureaucrat he had replaced.

"He spoke in this dialect. Three years in the circuit and we could barely understand him. Yet he loved to talk. So many evenings, I would just smile and nod at him."

Chen was smiling and nodding now. He stole a glance at Song Yi. Her lips were painted pink in a way he was certain he was meant to notice.

She ate in small, dainty bites while listening quietly to the conversation. His heart threatened to burst out of his chest.

There was a pause in the conversation as the servers moved among them to change out the plates.

"How are you?" he asked Song Yi in a low voice.

She regarded him through long lashes. "I'm well, Magistrate."

A frustratingly short answer, but it still felt good to hear her voice.

They continued on through the hot dishes, not speaking of anything relevant. Madame Shi kept the conversation flowing on neutral topics, like the accomplished hostess she was.

It wasn't until they were nearing the end of the night and Li Chen had convinced himself the whole evening was just a long way of showing their appreciation, when Madame Shi's smile faded and she grew serious.

"Magistrate Li, you have always been a welcome guest to our house."

"I have always been grateful for your hospitality."

"That last thing we would want to do is offend the magistrate."

The meal churned in his stomach. Offend?

"Our house has fallen on hard times. The magistrate must know we would never hold him to blame for our misfortunes."

"I will do my utmost to right such wrongs," he promised.

"Truly, we are undeserving of your generosity."

He frowned. Song Yi slid him a glance through her lashes and then stared down at the table. He stared at her. Madame Shi watched them both as she signaled someone with a flick of her fingers.

A server came in carrying a lacquered tray. The bank note he'd sent to Madame Shi lay prominently upon it. Dinner suddenly felt like a stone in his stomach.

"If my girls or I ever gave the impression that such payment was expected—"

"Please, Madam," he interrupted, mortified. "No apology necessary."

The tray with the money hovered luridly before him. Reaching up, Li Chen curled his fingers over the paper and attempted to tuck the money away with as much dignity as he could manage.

He was grateful for the silence that followed, as uncomfortable as it was. The servers had the wherewithal to pour more tea. He took a sip while Madame Shi remarked upon the quality.

The best quality, yes, he concurred.

"I hear that your family lives in Yu prefecture," Madame Shi said finally, searching for neutral territory. "Has it been long since you've returned?"

"Not at all, Madame," he replied quickly, hoping to put the prior conversation behind them. "I return to my family home at least once a year."

"Is it pleasant there in the autumn?"

"It's gray from the fog," he replied. "All spring and fall, I remember months would go by without a blue sky. There are days you can't even see five fingers in front of your face."

"Song Yi told us of the fog and the river." Madame Shi looked at Song Yi affectionately.

"That is correct. Miss Song Yi grew up in Yu prefecture as well."

It had been the topic of their early conversations.

"Very close to where your home is, I hear," Madame Shi went on, continuing to speak on Song Yi's behalf. "She was just telling me how homesick she's become lately. It has been a long time since Song Yi returned and we could never spare the time to go. However, with our house closed…"

Her voice trailed away tragically before she brought herself back. "With our doors temporarily shut, as you know, I wondered if Song Yi shouldn't use this time to go home and pay her respects to her ancestors."

Madame Shi looked at him expectantly and he had no choice but to say something, though he was uncertain of what was expected.

"I'm set to leave for Yuzhou in just a few days," he ventured.

Madame Shi pounced. "That would be perfect. I know my Song Yi would be safe with a magistrate."

Time alone with Song Yi. Was such a thing even possible?

"Little Sparrow can go as well," Madame Shi suggested. "She doesn't have much opportunity to leave the city."

"Miss Sparrow," he murmured, hesitating. There were practicalities to consider. "This trip is one I typically take alone…"

"A little music, a little poetry would make the time go by so much faster," Madame Shi pressed on. "When Minister Tan went to Hangzhou last year, he hired an entire troupe of performers. Remember, dear?"

A pause. Silence.

Chen looked to Song Yi, hoping for some kind of helpful hint.

"I remember," she echoed, her tone flat.

"So you needn't worry about impropriety or…" Madame Shi cast about aimlessly. "Or any sort of gossip."

"I want to help, Madame Shi, but I am going to see to family matters. My mother is awaiting my arrival. That certainly would not be a relaxing or pleasant journey for Miss Song Yi and Miss Sparrow. Perhaps at another time. The summer is much nicer in Yuzhou."

Madame Shi's eyes darted to Song Yi then back. "Oh, the magistrate can be assured my girls will not be any bother to him or his family. We would never impose. Song Yi would take her leave well before Li manor. Where was your home, dear? At the juncture of the Chang and Jialing river, right?"

"Umm, yes." Song Yi's gaze flickered toward him. "Jialing."

"Song Yi has relatives who will take her in."

"If that arrangement would be suitable to Miss Song Yi and Miss Sparrow," he replied.

"Yes, my girl is very happy for this chance to go home."

Song Yi played her fingertips along the edge of her teacup, biting down on her lip. She didn't want to go with him, he realized, his heart sinking. If he could just have a moment alone with her.

"This is a journey that has been delayed too long," Madame Shi pushed on. "With all the bad fortune we've had lately, I feel it's important that Song Yi go and make peace with her ancestors."

He wanted to retort that perhaps Madame Shi should consider making peace with her own ancestors. It wasn't Song Yi who had brought misfortune to the Heavenly Peaches.

Was that the real reason Madame Shi wanted to separate herself from Song Yi and Sparrow? Was she actually trying to protect them from the current scandal brewing in the quarter?

Li Chen could hear Magistrate Yang's advice to get Song Yi away from the courtesan house.

You don't need to ask for permission.

He tried again to catch Song Yi's attention, but she appeared to be lost in her own thoughts.

The engagement concluded shortly after with vague promises. His office would send word. Chen rose and politely said his farewells before leaving.

About twenty steps from the pavilion, the chilled air bit at him and he realized he'd left his cloak. He turned around to see Song Yi running toward him with a bundle in her hands, the ivory silk of her robe pale as evening jasmine. She looked like moonlight.

"You don't have to take me," she said in a rush as she halted before him. Color rose high on her cheeks.

"I don't mind."

"My ancestors don't care whether I pay my respects or not," she said with a bitterness that struck a chord in him. "And Sparrow and I can take care of ourselves if we really needed to go anywhere."

She thrust the cloak into his arms, her teeth chattering. He so wanted to enact some grand and highly improper gesture. Throw his cloak around her. Then what? Take her in his arms and warm her against him? Kiss her hard right there in the street beneath the lanterns?

"Maybe it wouldn't be a bad idea for you to come," he suggested. "Get away from the city for a while."

She looked up at him, waiting. His heart was pounding so hard he swore she could hear it.

"This case—"

"This case," she echoed blandly, her eyes darkening.

"Maybe there are answers in Yuzhou. Your relations there might know of something. Some information to lead us to who the stranger was."

He could feel her slipping away. Song Yi really didn't want to go with him. He could see it plainly in her eyes.

"My carriage will be leaving from the yamen in two days at the fifth hour, right after dawn," he offered. "If you're there, I would be truly happy to escort you. It's no trouble."

Song Yi nodded, but it was a nod of acknowledgment rather than affirmation. She hugged her arms closer to herself, shivering.

This case. He was such a fool.

"Go inside," he urged. "It's cold."

It was selfish to keep Song Yi out here just to have a few more moments with her. He waited until she had disappeared into the pavilion before throwing his cloak over his shoulders and heading home.

CHAPTER 10

Chen stared down at the cracked bowl of yellow millet and boiled radishes. His dinner this evening was night and day from the opulent fare he'd had at the Lotus Palace. The table was small, the wood bare. The packed dirt floor was tamped down with water to keep dust from rising.

He dipped his spoon and lifted a bite to his mouth, chewed methodically, then swallowed. It tasted like heaven and earth. Which meant the food tasted like air and dirt. He looked up to see Constable Gao's wife peering at him expectantly. Bai Wei-ling had her chin propped up onto her hands as she regarded him with an almost feline intensity.

He swallowed with some effort. "It's very good, Lady Bai."

Her phoenix eyes narrowed. "*That* is how they got you. They used your insistent politeness and utter sense of decorum against you."

"I don't know what you mean, Wei-wei," Gao said, taking a generous scoop of millet. "This is very good. Best I ever had."

Half of Gao's bowl was already gone. Chen took another

spoonful and washed the mouthful down with tea to keep from having to respond.

"They brought you to that glittering pavilion to distract you." She jabbed the air elegantly with an accusing finger. "Then they set you off-balance in any way they could. You were helpless in that situation, desperate to make things right. The only defense you had was to be exceedingly polite, saying yes to *everything*."

He glanced at Wei-wei over the rim of his tea bowl. If it was only bigger, he could hide behind it. She was waiting for him to say something.

"Politeness can win the confidence of kings," he ventured.

"Excessive politeness conceals deceit," she countered.

"One can forgive murder, but not impoliteness."

Gao looked back and forth between them. "Do you study these sayings?"

"Yes. We do." He had memorized over a thousand proverbs in the course of study. Lady Bai must have done so as well. Wei-ling came from a highly educated and well-respected family and, judging from the books stacked all throughout her home, she was no exception.

"We were almost wed to each other out of sheer politeness," she pointed out gently.

It was true. Both of their families had wanted it. It would have been an unobjectionable marriage and an advantageous match for him. He would have gone along with it and life would have been fine—as long as he didn't mind being the cause of Wei-ling's unhappiness for the rest of their lives. Chen knew what it was like living in a house where sadness had seeped into the walls.

Since they had mutually agreed to dissolve the betrothal, he had also discovered that Wei-wei could be a little sharp-tongued sometimes.

"Manners can be a very effective weapon," Gao agreed, finishing his bowl. "And you are being played, Li."

"I just agreed to do a small favor," he protested, his face heating. "I was already going that way. It's no extra effort to allow the ladies to come along."

If Song Yi actually showed up when it was time to go. They hadn't communicated since the Lotus Palace.

"You are being asked to escort a helpless courtesan traveling alone, unprotected. Because you're so *honorable*," Gao pointed out.

"Song Yi won't be alone. Sparrow is accompanying her."

"*Little* Sparrow?" Gao asked. "So the two of them can attack you from both sides."

"Like Liu Bei and Sun Quan," Wei-wei added emphatically.

Two legendary generals against a common enemy? That characterization was completely unfair.

"I'm not some pale-faced scholar," he pointed out. "I've seen things. I've done things. Once, I was trying this case in Hubei and the defendant ran at me with a knife made from an ox-bone. I had to fight him off with a ledger book. And the cases in this city aren't so straightforward. I've dealt with all manner of people."

Chen took another bite followed by an indignant swig of tea. In terms of politeness, he didn't want to be rude and not finish the millet, but maybe if he ate faster so the process could be over and done with, that would be an acceptable compromise.

"The important thing is you come back and deal with this other magistrate," Gao replied. "I don't trust him. He's ordered us to stop all inquiries into the courtesan house strangler case."

Wei-ling shuddered. "That description..."

"Wait," Chen interjected. "Did that command come through my office?"

"It came through the streets. A couple of yamen runners from the western circuit have been shoving our men aside and taking over patrols in the Pingkang li."

That was odd. The senior magistrate did have the authority to handle the case as he saw fit, but Yang hadn't said anything to him about this. It made sense he would want to work with his own constables and runners on the case. After his early missteps, Chen was reluctant to question Yang again.

Which was another example of him being a slave to politeness.

"I will certainly discuss this with the magistrate," Chen promised.

"And bring a ledger book on your trip in case Song Yi has an ox-bone hidden under her skirt," Gao suggested, grinning.

Chen gave him the eye.

"Don't torment him, Gao," Wei-ling murmured, spooning up a boiled radish. "The magistrate wants to be played."

SONG YI LOVED the full moon. Not because it was beautiful or ethereal or uplifting. She loved it because the literati in Changan loved it. There were full moon viewing parties where scholars and bureaucrats could drink and compose verses. She could recite five poems and play ten songs from memory inspired by the moon.

The full moon was good business. Song Yi was grateful the trip Li Chen had planned would be after the last full moon in autumn. She had a chance to earn a little more money before leaving.

The party was to be held in an outdoor pavilion in one of

the city parks. They started their preparations early. The walk there would take them over an hour, but they couldn't spare the coin to hire transport.

Sparrow was uncommonly excited. The appointments for the party had been set at the beginning of the month and both Song Yi and Pearl had been hired, but Pearl was obviously unavailable.

"There will be many entertainers there," Song Yi counseled as she helped Sparrow with her makeup. "Play softly if you're not sure of the song."

Sparrow was sixteen years of age. Pearl was three years older than that, but hopefully no one would notice and they would both be able to earn that evening.

Pearl hadn't made a name for herself yet and Song Yi had just begun taking her about for introductions. In a setting like this, all of the musicians would blend into an ensemble, like a flock of colorful birds. Sparrow wouldn't be expected to speak to anyone or carry on clever conversation. And if any of the other girls noticed their subterfuge, they'd stay quiet. No one would interfere with another girl's livelihood.

She outlined the shape of Sparrow's eyes, drawing out the winged edge and tapering it gracefully.

"Do I look older?" Sparrow asked.

"It will be dark," Song Yi replied. Sparrow pouted at her.

As she brushed rouge over Sparrow's cheekbones, the memory came of another "big sister" doing the same for her. It had been Ruozhong, who was hired into a governor's household several years ago.

It didn't escape Song Yi's notice that Pearl had come to misfortune while pretending to be her. Now Sparrow was pretending to be Pearl. They were all so interchangeable, one girl the same as any other.

"What's wrong, *a-chi*?" Sparrow asked.

"Nothing."

"You look sad. Is it the magistrate?"

Li Chen. He didn't think of her as any other girl. Li Chen hadn't been ever known to visit any other houses. Song Yi had checked.

It didn't mean anything. So she was a favorite. Regular patrons of the Pingkang li liked to single someone out. He could then show favor and be favored in kind. The game of romance required it.

"It isn't the magistrate," she replied, trying to banish away the gloom that clung to her. "There's more."

"Look at my girls," Mother cooed proudly. She came to stand beside them, peering over Song Yi's shoulder. "Make sure you're back in time to get to the magistrate's yamen tomorrow morning."

"Maybe we shouldn't go." Song Yi focused on drawing Sparrow's lips into the shape of two red peony petals. "The trip will take weeks and these are the last outdoor gatherings before the weather gets cold. A lot of bookings to miss."

"Opportunities to earn a coin here and there?" Madame argued. "That's like bailing out a boat one teacup at a time. We need to plant seeds, prepare for a harvest."

"There is no guarantee of anything if I go with Li Chen. He didn't offer to hire me for this trip. I know that's what you were hoping for, Mother, but Li Chen doesn't think like that."

"Well, maybe we need to think bigger too," Mother said, refusing to stand down. "That man couldn't take his eyes off you. Perhaps he wants more."

Li Chen did want more. Scholar Zhao and her other patrons had wanted her company only when the mood struck them. They wanted music, a sympathetic ear, the occasional mistress. The arrangements had at least kept them all fed and clothed.

Li Chen wanted the fantasy of romance and gallantry, but

once the illusion shattered, it would leave all of them with nothing. And her with a wounded heart.

But only if she got swept into the dream. Song Yi was too practical for that.

"Song Yi doesn't need me to go with her," Sparrow said. "I can stay here and play at small gatherings."

"Nonsense. I'm not sending Song Yi out on her own," Mother said grimly. "I made that mistake once before."

AN HOUR LATER, the sun was setting and they were walking out between the wards on the way to the party.

"How much longer?" Sparrow asked. She shifted the pipa in her arms. "This thing is getting heavy."

Song Yi was carrying her own instrument as well, but she had the advantage of having had to endure much worse for a booking. "At least it's not summertime. All of your makeup would be melted away by the time we arrived."

"Do you think Magistrate Li will be at the party?" Sparrow asked. They had already gone through most of the ward gossip. Time slowed down when there was no more gossip.

Song Yi kept on moving. "Magistrate Li will not be at the party."

"How do you know?"

"I always check who is on the guest list and he is not going to be there."

"Oh." Apparently, Sparrow was disappointed to miss out on the potential drama. "You do like him, right?"

Song Yi let out an impatient sigh and didn't reply.

"It's easier if you like them, isn't it?"

"It's easier if they're interesting to talk to."

"Will we be walking back afterward too?"

"Yes."

"The ward gates will be closed tonight," Sparrow remarked.

"We have a pass. The host issued all of the entertainers ward passes so we could return at night."

The reminder that Sparrow was doing something she'd never done before re-ignited the girl's excitement. Song Yi didn't tell her that it was going to be a very long night.

A while later, the city drums began to beat. They could hear the faint rumble coming from the signal towers in the outer wall.

A passing sedan came to a halt on the opposite side of the road.

"It's the magistrate!" Sparrow said excitedly.

Song Yi's pulse jumped, but it was only Magistrate Yang Yue. The one who'd issued the injunction against their house.

"Keep walking," she told Sparrow.

But the magistrate waved them over and as they were the only people on the road at that time, it was hard to ignore him.

"Miss Song Yi," he greeted. "Are you headed to the Pear Garden pavilion? Please do rest your feet and join me."

She wanted to refuse out of spite, but Sparrow's eyes widened hopefully.

"Thank you, Magistrate," Song Yi replied with excessive courtesy as they climbed into the sedan.

They rolled forward, the transport swaying over the pressed dirt road. The compartment was large enough to seat the three of them, yet the magistrate traveled alone. Perhaps Yang did so as a display of status, but it was also possible he had planned to intercept them all along.

"There are easier ways to set up an interrogation," she said coolly. "We cannot by law refuse your summons."

"You mistake my intentions. These questions are of a

personal nature. I realize you may not want them written into record, but they may prove useful for the inquiry. It is in your interests for the inquiry to be resolved as soon as possible, of course."

So the injunction against their house could be lifted.

"I'm willing to help in any way possible," she replied woodenly.

"Good. The record indicates that you came from a good family, left unnamed. It's not uncommon, leaving off a family name if it is no longer relevant or involves matters of a sensitive or damaging nature."

"My family is not important."

"Family is very important."

"I don't even remember it."

His eyes were like steel. "I don't believe that, Miss. There are a handful of wealthy families in the region where the Chang and Jialing rivers meet."

Her gaze darted to him. "How did you know that?"

Mother was the only person who knew anything of her past life. Except for Li Chen.

Magistrate Yang paused before continuing in the same calm tone. "It is possible to trace the family records. Which of those families suffered a misfortune about the time that you came to Changan. Which of those families had a daughter who is unaccounted for. But that will take time. It may be months before we find that information. It may be a year before we identify the man who was killed in your very house."

Sparrow gripped her instrument and looked to Song Yi with wide, frightened eyes. Song Yi wanted to reassure her. Men would promise things. They would threaten. They would offer protection. They would betray confidences. They would do it in this same civil tone.

The magistrate could have questioned Mother to find out

where Song Yi had come from. Or he could have simply gotten it from his esteemed colleague, Li Chen.

It had taken a long time to build her reputation. The process had started even before she'd ever come to the capital. The tragic nobleman's daughter, as the story went, written on the thinnest of paper.

"There's no need to search through any names," Song Yi admitted. "My family is none of those. I came from nothing."

Magistrate Yang fell silent, searching her gaze with the cold eyes of a bird of prey. There were men who prided themselves on being astute. Their eyes could see all. They could bend the will of men.

She'd once thought the truth had value. If any of the wealthy and influential scholar-gentlemen who frequented the pleasure quarter knew of her humble origins, she would be discarded.

But the truth was, these men really didn't care.

"My compliments, Miss Song Yi." Yang said finally. "You do a fine approximation of gentility. The posture, the diction. It's a very convincing picture. Even to a magistrate."

She thanked him calmly for the compliment. "It's not difficult when no one ever tries to look very far beneath the surface."

Why would the truth about any of their upbringings matter? The women of the Pingkang li were as real as the stories traded back and forth over wine.

CHAPTER 11

*L*i Chen was standing beside the carriage when Song Yi and Sparrow arrived. They had left with the ringing of the morning bell to travel by sedan chair. It would have been undignified to be seen arriving on foot. She had already suffered from being caught at such a disadvantage.

Li Chen appeared anxious before seeing them and relieved after. Even her jaded heart found it endearing. By the time he had straightened from his bow to greet them, all signs of nervousness had faded. She would have never known if she hadn't been watching with special care.

"Miss Song Yi. Miss Sparrow."

"Magistrate Li."

Song Yi kept her expression neutral. The glass surface of a peaceful lake. Hoard your smiles like coins, Mother had once told her.

The sun was rising behind him. Their belongings were few and soon after the attendant opened the carriage door for them to enter, they were on their way.

She and Sparrow seated themselves on one side while Li

Chen sat opposite facing them. It was as if they were sitting down for tea, though closer and more private as well enclosed as they were. Mother had been insistent about pressing this advantage.

"It will be three days from here to the ferry," Chen said to fill the silence.

"I've never been on a ferry," Sparrow piped up. "Or been away from the city for so long."

"There is poem about travel," Chen offered. "'The Hard Road'. *With sword drawn, I look anxiously in all directions.*"

Song Yi picked up the next lines. *"I want to cross the Yellow River, but ice blocks my way; I want to climb Mount Taihang, but snow fills the sky."*

"A great enterprise must find the right moment," Li Chen concluded.

"The poet Li Bai," she said. "A relation of yours?"

He smiled, more at ease now that they had found a familiar rhythm. "Perhaps distant cousins somewhere down the line."

She turned abruptly to Sparrow before she could dwell too long on the warm look in his eyes. "It's not difficult to carry on like this. One only has to learn a handful of poems from a handful of names. Then quote a line here or there and even someone as astute as the magistrate will heap praise on you and consider you accomplished." She looked back at him. "Except you were never fooled, were you, Magistrate?"

"You never tried to fool me."

"You knew better than to ask too many questions."

He was taken aback.

When they'd last met at the Lotus Palace with Mother intervening between them, she had been uncertain and tentative. Her defenses were fully in place now.

She wasn't angry at him for sharing information about her to the other magistrate. It made things clearer. To him, the magistrate, she was sometimes Song Yi, but she was always a supplicant, part of an inquest. To her, the courtesan, he was sometimes Li Chen, but he would always be a potential patron, a source of income and access.

After their exchange, the conversation waned. Sparrow's eyes drooped and she fell asleep on Song Yi's shoulder. Song Yi drifted off as well. She had had a very late night with only a few hours to sleep before the journey.

When she awoke, they were far outside of the city, with open road as far as the eye could see. Sparrow had laid her head on Song Yi's lap and continued to sleep. Chen was watching her, his eyes dark and troubled.

"Song Yi," he said gently. "We never speak in riddles like this."

"It was all riddles," she tossed back at him. "All strange tales and legends. I can quote Li Bai for four lines, but don't ask me the fifth."

"That doesn't matter. Those things are just—diversions. For people who have nothing else to talk about."

If he only knew. What had they ever talked about that either one of them truly valued?

"You'll know soon enough that I don't come from a wealthy family in Yu prefecture. I was never high-born and educated. Or you may know these things already, given how you and Magistrate Yang collaborate with one another."

He fell silent.

"I was afraid to associate with you when you first came to the Heavenly Peaches," she confessed, quieter now. "The brilliant young magistrate who could see through lies. He's from Yuzhou, same as you, everyone told me. I knew you would seek me out one day. The one person who would know that everything about me is a beautiful lie. A noble family's fall from grace. An innocent and talented orphan thrown into the cruel world."

"Then who was that man who came looking for you?"

"No one, because I'm no one," she said wearily. Song Yi wished she had an answer so the inquiry could be done. She wished she knew where Pearl had run to, but it wasn't because of her. "There's no one left to come looking for me. No wealthy relations searching for a lost daughter. Everything I am is an illusion and that stranger was an unfortunate soul who heard a good story one day."

She'd been so afraid to journey back to Yu prefecture. Back to the truth. She'd been afraid of having to lie and lie until it all fell apart. Now she'd just torn everything between them apart rather than wait. They were close enough to Changan for him to send them home.

When Li Chen said nothing more, Song Yi closed her eyes and pretended to sleep.

Li Chen secured them lodging at an inn for the night. Sparrow retired to the room they would share. Song Yi started after her when Li Chen stopped her, touching a hand gingerly to her sleeve. A deep line cut through his brow.

"Song Yi, I have always known."

She'd always suspected. Pretty lies are so pretty, and men wanted to believe.

"I always knew you had your secrets," he said, his voice low.

"But you went along."

His gaze pinned her in place. "You told me many truths as well."

Had she? She'd tried for so long to forget.

"Scholars are illusions too," he admitted sheepishly. "We love stories so much. Most of all, we love legends about ourselves."

Suddenly the hard line of his jaw relaxed into a grin. His long, serious face took on a boyish quality. Li Chen was different here, outside of the city. She found him most appealing when he was like this, not overthinking every word and action.

"I always knew your reputation was made up because mine is as well," he admitted.

"So you're not distantly related to the Emperor?" she challenged. "You didn't earn your imperial degree at only twenty years of age? And you don't come from an honorable and noble family?"

He waited for her to finish. When he answered, it was without a trace of humor.

"Only one of those things is true."

THE FIRST TIME Li Chen had come to call on her, they had spoken for hours.

After that, Li Chen limited his sittings to only an hour, but started visiting more frequently. Song Yi began watching the entrance, anticipating the moment the tall and serious magistrate would walk through the door.

They didn't duel over poetry or play parlor games. He wasn't there to have her play him songs so he could undress her with his eyes as so many proper gentlemen liked to do.

He said he liked her voice and he wanted to reminisce about Yuzhou and life along the shores of the river.

What do you two talk about? Mother had wondered.

I can barely remember, she'd say, downplaying the feeling growing inside her.

Rumors said he had passed the keju exams on his first try and was awarded the highest degree at only twenty. He shared the surname Li with the imperial family, leading to all sorts of other speculation about his fast rise through the bureaucracy. Certainly you had to know someone to be appointed to magistrate in the capital at merely twenty-six years old.

Courtesans knew an exorbitant amount of information about officials in Changan. Li Chen did not take bribes. Li Chen did not gamble. He didn't drink to excess or carry on with affairs. He was universally expected to be a paper magistrate. There was some sort of rivalry between two factions in the capital and it was said Li Chen was moved up to be exploited by one side or the other. Despite this, he'd managed to make a name for himself.

Song Yi had memories of reclining against silk cushions, listening to his voice, deep, steady, and impassioned. He told her of his youth, his first time in the capital to sit for the imperial exams. And she told him of her childhood, the fabricated one she had made up to become the celebrated courtesan she was. But there were times when she'd forget and the truth would slip out.

He had always kept her at arm's length then as well. What he didn't realize, what men never realized, was that she was learning more intimate secrets than the ones he revealed. She knew how he tried to keep up a strict countenance as the city magistrate. She could decipher the tiny lines that creased his brow when he encountered a topic he was resistant to discuss. He tried to be stingy with his expressions, but occasionally failed.

She had missed Li Chen when he'd stopped coming by.

He's forgotten you, she'd told herself, fighting the ache growing in her chest. And of course he'd forgotten. Li Chen was meant to be wed to someone like Lady Bai, whose family was so rich she could ignore the scandal of marrying below her station.

She missed Chen now, even though they had spent the day just beyond arm's reach. She lay in the darkness with Sparrow sleeping on the bamboo mat beside her. Outside of the city, the night was too quiet and she didn't know what to do with this sense of nothingness surrounding them.

Li Chen would *still* marry someone like Lady Bai. All Song Yi had was a small window of time to make her memories burn as bright as possible.

CHAPTER 12

*T*he next morning Song Yi and Sparrow awoke shortly after dawn to ready themselves. An attendant came by with a bowl of tea and steamed rice cake. By the time they emerged, the carriage was already hitched. Li Chen stood beside it, impeccable in his dark scholar's robe.

He first helped Sparrow and then Song Yi into the transport. The conversation from the end of the day remained with her. How much did she know of Li Chen beyond his reputation?

He was reserved, courteous, and careful with words. He was an accomplished scholar and official. They'd danced around their memories of Yuzhou and their very different lives. She suddenly wanted to know more.

"Magistrate, you need not keep so far away," she teased after he ducked inside the carriage.

He had positioned himself against the door with his shoulder practically pressed against the frame.

"That we women should accompany you on this trip is scandal enough," Song Yi continued. "Everyone will already assume that either you've seduced me—or I've seduced you."

Beside her, Little Sparrow suppressed a giggle.

The corner of Li Chen's mouth lifted. "It's not what *everyone* believes that concerns me. What is truth is still truth."

As if the arm's length between them in the tiny carriage made the difference between propriety and scandal.

"I forget. Rules are very much the magistrate's domain," she conceded airily.

Li Chen said nothing, but as the carriage started forward, the rigid set of his shoulders relaxed.

"Is Yu prefecture as big as Changan?" Little Sparrow asked him.

He chuckled. "No place is as big as the capital, Miss Sparrow."

The girl's cheeks flushed pink at being addressed so importantly. "What city were you born in, Magistrate?"

"It's called Shijing. My family has been there for many generations."

"What about you, *a-chí*?"

"I lived in the small village of Longyin. Our home was in the foothills, close to the riverbank."

Chen watched her, eyes lit with interest as she spoke. He was familiar with parts of the story, though she'd never given details. Sparrow knew nothing of this at all, despite them being sisters in the same courtesan house.

"That's not far from Shijing."

"You could have known each other as children," Sparrow proposed.

Song Yi smiled at her indulgently. "The magistrate's family is too wealthy and powerful to have moved in the same circles as mine."

"Not so wealthy," Li Chen said with the humility of those who lived in mansions. "Or powerful," he added quietly.

He glanced out of the window of the carriage, his jaw forming an unbreakable line.

The Li family was influential in the region and involved in land governance. They'd been there for generations and held positions and land and wealth that had been passed down from father to son.

Song Yi certainly hadn't known Li Chen. Her father had brought their family to Yu prefecture when she and her brother were children. They hadn't been there long, just a few years, before tragedy struck. It was long enough to learn a place, but not enough to truly know it.

She used to play along the banks of the same river where Li Chen had once sat and studied. Was it possible they had once stood on opposite sides of the river, unaware? He, a dark-eyed, studious boy with a book in his hand. She, wading into the shallows to try to catch fish with her bare hands and failing.

But it was a very long river.

Li Chen was telling Sparrow about the ferry and the villages they would see on their journey now. His gaze shifted to Song Yi as he spoke before returning to answer another question from Sparrow. Her pulse skipped every time their eyes met.

The carriage stopped by a roadside tavern for tea and something to eat, but it was only a brief pause before they were back on the road. Song Yi recited a famous poem about the meeting between a poet and a pipa-playing girl.

This was one of the reasons it was typical for noblemen to hire entertainers for long journeys. There was idle time to be filled. But Li Chen was too earnest. To him, the suggestion of a journey meant a journey. Or perhaps he was too frugal to pay for such pleasures.

Eventually, Sparrow dozed off again. The sway of the carriage tended to do that.

"You can recite more than four lines," Chen pointed out to her, speaking just above a whisper. He was sitting closer now, edging over bit by bit as the day progressed.

"As they say, even an old woman can understand that one," she said dismissively.

"I like the way you recite it."

Her heart beat faster. Chen knew this poem and likely a thousand others, but he didn't wrap his intentions in them as so many others tried to do. She was quite impervious to poetry, but not to Li Chen.

"I thought of you," she confessed. "All the time while you were away."

His breathing deepened at that. How many days had it been since they'd kissed? Li Chen wouldn't do anything so forward as that here, but he reached across the seat to brush his fingers against hers. She felt the touch all the way in her toes.

"Is this permitted?" she whispered.

"By whom?" His touch ran along her hand, grazing over each knuckle.

"By who else? You're the magistrate."

Little Sparrow stirred. Li Chen immediately withdrew and sat back, shoulders straight.

"How much longer?" Sparrow asked, yawning.

"Not long," he replied, looking only at Song Yi.

THE DAY PASSED QUICKLY. By sundown, they had secured lodging in a small port town along the river. Li Chen lingered in the courtyard, too aware of the room Song Yi had retired to. He didn't intend to do anything with that knowledge. He just simply could not make himself unaware.

He was staring at the door when Little Sparrow emerged from the room to move toward the gate.

"I have a message to post to the capital," the girl explained, waving a letter.

Li Chen blinked, embarrassed at being caught. "Allow me to escort you to the relay station."

He moved to go with her, but Sparrow raised a hand to wave him back. "Really, Magistrate, there's *no* need," the girl replied forcefully, her eyes narrowing on him before disappearing through the gate.

Li Chen was left alone in the courtyard with the truth that was still truth, even if he wouldn't speak it aloud. He looked toward the door, his chest growing tight.

He took one step, then another. The door opened after a soft rap.

"Magistrate," Song Yi greeted, a mild question in her eyes. The same luminous eyes that haunted his nights.

Li Chen started to speak, but his throat had gone dry. He thought wildly of telling her he was there to seduce, or to be seduced. But he didn't need to say anything.

Song Yi's expression softened as she reached for him. Her graceful fingers curled over the neck of his robe to draw him forward, and he closed the final distance between them to take her into his arms.

Her lips were soft. So warm. Song Yi tasted of tea and clove and his heart had never beaten so hard. He pressed against her mouth hungrily, his movements growing rough in his eagerness.

She was the one who remembered to close the door. Who drew him into the chamber. She showed more skill than he did when she pressed a kiss to his lips. Because there had been others, came the distant, unbidden thought. All thoughts swept away as his tongue found hers. He pulled her tighter and Song Yi pressed against him, arms encircling his shoulders, soft curves fitted to him.

There wasn't a proper bed in the chamber, just a sleeping mat woven from bamboo. As he lowered her to it, Chen tried to support her weight in his arms. Song Yi looked up at him as her hands stole to his belt. His pulse surged as she undid the clasps.

He took over, pulling the belt off and opening his robe, breath ragged. Then he reached for her. He shifted through layer upon layer of silk until Song Yi's hands joined his, pulling up the edge of her skirt for him. His hands finally found the smooth curve of her thigh. So much bare skin. He was hard, his body straining.

The crudeness of the moment struck him as he pushed up the volume of silk and angled her hips. He positioned himself over her and his heart pounded. So much restless motion. His fingers, thick and searching, slid over slick flesh and then still as he finally sank into her.

There was nothing else like it. He closed his eyes, overwhelmed.

Song Yi gave a soft gasp as he eased deep. Heat and searing pleasure gripped him. Vaguely, he felt her arms around him. Her legs around him. He thrust, then withdrew, each movement heightening the pleasure until every muscle in his body locked and release came.

"Darling…"

A gentle voice came to him in the darkness. Song Yi had never called him that before and there was a thrilling strangeness to it. He supposed it made more sense than calling him magistrate.

He'd closed his eyes as the moment swept him and opened them now. Song Yi's cheeks were flushed and her lips pink. He didn't know how much time had passed, but he sensed it was mere moments.

"Am I too heavy?" he asked, which was apparently what decades of study and a thousand books were able to inspire at this time.

His voice sounded thick and rough. She regarded him with a heavy-lidded, indulgent look. "No. Not too heavy."

He lifted himself onto his elbows. His body, tense and straining just moments earlier, was now lax and boneless. It was the feeling of being drunk, but with the best of wines. Song Yi was crushed beneath him, but he didn't want to let go yet.

The aftermath of coupling was as absurd as it was profane. They were half-dressed, clothes disheveled and hanging open. Their bodies remained intimately pressed together. Even in the aftermath, he couldn't yet bring himself to pull away.

"What is it?" she asked, watching his expression.

"This wasn't as I intended."

"Oh?" She seemed faintly amused.

His frown deepened. "I was supposed to woo you first."

Song Yi looked up at him and something shifted in her gaze. It was a measuring look, one that caused his heart to beat faster. What did she see when she looked at him like that?

Her fingertips rested against his cheek. "You can woo me now."

~

CHEN DID his best to woo Song Yi.

"You're beautiful," he told her, touching his lips to her neck, then the curve of her ear. "And kind. And caring of others. Those aren't illusions."

He lifted his head to look at her and found Song Yi

watching him in that careful way of hers. But the watchful look dissolved immediately into one more pleasing.

"You must be used to compliments," he said.

"Not at all," she replied with a smile that hooked into him. "Tell me more."

His next ones were new, at least from him. He hadn't known before how soft her skin would feel. He kissed along the line of her shoulder. Or how her embrace was like the warmest of summers. She laughed at that and he found himself grinning at his own expense. Song Yi's laughter was never meant to wound.

"My talents never tended toward poetry," he admitted.

He kissed her forehead, the bridge of her gracefully curved nose, her eyelids. Confessed to her how long and how often he'd dreamed of doing exactly that.

"Why then did you make me wait all night last night?" she scolded.

Song Yi. Waiting for him. His heart pounded.

"I didn't want to overstep my bounds."

"Because honorable Li Chen and the *rules*," she said silkily, reaching up to finish removing his robe. He'd failed to do more than loosen it in his haste earlier.

"Yes, rules," he agreed, finding his voice hoarse when he spoke. Her hands were moving down his back. "I did promise Madame Shi to escort you."

"And you really, truly did not think this is what she meant?" Her hands had reached his waist and moved around to the flat of his stomach, trailing heat in their wake. He longed for her to move lower but didn't mind too much when her touch traveled up over his chest. Song Yi could do anything she wanted with him at the moment.

"I had an idea," he said honestly. "But it wasn't exactly certain."

"That's what this business of the clouds and rain will do. Make everything certain, and yet uncertain all at once."

Chen swallowed hard. Her fingers traveled down his body again. His organ hardened before she ever reached him, but when Song Yi took him in her perfect hands, his flesh became engorged beyond belief. Desire flooded hot into his veins.

"Not yet," he said.

A look of surprise flickered across Song Yi's eyes as he gently pushed her hands away. He was determined to take things slowly this time.

He found the various ties and knots that held those mystical layers of silk onto her and pulled them away until she was bared beneath him. He drank in the sight of her. So many secrets revealed at once. Graceful shapes and curves. The shock of dark hair at the apex of her thighs.

Once again, she was the one who guided him to her, her delicate fingers circling his wrists to place his hands onto her. He explored all the places where his eyes had lingered. The shape of her breasts, the slope of her stomach.

At first, she watched his face, her eyes darkening as her breath quickened. Then when his hand slipped between her legs, her eyes closed as her head tipped back, as if focusing on the sensation. Her lips parted with the first intimate touch against her sex. There was a soft, hidden pearl beneath the delicate folds. He found it, found her with his fingers brushing lightly, and watched the play of emotions across her face.

Beautiful.

Song Yi's expressions were always schooled, practiced, perfected. He knew this, it was in his profession to read these things and he appreciated her artistry in it. Cherished the moments of surprise when he caught her off guard. But all of that artifice disappeared now. Her back arched, her mouth opened, her breathing became labored. Gone was all the prettiness and perfection. Her expression became raw and strained. Her hips churned restlessly as she raised them to seek more of his touch.

Had he complimented her for being caring? He loved this even more, when she was greedy and demanding.

And he was the one doing this to her. He could do this forever.

Her eyes opened. She reached up and dragged his mouth to hers as she strained and arched against him, flooding his fingers. Her cries of pleasure were swallowed in their kiss.

Patience spent, Chen positioned himself and sank deep, knowing this time where to find her. And where to lose himself. Song Yi's body tensed at his entry with a sharp cry that sounded like one of pain. Her flesh was swollen, tight, and throbbing around him. Her nails dug into his shoulder, but she pushed her tongue into his mouth.

It was impossible to stay in this moment. The pleasure was too intense. Several thrusts and he was lost in it.

Afterward, he was suddenly as tired as he'd ever been. Chen rolled onto his side and his head sank onto Song Yi's shoulder. He had just enough left to kiss the side of her neck before he collapsed into dead weight.

She laughed softly, her fingers stroking the back of his neck as he drifted off. He slept, but not for long.

CHAPTER 13

*T*hey reached the river late the next morning. Li Chen went to secure the ferry while Song Yi and Little Sparrow waited by the bank. Song Yi's attention drifted to Li Chen and the confident way he moved along the dock.

She'd never thought of him as particularly tall or imposing, but he certainly had a presence about him. Even when he wasn't wearing a magistrate's uniform, everyone along the dock sensed he was somebody. It wasn't so much command or authority as it was a quiet sort of conviction.

"You *do* like him," Sparrow remarked soundly.

Song Yi looked over at the girl and smiled. The start of an affair was always the best time, full of wonder and promise. All the usual routines, sleep, food, even conversation became secondary. She and Chen had barely slept last night.

"Do you know they used to call him *daoshi?*" Sparrow said.

"That's an odd nickname."

"I heard it from the girls at the Lotus Palace. They think

it's because he was like a monk. You probably know the answer to that."

"Sparrow," Song-Yi chided beneath her breath.

She couldn't fault Little Sparrow. The girl was curious. What was a big sister for, if not guiding the younger ones through complicated matters like the dance between men and women?

Little Sparrow wasn't ignorant of what happened in the bedchamber. The girl had known to retire quietly to the second room as to not disturb Song Yi and her newfound lover.

A lover who she would say was far from austere and moralistic.

Chen was making arrangements with the ferryman. His gaze strayed momentarily to her and she rewarded him with a smile. It was enough to make his chest puff out just a bit more, his head lift higher. It was good of him to notice.

When he had first come to the county seat, people had said the new magistrate was timid. He was youthful and seemed to prefer the company of fearsome constables to make up for a lack of presence.

As soon as she'd met him, she knew the rumors were untrue. Chen wasn't timid; rather he was reserved. Careful in thought and action.

Chen finished his negotiations with the ferryman and beckoned the carriage-driver over to transfer their belongings to the riverboat.

He came to stand beside her as the driver loaded the ferry.

"It will be much faster by boat," he said. "We'll be there in a week."

"Last night, I wished that this journey would go on forever."

They had been naked in each other's arms, warm in the

first flush of discovering one another. These were sweet words to say, but they were also true.

"I feel the same," he confessed quietly.

His fingers twined through hers beneath the cover of her sleeve. For a moment, the rest of the world faded away.

Then came the guilt. Song Yi had voiced her concerns about leaving Changan, but she'd also longed to be free of the weight of the house for just a little while. Over the last week, she had played banquet after banquet with hardly any sleep.

They hadn't found Pearl, and Mother was already acting as if Pearl wasn't just missing. She was acting as if Pearl would never come back to them.

If she asked Li Chen about Pearl, would he see such involvement as interfering with the case?

Maybe it was true that Pearl didn't want to be found. If she came back, she would face the tribunal for the killing. Maybe she had indeed run away to lose herself in the arms of a lover for as long as she could before the consequences caught up to her.

The ferry was ready and Chen stepped onto it first before extending a hand to help Little Sparrow. Then he reached out to her.

Song Yi paused on the bank. A look of concern flickered across his face before she finally took his hand. Their touch lingered for a moment longer, his fingers sliding across her palm in a hidden kiss.

The boat swayed beneath her feet. For the first time in fourteen years, she was back on this river.

"Miss Song Yi, are you alright?"

She was Miss Song Yi again out in the daylight, but she alone could hear the catch in his breath as he said her name.

She would think only of him and not where the ferry was taking them.

"I'm fine, Magistrate."

There was no privacy out on the water to do or say much more, but the moment the ferry embanked that evening and they retired to their quarters, she was in his arms. Her robe was nearly removed before they reached the mat. Li Chen was a quick study with deft hands.

He parted her legs, finding her already wet. Then he was inside her, hard and unyielding. His mouth crushed to hers.

He groaned and kissed her harder as she clenched around him. He rutted harder into her as well, his hips thrusting relentlessly toward release. She was there with him. Throbbing and undone.

Afterward, he rolled onto his back and pulled her on top of him.

"This room is awful," he said, looking about at bare walls, chest heaving.

She bit his neck. "It's perfect."

The second time was slower.

"This?" he asked, caressing.

"Mmm," she murmured, nodding.

"This?" he'd ask again after more exploration.

"Yes," she would tell him. Then again, *yes* as he explored her with his hands and his lips. Li Chen had a delightful scholar's mind in the bedchamber. She recoiled, giggling as he ran a finger along her instep.

"No?" he asked.

"Sometimes," she relented.

He planted a kiss on her inner thigh. "This?"

"Yes," she agreed, her heart racing.

His breath was warm against her skin. "This."

His voice was barely audible, but she could *feel* the words. She murmured her assent and then her head fell back and she could say nothing. He parted her with gentle fingers and then his mouth was on her, hot and wet. His tongue caressing deeply.

Always, she wanted to weep. Her eyes closed so she could think of nothing else. She came with his mouth on her and it was like they said. Clouds and rain. Lightning.

"When it's dark like this, I wonder if you know it's me," Chen said.

He was inside her once more, thrusting slowly. So much time had passed, yet none at all. Lovers' time. She was drowsy, her body sore from their activities, but she didn't want to stop.

It was the first vulnerable thing he had said.

"It's always you," she whispered, not sure if it was what she meant to say. "For a long time now, it's been you."

There was a danger to talking during sex as she was learning Li Chen sometimes liked to do. One became daring during the act. One could also become very fearful.

He kissed her, his hands threading into her hair.

She didn't know if they finished that time. She fell asleep with Chen still inside her, around her. Surrounded by the scent of sweat and skin.

SONG YI REQUIRED Sparrow the next morning to help her re-pin her hair. Perhaps Mother had thought of these practical matters in sending Sparrow along with her.

She sat while the girl combed and parted her hair. "How does he like you to wear it?" Sparrow asked.

"I don't believe the magistrate gives much thought to that."

He had certainly undone all of her elaborate work last night with hardly a pause.

"Nothing too complicated," Song Yi added as an afterthought, her pulse skipping from just the hint of what the next night might bring.

"What is he like, *a-chî*?" the girl asked curiously while she braided and looped.

"A courtesan must exercise discretion. How else can she be trusted with secrets?"

"But not to her sisters!" Sparrow protested.

That might have been true in the past, but Song Yi wanted this new spark, this tiny promise of what could be for herself alone.

If Li Chen had been waiting impatiently for them, he didn't show it. He stood on the bank. He'd managed to fix his appearance without assistance. His hair was neatly back in its top-knot, his robe smooth and impeccable. His expression brightened as he saw her, with no sign of any long nights with little sleep.

"There's a story," she began as they embarked. "Of a scholar who went to sleep at night and faced all manner of ghosts and demons in his dreams. Yet each day he woke up without any sign on him that there had been any turmoil."

"Demons?" he questioned.

"Do you not require sleep, Magistrate?" Song Yi cast a meaningful glance at Li Chen which made him blush.

"It must be a habit from my academy days."

"I hear they called you *daoshi*," Sparrow teased, enjoying his struggle.

For a moment, Chen appeared startled. Then he burst out laughing. "I suppose they did."

The laughter changed his face. The deep, serious lines eased away and his eyes were alight. There was a boyish quality to him Song Yi had never seen before.

Li Chen's smile actually made him quite handsome.

"Was it because you were so austere and disciplined?"

"I believe it was because they thought I was a know-it-all," he replied. "Which wasn't true. If I knew everything, I wouldn't have had to study all the time."

He was relaxing into the story now. "Did you know, Miss Sparrow, when I was younger and forgot my lessons, I would be punished."

The girl's eyes grew wide. "Punished?"

"With a willow switch. Smack across my hand."

"Perhaps we should try that method with Sparrow when she plays a bad note," Song Yi remarked.

"*A-chi!*" Sparrow wailed, affronted.

A ball of warmth grew inside Song Yi's chest. He was being so wonderful indulging Little Sparrow.

"You must have graduated first in your class, Magistrate, studying so hard," Sparrow pressed.

Song Yi shot her courtesan-sister a look which Sparrow, of course, ignored.

"Not first, Miss Sparrow. It was a challenging exam that year."

"Seventh," Song Yi chimed in. "Among all the degrees conferred in that period. And at only twenty years of age. All of Pingkang was delighted with him."

Chen's face grew even redder, but there was a glow in his eyes. Of course, he was pleased. All men liked to be flattered.

"I didn't realize you would have known anything of me, back then," he said quietly to her when it was just the two of them at the prow.

Song Yi looked ahead down the endless waterway. The river received its simple name from the distance it spanned, flowing through valleys and forests. Chang Jiang, the Long River.

"After the degree holders are named, that's all anyone talks about in Pingkang for months," she said airily.

The courtesans cared about the examinations because the scholars who sought their company cared about it. It was a courtesan's trade to validate what her patrons wished validated.

"Everyone was quite impressed. Someone so young, passing on his very first try."

Song Yi played off her knowledge of Li Chen as part of general parlor gossip. She feared he was gaining too much of an advantage already without knowing how much he was becoming a part of her awareness. Her world. She didn't let many into her circle.

It didn't appear that Chen was fooled. He touched her lightly against the small of her back. A daring touch for him, out in daylight, with the ferryman and Sparrow not so far away.

"I knew of you then as well," he said, so low that only she could hear.

SONG YI DRIFTED through the next days as if in a dream. The ferry traveled down the river during the day and sometimes through the night as well. When there was nowhere to stop for the evening, they would remain on the water, sleeping huddled inside the small cabin while the vessel banked along the shore.

During the day, they filled the time with stories and songs and poems. Li Chen was better than a book of tales. He'd traveled to different provinces and solved all manner of cases. The many disputes and quarrels within the capital itself yielded enough stories for any journey.

Song Yi was able to teach Sparrow new songs. The girl's memory was poor for recitation, she was easily distracted, but her playing was progressing well and Li Chen was a receptive audience. Sparrow's conversation could be blunt and impulsive at times, but Chen was always patient with her. He laughed whenever the girl said something outrageous.

That was the art of it. Many topics, even taboo ones, could be forgiven if a courtesan was in someone's good graces. The trick was to find the proper balance—Song Yi had to remind herself more than once that this journey wasn't for leisure.

It was her responsibility to instruct Sparrow now that Pearl was gone. It was her responsibility to mediate the interaction with Li Chen. It was her responsibility to ensure that they establish a beneficial connection to the magistrate. It was fine that he know of it; Li Chen was too intelligent not to understand. At the same time, there had to be enough mystery and artfulness to make it not so cold of an exchange.

If they had an examination for the skills required to be courtesan, she imagined it would be more difficult to pass than the keju.

As the ferry traveled closer to Yu prefecture, Song Yi braced for the past to come back to her. Hadn't it been waiting there all this time like a stray animal, abandoned and hungry? But for now, the river remained just a river. And she had Li Chen to distract her.

On the nights when they were able to find an inn, he would take her in his arms the moment they were beyond closed doors.

"I missed you," he'd whisper, even though they spent their days practically within arm's reach.

That was new love. Hungry and impatient.

Some of the restlessness had faded. They were becoming more comfortable with one another. Secure that they would have more nights, more embraces.

She lay nestled against Chen afterward, head over his chest while her eyes drifted closed. The cold ghosts of memory couldn't come for her while he was there. A slow song came from the next room.

"Is that Sparrow?" he asked, his voice rumbling low beneath her ear.

"She's practicing."

He was silent for a moment. "If we can hear her, she can probably hear…"

Song Yi laughed at that. "Little Sparrow is well aware of what goes on when you pull me into your room."

He'd done exactly that this evening, reaching for her because they could not get into the room quick enough.

"I realize that," he said stiffly.

It was one of his endearing contrasts. So daring and uninhibited in the bedchamber, but so reserved when it came to public matters. She told him that.

"I don't believe you ever composed a poem about me," she teased, her fingertip drawing a wayward pattern over his chest.

"I did," he insisted. His hand stole possessively around her waist. "The very first time I saw you. You came through a curtain with red flowers in your hair and it was like a lightning strike. I went back to my rooms and wrote a poem titled, 'A Red Blossom in Winter.' That's how lovesick I was. Then I was so ashamed that I burned it to ash."

"After Guan's banquet?"

She couldn't remember ever seeing a more serious expression than the one Li Chen had worn at that banquet. The young new magistrate put in charge of the largest county in the empire.

"No, not then. The *first* time I saw you. You were playing the pipa at a winter festival. There was snow outside and the plum blossoms were in bloom. I was still studying for the examinations."

"The examinations…you were only twenty," she marveled.

"That seems so young now. I knew nothing then," he said, the seriousness falling back over him like a dark veil.

Song Yi would have been seventeen. She had already lived in Pingkang for five years. She'd already had her first patron. Come and gone. And her first lover, much like a patron, but chosen for her own fancy. Also, come and gone.

She'd learned something from every scholar and bureaucrat she met in the House of Heavenly Peaches. The ones she'd taken to her bed taught her even more. Not about the pillow arts. She learned about their ways of speaking, the allusions that were thrown about. Learned enough characters to write her name and a few choice idioms. Memorized enough proverbs to be playful with language.

When she was growing up, she'd tried to ask her father and mother questions, but she'd always been just "a simple girl." Not worth the breath it took to explain. But in Changan, in the Pingkang li, everyone had something to say. Everyone wanted to show off, even to a simple girl.

What would have happened if young Li Chen had tried to court her? She would have had no use for another young, bright-eyed scholar with nothing to give but broken promises. Song Yi was already, as Madame Shi had taught her, learning to protect her value.

The sounds of a pipa floated to them from the next room, mournful. The lingering sound of each note an unanswered question.

CHAPTER 14

*W*ithout argument, this was the most enjoyable journey home Li Chen had ever taken. The yearly trip was typically perfunctory. A string of hard beds and bland meals. He would read books to pass the time. When he was tired of reading, he would stare at the river. Then he would read again.

Presently, he hadn't opened a book in days. Which, for Li Chen, was something to be remarked upon.

And he could barely keep from grinning.

He wasn't entirely removed from his duties. His office was instructed to send regular reports through the relay system. Messages went out by horse from the capital and sent from relay to relay. At each one, there were fully rested horses and riders waiting to run messages to the next posting station.

It had been originally designed for rapid communications during wartime. Sometimes it was used to transport some luxury for the Emperor. For Li Chen's purposes, the relay was faster than he traveled. The reports from Changan he received were only a few days past.

By sundown, they went ashore at a well-populated settlement with a relay station. Li Chen left Song Yi and Sparrow at a tavern while he went to fetch his messages.

There was a report waiting for him as he'd expected. This was his third year making this trip from Changan and the functionaries in the yamen were familiar with the routine.

Chen opened the letter to glance quickly at the contents. Nothing out of the ordinary. There was no update on the courtesan house murder investigation, which he supposed was expected. Yang Yue wasn't required to report to him.

A separate piece of paper had been included with the report.

The weasel bids the rooster a happy new year.

It was signed by Constable Gao.

The note was obviously composed by Gao's more literate wife. Li Chen had come to recognize the signature features of Lady Bai's calligraphy. Was she trying to communicate something or was it Gao's message as the signature indicated?

Li Chen stared at the note for a full minute. Roosters... and weasels?

Eventually, he gave up and folded up the report, tucking it away in his belt. He returned to the tavern to see Song Yi and Sparrow sharing tea.

As soon as he seated himself, a server came with an armful of dishes to set before them. At the center was a savory stew in a ceramic pot from which a spicy aroma wafted up to surround them.

"I'm being treated well on this trip," Chen commented.

"It's because everyone thinks you're rich, Magistrate," Sparrow said bluntly. "Traveling with *yiji*."

Song Yi was occupied with the pouring of tea. She shot the younger girl a sharp look and Sparrow quieted.

He looked between them. Two women traveling with a

man could mean they were family or that Song Yi and Sparrow were servants.

How had he completely misread the situation? Madame Shi had even talked about some official employing *yiji* in his entourage. Entertainers were a status symbol displayed to show one's wealth. Director Guan liked to throw his lavish banquets with hired musicians and song girls.

Chen wasn't well-established or wealthy enough to hire household entertainers or surround himself with a retinue. He didn't even travel with a personal attendant because his needs were few.

Heat rose up his face. Under this new light, the travel arrangements suddenly seemed questionable. There was an uncomfortable lack of boundaries. Even the hint of scandal. He felt as he had in the Lotus Palace. Was he insulting Song Yi and Sparrow while thinking he was being helpful?

"Is there any news from Changan?" Song Yi asked, attempting to smooth things over.

"Just the usual report," he replied.

"Nothing about Pearl?" Song Yi was genuinely concerned.

He noticed how Sparrow's eyes became hooded. The chirping little bird was suddenly very quiet.

"Nothing, I'm sorry to say. These inquiries can take some time and the case is not under my authority any longer."

"I imagine there are cases where it's impossible to find the culprit. Especially in a city as vast as the capital."

"There are certainly difficult cases," he admitted. "The longer a case goes unresolved, the harder it becomes to find the offenders."

Song Yi ladled the stew between them and they started eating. Sparrow picked at her food listlessly.

"Are you not hungry, Miss Sparrow?" he asked gently.

Large eyes darted up to him. "I—I'm just thinking of Pearl. I wish she was home with us."

He had questioned Sparrow himself about the incident. Magistrate Yang had done so as well. Despite her young age and apparent nervousness, her story had remained constant. She had brought wine to the sitting room and left Pearl alone with the caller. She had been the one to later find the body.

"What happens with the inquiries that go unresolved?" Song Yi asked. Predictable, how she rushed to Sparrow's defense.

"It's unavoidable. There's a collection of such cases in the yamen. A magistrate is reviewed based on the number of cases where he is able to arrest the offenders as opposed to the ones where he does not."

"And if a magistrate can't catch enough offenders?"

"He can be removed from office. Or, if he is judged to have deliberately failed to pursue justice for a crime, he can be punished."

It was a somber topic. They continued the meal in silence for a few beats before Little Sparrow spoke again, food still uneaten.

"For the case involving the Heavenly Peaches, would it be you or the other magistrate who is held responsible?"

The question was like the shattering of a vase. A disturbance followed by the shock of silence.

"It is unclear what would happen in that case," Chen replied finally.

The meal concluded in subdued fashion. While they retired to the rooms after supper, he reached for Song Yi, his hand grazing lightly over the silk of her sleeve. Song Yi glanced back at him while Sparrow caught the gesture and continued on.

She followed him into his room but immediately set her back against the door once it was closed.

Song Yi peered up at him, mouth drawn and eyes flashing

fire. "You know we want for this case to be resolved as much as you do."

"I know you would do anything to protect your sisters."

Her armor splintered and he could see the vulnerability underneath.

"I know you can't separate that from anything you do," he continued, moving closer. "It's why you came."

This was a first for him. Saying something while hoping fervently for it to be denied.

She didn't deny it. "I wanted you before any of this," she said brokenly, closing her eyes.

Somehow her response was better than a denial. His pulse quickened.

What was it about Song Yi that had hooked so deeply into him? He touched a hand to her cheek and her breath caught, lips parting to beckon to him. He would never tire of looking at her. There were so many layers beneath the surface. A tangle of emotions warred within her.

"I wanted you even when they insisted we were ill-suited." Her eyelids fluttered open.

"Ill-suited?"

"You weren't the sort to ever—"

He was the sort. He kissed her, capturing her mouth with his heart beating out of his chest. Her lips softened and opened to him. Desire curled tight and low in his stomach.

His hands rounded her waist, pulling her away from the door to drag her to him. With a soft sound in her throat, she yielded, wrapping herself around him.

The heat that hit him was a force. There was too much silk between them so they did away with it, pulling at belts and ties and sashes until they were free.

Her skin was softer than any silk. He needed to touch her, taste her. Song Yi must have felt the same because her mouth was at his throat, teeth scraping in a way that made him gasp, then hardly a breath later she was lower. There her caress was softer, taking him into the sleek, hot depth of her mouth until he could do nothing, think of nothing else but what she was doing to him.

Though it pained him, he lifted her from him. It would be over too quickly that way. Over the last nights, he had learned much about the ways of pleasure, but there was always more.

They kissed again. Just that touch sharpened the dull, throbbing ache in his body to an insistent point. But he could be patient. There was a benefit to practicing discipline.

Song Yi moaned when he closed his mouth over her breast, tongue teasing gently at the hardening nipple. The other one was already raised with anticipation when he moved over. Down below, his fingers eased into the wet heat between her thighs.

Chen watched her face as he stroked his fingers deeper. Her skin was flushed. Her look tormented, but of a different sort than before. He hardened to the point of pain, the best kind of pain.

Now it was Song Yi who nudged his hand aside, making a soft purr of protest even as she did. Whatever she wanted, whatever she did next, he wanted it too. Blood rushed hot through him.

Song Yi pressed a hand to his chest. She wanted him on his back and he was more than happy to surrender. She climbed over him and his hands circled her waist a moment before she took him inside her.

His last thoughts melted away. Why was Song Yi here, why was he...It didn't matter. There was no discipline, no patience left in the hot, tight wetness surrounding him. With a soft moan, she drove him deeper.

She leaned forward, finding an angle that pleased her. The sounds she made. Primal music. Her gaze was clouded with desire, eyes half-closed as she moved. He took in the sight of her with the last light of the day.

Darkness took him as she tightened around him, legs trembling. Her body milked him in soft pulses. The day was gone. He was climaxing.

There was quiet afterward. Song Yi sighed as she fitted herself into the crook of his shoulder. There was just enough strength in his arm to circle around her.

A faint tumble of thoughts eventually emerged.

"Song Yi," he breathed.

"Hmm?"

He traced a fingertip down the curve of her spine. Her skin was damp with sweat. His was as well.

"Am I doing this improperly?"

"Properly?" her voice was muffled against him and laced with faint amusement.

"Not *this*," he clarified. Well, partly this. It was all woven, inseparable. "The gift that Madame Shi refused. She didn't intend to refuse it completely, did she?"

She made a sound of protest, nestling closer to him as if she would rather be talking of anything else.

"Was I supposed to hire you and Little Sparrow for this trip? I mean, not hire but..."

He couldn't forget what Sparrow had said about traveling with *yiji*.

That whole business with returning his money. Had it been a matter of saving face? Madame Shi wouldn't accept outright charity but some sort of exchange was acceptable.

"You have to tell me," he implored in all seriousness. "I'm not sophisticated about these matters."

Song Yi lifted her head and tried to kiss him. Which he of course allowed her for a little while before pulling away, still awaiting an answer.

She sighed and sank back down against him. "Darling,"

she chided, scolding, yet affectionate. This was a coldly practical and slightly uncomfortable conversation.

That was her way, always so careful to take his mind away from the cares and worries of daily life.

"I want to do this properly," he insisted.

He cared deeply for Song Yi. They had affection for each other. There was desire between them. It wasn't just desire, it was the best time of his life. But there were also realities.

"Ask me in the morning," she said, kissing him again as her hand slid down over his stomach then lower.

This time, Li Chen did happily allow himself to be distracted.

"What of your previous affairs?"

It was the first thing Song Yi said to him the next morning. He looked up at her with his head resting in her lap.

They'd woken up long before that. He'd made love to her before they said a word. Now she was running her fingers through his hair in the lazy aftermath of their coupling. He felt like a lord, a prince.

"There were no previous affairs," he replied honestly.

She paused mid-stroke. "None?"

"You're the first."

Had she not realized? *How* had she not realized?

"Not even during your carefree academy days?" Song Yi resumed her gentle stroking. Her nails traveled lightly over his scalp, each touch sending a warm ripple down his spine.

"I didn't have any carefree academy days."

Daoshi. Stiff. Reserved. Unbending. It wasn't that he wanted to be those things. He'd spent so many years alone staring at four walls and shelves of books. Then, after years of austerity and a strict regimen of the classics, he'd been unleashed upon the turbulent decadence of the capital. Instead of running wild enjoying the pleasures of Changan, he'd retreated back into what he knew.

"You were the studious sort," she affirmed, making it sound way more admirable.

"I wouldn't have minded carousing with pretty song girls," he added. "I never found the time. Or the opportunity."

Scholars and their exploits were the stuff of legends, mostly fueled by their own boasting. Bouts of heavy drinking and midnight revelry surrounded by beautiful women. Archery contests and polo fields. To him, these delights were farther away than Mount Tai.

"The opportunity isn't difficult to find," she said with a laugh. "Certainly not for someone young and handsome with gentlemanly ways. Who's so accomplished."

It was impossible not to feel his chest swell. Even if she was teasing. It was all done with such deliberate artfulness.

Lady Bai had said he wanted to be played. What man wouldn't want to be played, when the artist was so skilled? But still, he knew. He knew and Song Yi knew. And here they were.

"I'm not as wealthy as one might think," he began.

Song Yi stiffened. "That doesn't matter to me."

These were things not meant to be spoken aloud. This was the illusion Song Yi always spoke of.

He might be unschooled in the interactions between scholars and courtesans, but he wasn't ignorant.

Even the freedom of a liaison unburdened by obligation or monetary exchange simply meant the burden was removed from him to be carried by another.

"We should ready ourselves," Song Yi said. "It's getting late. The ferryman will be waiting."

Li Chen knew it wasn't the late hour or the ferry that had

Song Yi easing away from him. It was his unsubtle way of handling delicate arrangements.

They separated to see to personal matters. He called for the attendant to bring a basin of water. He splashed some over his face and dressed himself. Song Yi smoothed her hands over the front of his robe as he straightened his belt.

"Don't worry about these bothersome details," she assured gently. Her hair was unbound and fell in a dark spill over her shoulders. "They will be sorted out in time."

He supposed they would, even if he had no idea how. Taking his journal and his papers with them, Chen left Song Yi inside the room to finish her morning routine in privacy. After five steps outside, Sparrow appeared. He greeted her politely and started to step aside, assuming she was there to see to her big sister.

Sparrow cut into his path. "Magistrate Li, I wanted to speak with you."

He caught himself as he was forced to an abrupt halt. "What is it, Miss Sparrow?"

"Something happened that night the stranger came," she said, dropping her voice to a whisper. "I saw Pearl with something earlier. We had a fight."

Chen leaned in. She had his full attention now, but she was making little sense. "What exactly did you see?"

Her eyes darted to the closed door before returning to him. "Pearl received a letter earlier that day. I tried to pick it up and she snatched it away. She scolded me!"

"What did she say?"

"She called me meddling. And a brat. She warned me not to tell Mother." The girl was apparently still affronted.

"Who delivered the letter? Did you see what was in it?"

Sparrow shook her head. Again her gaze shifted toward the room. Song Yi was still inside.

"Why didn't you tell me or Magistrate Yang of this earlier?"

"You didn't ask," she replied smoothly, with an air of casual superiority reminiscent of her older sisters. But her confident facade didn't last. "I was worried when there was talk that Pearl could be arrested. The letter could have been nothing."

But Sparrow knew it wasn't nothing. Chen remained silent. Most people, including chatty courtesans-in-training, could not manage prolonged silence.

"I think she might have had a lover," Sparrow said with eyes downcast. "The way she looked when she saw that message. Why else would she make me promise not to tell Mother?"

"Is that Little Sparrow?" Song Yi called from inside the room.

The girl's eyes grew wide. "Please don't tell Song Yi any of this!"

"Why not?"

"*Send her in...*"

Sparrow looked to be in a panic. He hadn't dismissed her and the threat of Song Yi overhearing their conversation had the girl in knots. These were the sort of conditions that elicited confessions.

"Isn't she your *a-chi*?" he pressed.

"Song Yi keeps all kinds of secrets from us. She's so much like Mother sometimes."

Sparrow practically tore herself away from him to rush to the door. After taking a moment to compose herself, she slipped inside.

Li Chen thought over what he'd just heard. It changed little, other than strengthening the suspicion that someone else had entered the house and killed the man. Still, every bit of information was important.

He went to the innkeeper for ink and paper to write a message, which he sent to the posting station through an errand boy. The relay would have it in Magistrate Yang's hands by the time Chen reached Yu prefecture.

In the remaining time, he called for tea and reviewed his reports again. All the while considering whether Madame Shi had sent Song Yi and Sparrow away with him to protect them or had she sent them to get in his good graces? It couldn't make a difference with the investigation when it was no longer in his hands, could it?

As soon as Chen considered it, he knew it wasn't true. They were clever women, but they were still only women and of lower standing. They needed any protection, any influence they could gather.

He had just finished looking through the messages he'd received the day before when Song Yi and Sparrow appeared in the common room. He folded away the message from Constable Gao as they seated themselves beside him.

"Did you sleep well?" he asked Song Yi perfunctorily as if they hadn't spent the evening skin against naked skin.

"Well enough, Magistrate," she replied, holding back a smile. His face heated.

He watched Song Yi's face as she took tea. She glanced at him, little looks, even while she spoke to Sparrow. The girl was a touch more sullen than usual.

Song Yi had told him she wanted the murder investigation resolved as much as he did and he'd believed her. The case had shut down her house and taken away her livelihood.

But one of her courtesan-sisters was involved and Song Yi was loyal to her den mother and her house above all else. They were her family. He understood that sort of flesh and bone loyalty. It demanded sacrifice.

Song Yi glanced at him, lashes fluttering. His chest

swelled. Whatever she'd just said was the most interesting, intriguing thing in the world because she had said it.

"Were you writing something this morning?" she asked.

He followed her gaze down to his hand. "A letter to the yamen," he said, rubbing at the dot of ink that stained his finger. He must have been distracted for that to happen. Li Chen could write a thousand characters without a single smudge.

"Tending to your duties even now," she teased.

Sparrow glanced at him before looking away. Song Yi missed the gesture, but she detected something was amiss.

"You seem occupied, Magistrate."

"I'm always...pondering something."

She nodded. "I know this about you. I used to think that was why all you ever wanted to do was talk."

"I enjoy our talks."

Her eyes warmed. "I do as well."

He'd enjoyed all of their conversations, even though he'd been working up the courage the entire time to venture further. How did an inexperienced admirer go about courting a woman one was hopelessly smitten with, but shouldn't be?

How did one perform his duties as a magistrate when she was involved, even secondarily, in an inquiry?

From a young age, he was used to having to give answers and being beaten when he didn't have them. The switch wasn't painful. It was more the shame of not knowing that served as punishment. Li Chen always wanted to know the right answer. The number of cases he'd left unresolved in his career as magistrate were remarkably few. And there was only one case where he'd shifted the responsibility to someone else.

"Have you ever heard of a phrase about a weasel sending New Year greetings to a chicken?" he asked Song Yi.

She chuckled and looked to Sparrow. "Do you want to tell this one?"

"You do it, *a-chi*," the girl demurred.

"The proverb goes that the weasel didn't have food, so he went to the chicken's house to wish him a happy new year. Being a gracious host, the chicken invited him inside only to have the weasel steal away with his eggs."

"Ill-intent masked with good cheer," he summarized.

Or good manners leading to bad outcomes. Was Constable Gao trying to once again warn him not to be taken in so easily by peach blossom eyes and a sweet voice?

Song Yi smiled pleasantly and finished her tea.

Maybe Song Yi had wanted to seduce him. Maybe he'd wanted to be seduced, but they were more than that. He felt it in the pit of his stomach. He felt it as sure as his heart was beating.

He still believed her. Multiple truths could live in the same person, the same way they lived, day in and day out, inside him.

CHAPTER 15

*S*ong Yi knew they were getting close by the fog. It came in the mornings now and again in the evening. The world in gray, much like the last memories of her childhood.

"What would happen if a courtesan had an affair her mistress didn't approve of?" Li Chen asked her the next evening.

The directness of his question surprised her.

They sat after dinner together overlooking the water with a lantern between them. Yuzhou was warmer than Changan, by virtue of the wide rivers that surrounded it. Sparrow was nowhere to be found.

"Do you mean, like the two of us?" Song Yi asked, casting him an impertinent look.

He swallowed nervously, and she wanted to laugh out loud and throw herself into his arms. Heaven and earth, after the things they'd done, how could Li Chen still get so flustered at the smallest of talk? Especially when he'd asked the question.

"You're not as unwelcome as you once were. I think even Old Auntie likes you more than she admits," she told him.

"It's not about us," he managed. "What would happen?"

"No madame wants a disobedient courtesan and no courtesan wants to be completely under her mother's rule. You should hear some of the screaming matches. Not glamorous."

She said it with a smile, hoping to amuse him, but Li Chen was in one of his serious moods.

"There are more serious implications," she added, in a subdued tone. "A disastrous affair could ruin a girl. If she trusted the wrong person. If her lover turned out to be someone powerful and vindictive. Sometimes the consequences don't even come from someone else. A girl can become heartbroken and fall into despair. Stop eating, stop wanting to continue with this life."

Song Yi had said too much. Chen was listening patiently, as he always did, but these weren't the stories he was looking for.

"A courtesan isn't free to do as she pleases. We're indentured to the house."

"You don't even own the silk you wear," he murmured.

A crack formed inside her heart. Li Chen already knew too much to be enchanted by the illusion, but he was still here, wasn't he? For now.

"A girl who won't listen to her mother, who is defiant, who might run away can threaten the survival of the whole house."

Pearl leaving had torn a hole into the thin cloth of their existence. The rest of them had been fighting to hold the ragged edges together.

"There was another girl at the Heavenly Peaches," he said. "Ziwan. She was sold to another house."

"You *have* been talking to Sparrow," she accused, sighing.

The girl had spent a long time outside her door before coming to her that morning. And now Sparrow was off moping somewhere.

"Miss Sparrow didn't tell me this. I saw it in the indenture records," Chen admitted. "A transfer from the Heavenly Peaches to a smaller house earlier this year."

"Not a smaller house," she corrected. "A lesser one. One where men don't come to be distracted by music. Ziwan and Mother didn't get along. When we started falling into debt— it's what happens, Magistrate."

Her use of the honorific raised his hackles. Her skin prickled defensively as well. The evening was taking a bad turn.

"Would Pearl have feared the same thing if she had a secret lover?" Chen asked.

"Mother cherished Pearl," she denied, agitated. Cherished her so much that Pearl was left alone as an offering at the sight of silver. Song Yi pushed the thought away and calmed herself. "Sparrow did speak to you, didn't she?"

"She did," he acknowledged. "She told me Pearl received what might have been a letter from an admirer the same day she disappeared."

"Was she certain?"

"She wasn't certain."

Li Chen really could not lie. At least he couldn't seem to lie to her—which she should be happy for. She was far from it at the moment.

She angled her shoulders away, forming a barrier between them as she stared at the river. The light from the lantern created dots of light over the water.

"Not as unwelcome as I once was?" Chen echoed into the silence.

She held her breath for a moment before sliding a glance

at him over her shoulder. "I may need to rescind that remark."

The corner of his mouth twitched. "When was I unwelcome?"

Mother and Auntie and even Pearl thought he was stiff, cold, too reserved. Li Chen was none of those things. When he'd first come to her parlor, Song Yi had been surprised to find that his reputation was well-deserved, though not in the way everyone assumed.

Li Chen was uncannily intelligent. It wasn't just the books. He watched and noticed everything but only admitted it in part. Everyone said he was too controlled and hid his emotions, but half of what he hid was curiosity and amusement.

"Mother thought I was wasting my time with you."

"What do you think about that?"

A feeling of warmth blossomed within her. "I wanted to waste my time with you."

She turned to face him. "I wanted nothing to come of us being together. I longed to be one of your indiscretions. I didn't realize I would be your only indiscretion."

Li Chen held onto her, his eyes searching her face with wonder. Now she had certainly said too much. It was her turn to blush.

"You're not an indiscretion, Song Yi." He cradled her face in his hands, his touch warm against her skin.

"Am I not?" she asked crookedly. It was too much, sitting here with Li Chen looking at her like that. So close to the place she'd left behind.

"Weren't you the one who was concerned what it would look like, you traveling with two unmarried women?"

"Well, that—"

"You don't want to be seen with me at the gates of your family mansion," she teased. "You're even worried my presence might threaten your pious ritual. Why else would we be out here by the river, listening to the lonely crickets, instead of retiring to your bed?"

Jìchén was observed as a day of abstinence from earthly pleasures. No spiced food, wine, and, of course, sex. She sensed the change in Li Chen's manner as they drifted closer to his home. How scandalous, enjoying the clouds and the rain with his courtesan lover where the ancestors might see.

"It's not true," Chen denied, though she could see her words had struck against something in him.

"I apologize," she said immediately, regretting her flippant tone.

"I'm not offended," he said, trying to pull her to him. "I like it when you throw me off balance."

"I didn't mean to make light of your family."

Scandalizing the ancestors? How could she even think it? She was just so afraid they would part and he would go home and remember who he was. And forget her.

He was being gentle now. Holding onto her as if she was the thinnest gauze. He tried to ease her closer while she tried to slip away.

"I'm going to kiss you now," he said quietly. "Just a kiss."

"You'll want more," she warned, not deserving the kindness he was trying to show her.

But she let herself be held, let herself be drawn into his arms. When he touched his lips tenderly against hers, she kissed him back.

He did want more. She could feel it in the tension that ran through every part of him.

She wasn't wrong. Li Chen was holding himself back. She was a temptation he was trying to control.

So they stared at the river instead of retiring to his bed.

"I like this river," he began woodenly. "I used to stare at it and let my thoughts wander. I forget how much I miss it when I'm away."

"I don't miss it," she said, then made herself stop talking.

She hadn't wanted to come back here, but she didn't regret the journey. At least not yet.

"The crickets are always so loud this time of year," Chen remarked.

They sat together, listening to the incessant chirping. The drawing of a thousand bows across tiny instruments.

He tilted his head to listen. "I wonder why they sound like that in the autumn."

Did he really not know? It was a last desperate call before dying. The autumn was a cricket's final chance to mate before freezing from the winter frost.

Song Yi kept that story to herself.

THE NEXT MORNING, Song Yi opened the door to find everything had gone ghostly and gray. Fog hung thick in the air, blurring the world at a distance into nothingness.

Sparrow emerged immediately behind her, darting her head left then right. "Is it morning yet?"

Song Yi and Sparrow had slept in the same room last night. Song Yi had tossed about restlessly, realizing with dismay she had become accustomed to having Li Chen's warmth surround her. Without him, she was in a strange place, traveling blindly toward a past she had long left behind.

"This is how it is most days in the autumn here," Song Yi told the girl.

Li Chen emerged from his chamber a moment later, and also glanced around with a look of familiarity.

"Magistrate Li."

He met her eyes for a long time. "Miss Song Yi."

The boat ride was a silent one. The vessel cut through the water, shrouding them in mist. It had been like this when her family had first come to Yu prefecture.

She'd been nine, her brother two. He'd held onto her hand as they stood like tiny ants upon the boat, looking up into the vast gray cloud around them. It was as if they'd reached the end of the world.

Song Yi shut her eyes. All of that was gone now. Her brother was gone. She was also gone, transformed into something else.

"Song Yi."

Li Chen was close but she didn't want to open her eyes.

His voice dropped lower, until it was barely above a whisper. "Song Yi," he repeated. "Are you alright?"

She nodded wordlessly, her eyes still squeezed shut. Maybe if she kept them closed, the memories would stop flooding in. Maybe Li Chen would stay beside her.

"The ferryman tells me we will reach Shijing mid-day," Chen reported. "Your village is north of there."

She did open her eyes then. He was looking at her, not with wonder or hunger or anticipation. Instead, there was reservation. What was he to do with her?

A courtesan wasn't a mistress or a concubine. She wasn't the sort to resort to dramatics or cause trouble.

"You said you have family in Longyin?" he asked tentatively.

"Madame Shi said I had family there. She was mistaken."

Mother had lied. Whatever it took to get Mother's way.

By now, Li Chen must have figured out that the story about making an offering to her ancestors was a ruse. She wished she had thought to name another village. It would have been better to set foot into an unknown place where she was a complete stranger.

"I never had any ancestors in Longyin," she told him.

It had been just her mother and father and she and her brother. Her family had been uprooted and brought there. She had started to think of this gray and clouded place as home, but when their family had fallen into hard times, there had been no one there to help them.

The fog had not dissipated by midday. It hung like a curtain over the shoreline, occluding their view. Behind the veil, Song Yi could see walls and buildings emerge.

"The Li mansion is there somewhere," she remarked, looking to the cluster of buildings at the fork in the river.

Li Chen nodded, his expression flat. To Song Yi's surprise, the ferry didn't dock in Shijing, but instead continued northward. She'd thought Li Chen would disembark at his hometown.

Within the hour, the cool air and the smell of the water started to tug at her. The shape of the cliffs overhead had been imprinted in her memory. Houses crowded along the shoreline, raised high up on the bank. The foothills beyond were lush and green.

A tight fist closed inside her chest. She'd waded along the riverbank. She'd climbed those hills.

Song Yi hadn't realized how close her village was to Chen's family home. Just a few hours by water. By foot, she knew the journey would take up the good part of a day.

The ferry docked along the bank. Li Chen climbed onto the dock and turned to assist both Sparrow and her. Song Yi stared upward at the cliffs before stepping from the boat.

She was here. Back in a place she thought she'd never see again.

Li Chen walked ahead. She let herself be led through streets that were both familiar and not. She had been young when she'd left the village. The streets were dirt and the houses small and weathered. The market was along a single lane. Not much had changed, yet it all seemed different. Song Yi's gaze darted through the street, searching for signs of familiarity. Mother with her sad eyes and her hair fixed in a knot. Her brother, long-limbed and thin-faced.

They wouldn't be there. She knew they wouldn't. If she could have returned to them, she might have at least tried to make the journey back. She was indentured but not enslaved.

But she had been honest with Chen. She had no people here. Her only family was Mother and Auntie and Sparrow. And Pearl until the last hope of her return faded.

Chen didn't ask any more questions. He seemed to know she wouldn't have more answers. Instead, he found his way to the village inn and spoke to the proprietor to secure their rooms.

When it was settled, Chen pulled her aside into the corner.

"The proprietor will see to anything you need," he assured her.

"Thank you, Magistrate."

She was under Li Chen's protection here. It was too much like other conversations she'd had. Other arrangements.

"I will come back in three days. Will that be enough time for you?"

Three days. A lifetime. "Of course, Magistrate. I am grateful for your generosity."

"Generosity? Song Yi," he sighed, sinking his forehead onto hers. The gesture was scandalous in its intimacy. Her heart raced.

Why was this so difficult? Why was she making this difficult? She was the one who was experienced in these matters.

"Send a messenger to me if you need anything," he said, still standing too close.

"I'll count the days," she whispered, hating that she'd said such things so many times before because they were expected of her.

She watched as Li Chen left her, carried away by the ferry. She was farther away from him now than she had ever been.

CHAPTER 16

*L*i Chen entered the gates of his family home to the faintly sweet and herbal smell of incense. The servants greeted him in subdued tones. He inquired about his mother and was told she had gone to make an offering at the temple.

The eerie quietness of the house settled over him. His mother had lived there alone while he moved from one assignment to another throughout the empire. It was too large for one woman and the three servants she kept on, but the place had been the family home for generations. It was where Chen had been born and where he was expected to return one day.

He went to the altar to pay his respects, circling around the garden in the courtyard to avoid the study. The altar was set into an alcove in the back of the house. A set of plaques were situated there, his grandparents and their parents. And the one for his father.

Selecting three incense sticks from the holder, Chen held the ends against the candle that burned on the altar. A coil of fragrant smoke rose from the sandalwood. He lifted the sticks to perform the proper obeisances. One bow, two, three. A prayer for the ancestors. A word of respect for his father.

Chen had once thought his father was listening. He'd thought when he stood here, surrounded by candlelight and scented smoke, that his father could hear his thoughts. As a boy who was not yet a man, he'd tried to ask his father questions. What should he do to honor their family? Did his father have enough to eat wherever he was?

Was it dark there?

Was he alone?

Sometimes the questions became more desperate. Why?

Why, Chen would ask, then back away in shame. It was not a son's place to demand answers from his father when his father was alive, let alone after he was gone.

It occurred to Li Chen that he'd spoken more words to his father in spirit than he had while his father was living.

At some point, he had stopped asking questions of the dead. It was better to seek out questions that could conceivably be answered. He did believe his father was still watching over them, but it was up to Li Chen to figure out what it was his ghost wanted. Even if he would never have that answer.

After setting the sticks into the urn, he stepped back out of the alcove and went to reacquaint himself with the house.

He'd made the journey home every year since his father's death, with the only exception being his examination year when every moment had been dedicated to studying.

His bedchamber had been prepared by the servants. There was a proper bed rather than the mats and pallets he'd slept on during the journey down the river. Yet he already knew it would be a cold night. The house was always cold.

And Song Yi wasn't there, breathing softly in the darkness beside him.

"Master Li, these came for you."

The house steward brought the packet of letters directly to him. More reports from Changan. And another letter from Lady Bai Wei-ling on behalf of Constable Gao.

All friendship is deception.

Likely a play on Sunzi's text, *All war is deception.*

Chan wondered if the constable and his wife were engaging in some elaborate prank.

The rest of the operations in the magistrate's yamen were running smoothly.

It was dinner time when he finally saw his mother. They sat across from one another at the family table, sipping tea. Like the house, the table was too large for the two of them. It had been that way for a long time now.

"You arrived later than I expected," his mother said. "Were there delays?"

He'd taken the time to accompany Song Yi to her village. Perhaps he'd lingered longer each morning in Song Yi's arms. "No delays, Mother."

"Did you light incense for your father?"

"Yes, right after I arrived."

The housekeeper brought soup in decorative porcelain bowls. His mother preferred to maintain a formality around their routine. She insisted on dressing in an embroidered robe with her hair pinned and jeweled, even if the only guest she received was her only son.

She waited for him to dip his spoon into the soup and take the first taste.

"Too salty?" she asked.

If there was any salt in the dish, he couldn't detect it. "No. It's fine."

They ate in silence for a pause before Mother started her usual inquiries. His work in the capital. The well-being of various acquaintances she'd made in her trips there. There was a sly, offhand inquiry into the Bai family without mentioning their daughter whom he had defiantly not married despite his mother's best efforts to arrange a betrothal for him.

She'd become so upset by his failure that she'd left the capital to return to Yu prefecture in protest. Yet one wouldn't know there was any lingering enmity at all given his mother's utter composure. But Chen could read the signs clearly.

He understood why his mother was upset. Seeing to his future was his mother's singular calling. Cultivating a relationship with the Bai family had taken time and effort on her part. Even though he didn't regret how things had ended, Li Chen hated to disappoint.

Dutifully he inquired about his mother's health. How she was sleeping. The minor happenings of the neighborhood.

"Have you called on Prefect Guan recently?" she asked.

"He's a director now. In the Ministry of Personnel. Director Guan invited me to a banquet earlier this month."

"That's right. Director Guan kindly sent a basket of pomegranates, all the way from the capital. We must put some on the altar for your father. You should thank the director."

Chen nodded. "I will."

"We are forever grateful to him for seeing to your education."

"We are." His participation was hardly needed in this conversation.

Again, Mother was seeing to his future.

For climbers, the closer to the capital, the better. In his mother's eyes, Chen had behaved like the perfect son, honoring his father by dedicating himself to his studies, by passing the keju, by building up a good name in service to the empire as a magistrate. He had done everything right until his failure to marry Bai Wei-ling, whom Mother had selected to be her daughter-in-law.

Unfortunately, Lady Bai was not as obedient as he was.

The next course was whole steamed fish shared between them.

"Master Li's favorite," she said quietly, referring to his father in her formal way.

She reached with her chopsticks to separate a choice morsel from the collar of the fish. Wordlessly, she placed it into his bowl.

"Eat more," Mother urged, even though he was already eating.

CHEN HAD ALWAYS ASSOCIATED the anniversary of his father's death with the coming of winter. With darkness and a chill in the air. The practice of *jìchén* in their household involved the extinguishing of all fire save for the candles on the altar. Meals were served cold without meat and salt. At night, they wrapped themselves in blankets to keep from lighting the hearth.

As oldest son, as only son, Chen led the mourning rituals. The day started with the burning of incense at the altar. Fresh dishes of food were brought to replace the old ones. Chen placed the pomegranates his mother had received from Guan He onto the altar in a prominent location, stacking the red fruit high into a pyramid.

They prayed for his father's spirit to remain in peace and for him to bless their family with good fortune. "For honors and offices," as the prayer went.

To his mother, Li Chen's success at his studies, his appointments and promotions were a sign that her husband's spirit was at peace.

"Your father was never able to pass the imperial examination," she told him quietly when he earned his *jinshi* degree.

And here was Chen, successful on his first try. Surely that was due to his father's benevolent grace. It might also be due to how the family had mourned for three years after his father's passing. They'd worn coarse clothing and eaten the plainest foods without salt or other spices.

He'd always been a serious student, but there had been nothing to do during those years but read. He'd studied every book in the house backwards and forwards. He didn't need the threat of a switch against his palm to motivate him. His studies became an escape. He could absorb himself into something besides the ritual of death.

Once the morning rites were completed at the house, they traveled to the Li family mausoleum where his father was buried along with their ancestors. The mausoleum was located on the outskirts of the city in an auspicious location where the elements were balanced.

There he burned more incense along with stacks of thin, decorated joss paper. Money for the dead. For this father and all of their ancestors who were entombed on the family site.

One day, he would rest there as well, Chen thought, watching the papers burn.

They swept the tombs clear of dust. Said more prayers. Chen stood by respectfully while his mother bowed her head before the tomb, giving her time to say whatever she needed to say to the spirits before she deemed them ready to go. It would be another year before he returned to this place. He could spare the time and the patience.

There was a time, not immediately after this father's death, but several years after, when he had wondered if this cloud of mourning would ever lift. Was he meant to mourn his father this way forever, as a good son, as a sign of filial piety?

It wasn't the rituals. The annual observance. The days of abstinence. These were fitting acts for a dutiful son and wife.

Chen had started to feel as if an oppressive weight had fallen over them. Mother had changed. She was once bright and filled with stories. It was said she was clever and quick-witted, but all of that cleverness had become singularly focused on honoring and building up the Li family name. Chen changed as well. At fifteen, he was already head of the family. His reputation was the family's reputation.

He hadn't questioned the long mourning period. Parts of the ritual were even comforting. It was acceptable, even a sign of how good of a son he was. He didn't have to decide what to do next. He had just thrown himself into his studies.

Death was taboo. No one spoke of it other than in hushed tones and few words.

On the day his father had passed away, exactly fourteen years ago, the house had been quiet when he woke up. Mother had shut herself away for some reason and had not come out for tea. The door to his father's study was closed and when Chen approached to knock, the servants had quickly intercepted and ushered him away.

It was Prefect Guan who had come to the house to tell him that his father was gone. The rest of the days after that and for the next three years blurred together like ink in water.

The smell of smoke and incense had taken over the house. Monks had come to chant and pray. Professional mourners wailed on both sides of the street during the funeral procession. People who weren't family, whom he didn't know, crying in anguish for his father.

His mother had told him to hold back his tears. It would upset his father's spirit to see them weeping. As with all things, he'd obeyed.

There was only one time when he hadn't listened. Before the funeral, there had been a single act of disobedience, one Chen had never told anyone about.

Prefect Guan had taken him aside to tell him his father was a good man. To assure him that he and his mother would be taken care of. He had asked to see his father one last time. All he knew was that his father had gone into his study one night and never came out.

Guan, with full authority and wisdom, had refused. "It is of the utmost importance that your father not be disturbed."

A servant was assigned to watch over the door where his father's body was laid out before burial. Yet late one evening, two days after his father's passing and the night before the burial was to take place, the door was left unattended.

Chen had never disobeyed a command from an elder his entire life, but something compelled him to open the door and slip inside. He saw his father laid out on the floor of the parlor. Dread filled his stomach and clenched at his chest, but he stepped closer.

Father's skin was colorless, so gray that the purple, black marks on his jaw stood out dramatically.

Chen only had one brief glimpse before the servant's hand closed over his shoulder to drag him out. It was impertinent for a servant to grab him like that. The man apologized profusely once they were outside.

"Master Li, have mercy. Don't tell anyone."

Chen could barely understand the servant's babbling. It took him a moment to realize that he, not his father, was now Master Li.

His mother had dismissed their servants shortly after the burial. She bade them to go home to their families. Over time, his mother had replaced them with new servants who had never served Old Master Li in life.

Anyone who spoke of his father only did so in a whisper. Chen had thought that was the proper way with the deceased.

He never told anyone what he'd seen and the servant who

had dragged him out of the parlor was long gone by the time Chen was curious enough to ask about it.

Only years later, after he'd earned his degree, did he discover the answer he'd been wondering about for so long.

Chen had been appointed magistrate in a remote county. The former magistrate had passed away and he was sent to take over. The constable was a fearsome man named Wu Kaifeng who also served as examiner. It was only then that Li Chen finally understood what he'd seen in that room where his father was laid out.

Constable Wu had no time for taboos or superstitions. Wu was able to examine corpses and openly describe the stories that each mark and injury told.

Wu Kaifeng educated him about bruises and ligature marks and strangulation in great detail. And then Chen had seen evidence for himself, as he continued to serve as magistrate. The same darkened marks he'd seen on his father were caused by rope and appeared on people who had died from hanging.

Now each year, Li Chen journeyed home to show his respect for his father. He allowed his mother her grief in any way she required. He continued to do his best to honor their family name, but in his heart, he knew it would take more than incense and burned paper and a dutiful son's humble accomplishments to put a soul in so much turmoil to rest.

CHAPTER 17

"Is it how you remembered?" Sparrow asked as she and Song Yi lay on their sleeping mats that night. The lamp was extinguished and the room dark.

"A little. My family lived on the outskirts of town, close to the river."

She had come to the center of town to go to the market or the temple with her mother, but everything had seemed different through a child's eyes.

They had spent some time that evening wandering down the main lane before returning to the inn. Song Yi had still searched through the faces in the street, knowing she wouldn't find what she was looking for.

"How old were you when you left?"

"Twelve."

"It must be comforting to have a place to go back to," Sparrow said wistfully.

"I suppose it is," Song Yi said, trying not to be unkind.

The place might be familiar, but there were no warm memories of home or family for her here. Just unanswered questions.

"Sometimes I wonder if I ever saw my mother's face, would I recognize it," the girl confessed.

"I think of Madame Shi as my mother now," Song Yi said. "She's taken care of me for so long." Though the roles at some point had become reversed and she was now taking care of Mother and Auntie. Song Yi didn't resent it. She had a debt to pay the house.

"I think of Mother that way too," Sparrow admitted. "But at least you have an actual mother."

Song Yi had been so absorbed in her own thoughts, she hadn't realized how the journey affected her little sister. Sparrow had been abandoned when she was little more than an infant. Madame Shi had taken her from a temple orphanage to begin training her when she was only five.

"Do you think there is any chance your family is still here?" Sparrow asked.

"I don't believe so."

Song Yi had tried to send letters home to her family. She had learned just enough to write simple messages, but her mother wouldn't have been able to read them. Her brother, Little Jie wouldn't know more than a few characters, even if he had been able to continue studying, which was unlikely without their father to teach him.

There were never any letters in return.

Song Yi had sought out news whenever a visitor had come from the region. She wasn't free enough then to move about and do what she wanted. She barely had such freedom now.

One day a courier told her of the flood that had swept through the village not long after she'd left. The low-lying houses had been washed away.

Her family's house had been close to the river's edge. For years, she'd continued to send letters, but she'd stopped after that.

"Do you think you will ever forgive them?" Sparrow asked finally.

Song Yi thought the girl had fallen asleep, she had been silent for so long.

"Forgive them for what?"

"For selling you off," Sparrow replied.

Her family had never sold her. That was just the story she'd created for herself. A daughter from a wealthy clan, sold off when the family had fallen from grace.

"I don't blame them," Song Yi said flatly.

If there was any question of forgiveness, it would be whether her family would ever forgive her. She was the one who had abandoned them.

SONG YI DREAMT she was walking along an endless road that night. One of those dreams she knew was a memory, but it was different in dreams. Her feet weren't sore.

When she woke up the next morning her eyes were dry. She rose and washed. Took the time to comb and braid Sparrow's hair before Sparrow tended to hers.

She had to ask around to find the temple. Her father hadn't been particularly devout. Her mother went occasionally to give offerings on festival days.

Their ancestors weren't here to watch over them. Her family had come from far away to settle here and only briefly.

Still, Song Yi lit incense at the altar of the enlightened Buddha. Sparrow did the same. Then they moved to the ancestral altar where the plaques and names of the local villagers were kept. None were familiar to her.

Her father's body may have never made it home. She had paid a corpse walker, a tradesman who specialized in transporting the dead, to take care of the body, but she was too trusting. The transporter could have simply buried the bodies to save himself the trips. Not everyone feared the retribution of ghosts.

The message Song Yi pinned to her father's clothing might have been similarly lost. And the money. Money sent alongside a corpse might be too tainted to touch. Her mother wasn't devout, but she was superstitious. Mother had seen nothing but ghosts after Father died. She had blamed them for stealing Little Jie's speech. Her brother was so shaken with grief that he couldn't utter a word.

She hadn't expected her father's name to appear among the dead any more than she expected to see her mother and her brother's faces in the streets of Longyin.

Song Yi left the temple, feeling at least that she had done what she'd told Li Chen she was here to do. Her ancestors weren't any less appeased, but as to the greater questions, the greater wrongs, she didn't expect to ever have answers.

She had been too trusting once that the world would do right by her. Now she knew that wrongs didn't right themselves so easily.

THAT NIGHT, the proprietor of the tavern asked them for stories of the capital. An elderly musician, a former *yiji* who was playing a song on the pipa was cast aside and ignored as the crowd turned their attention to the younger, more fresh-faced entertainers who had arrived.

Song Yi recounted several of the best tales of Pingkang, full of romance and sorrow and scandal. Sparrow was a particular favorite, so young and vibrant and pretty while she played. No one cared that her fingers weren't particularly nimble or that she skipped notes whenever she hadn't mastered a section.

The resident musician looked on silently without causing a fuss. Were she younger, she might have thought of them as rivals and glared at them with contempt.

Song Yi made certain to pay for the resident musician's food. Call her auntie. Treat her with proper respect as she engaged the woman in conversation.

"You used to live here?" the older songstress asked.

"I grew up along the shoreline, just outside of town," Song Yi replied.

"Ah, one of the fisherman's families?"

"The head surveyor."

Sparrow wanted to know what a surveyor was. Song Yi explained what she knew as simply as she could.

"They measure the land, how much area is there on the map, so the Emperor can determine who owns what and how much."

The older woman listened intently to her explanation. "There was a story about a surveyor in this village many years ago," she said slowly, cautiously. "There was an unfortunate tragedy."

Song Yi fell silent. She wanted yet did not want the woman to continue.

"It is said that he went up to the cliffs one foggy day. Some say he lost his way and didn't realize how close he'd come to the edge and slipped, falling tragically into the rocks below. At least that is one version of the story."

"What an awful story, old woman!" Sparrow reached for Song Yi and tried to draw her away, but Song Yi remained fixed in place.

"What is the other version told?" she asked woodenly.

"Some say he threw himself into the river. To hide his shame."

Song Yi frowned. "Shame?"

"The fog that always covers the area caused his instruments to not work properly. All the work he had done was full of errors. He was to be removed from his appointment."

"That's not the story at all."

The old woman's eyes glittered at her. Maybe she did consider them rivals after all.

"That is the story that is told," the woman said triumphantly, peering at Song Yi with lurid interest. "Perhaps your father knew this man, being a surveyor himself."

hen saddled the old mare and rode out early the next morning. After the day of fasting in the silent house with the locked study, he needed to breathe air that wasn't clogged with incense smoke. He needed to be away from the weight of his memories.

He kept his mount at a leisurely gait as he followed the turns of the river. As the sun peeked out, he wondered if he should return. Yet whenever he asked himself the question, it served to only push him farther.

He was stopped by a figure in blue silk looking thoughtfully over the water. Was that Song Yi?

He dismounted and approached slowly. The line of her neck and the way her hair fell over her face told him it couldn't be anyone else.

She turned then and saw him, her eyes widening with surprise. He moved toward her, leading the horse by the line.

"It hasn't been three days," she said, her eyes shining.

"I didn't realize I had come this far."

He must have been meandering for hours.

"There must be fate between us," she said lightly, but her

gaze was focused behind him at the horse. She tilted her head in its direction questioningly. He couldn't look at anything but her.

"I came up the river hoping to find you," he admitted.

Her smile warmed him to his fingertips.

"You're far away from Longyin as well," he said, turning to face the water as she had been when he found her. He'd expected to ride for another hour.

"The village used to extend out here. There were houses there, along that embankment." She drew her finger through a line just above shoreline.

"What happened?"

"They say the river rose and flooded one year. Everything was washed away."

She was calm as she recounted the tale. Almost too calm. Even though she was smiling, even though her expression was pleasant, there was a tightness in the set of her jaw.

He had walked into the midst of a reverie and he wasn't certain he was welcome there.

The embankment she spoke of had indeed once held some sort of structure. What remained were wooden stilts and what looked like an eroded platform. Whatever had once been there, he couldn't tell. Song Yi stared at the wreckage for a long time before veering sharply away.

"Imagine the amount of rain that must have fallen," she murmured. "How much water must have poured down from the heavens for the river to rise that high."

"It wasn't just the rain. There are dikes upstream." He gestured vaguely northward, not that he knew exactly where they were located. "If the barriers overflow and suddenly break, the water can come rushing all at once."

She looked at him with surprise. "You really are *jinshi*. Is there anything you don't know?"

"No, it's just that—" He hadn't meant to sound like he was

179

showing off. "This isn't something I've studied. My father. He was an official of sorts. A land administrator. I remember hearing of the floods."

Villages had been damaged and lives lost. His father had been alive at the time and had seemed particularly stricken by the devastation. Li Chen hadn't realized the villages were so close.

"Is this where your family lived?" he asked quietly.

She shook her head and turned to move down the river. He watched her back as she drifted away, the wind blowing her silk robe around her.

Oh, Song Yi. This was it, wasn't it? This was the cruel fate that had taken her family. She wasn't from a fallen, noble family, but it was still tragedy that sent her into indenture. Eventually, she would be taken to the capital, far enough away that she fashioned a new story for herself.

He quickened his pace to catch up with her. She was walking slowly, her expression a thousand li away.

There had been heavy rains that year. His family had spent nearly the entire monsoon season indoors. Father had received constant reports of damage. Of boats and houses swept away. People who were missing.

His father had become morose after the flooding. Long after the waters receded, the tragedy stayed with him.

"The two places really aren't that far," Song Yi said, interrupting his thoughts. "Where you lived and the village where I lived."

"Not so far at all."

"Can you imagine if we'd met then?" Her smile was once again forced.

"I would have never passed the exams," he replied, playing along. "I would have been too besotted to study."

"You wouldn't have noticed me, Li Chen," she said, suddenly serious.

The image came to him again of a girl appearing through the mist. Much like Song Yi had appeared today. He couldn't place where the memory came from.

"I was nothing when I lived here," she said.

"You could never be nothing."

Despite the sadness haunting her eyes, he was glad to be beside her. The last two days had been like moving under water, unable to breathe. As they continued along the bank, Chen felt the weight that hung over him lifting. He hadn't eaten in over a day, but the emptiness inside him disappeared.

"You looked sad before," he began.

She denied it.

"Whatever it was that happened all those years ago, it doesn't matter."

Her gaze on him sharpened. "To you, it doesn't."

"I didn't mean it that way. I just meant I cherish you as you are now."

She held his gaze for a long time, shapely eyes narrowed. Whatever she decided, at least she forgave him for not having the right words.

They continued walking together side by side, not touching. When they spoke, it was in fits and starts.

"What did you and Little Sparrow do?" he asked. "In the village?"

It felt good to be asking about someone else's day. The period of observance and abstinence were meant to be empty and indeed they were.

"We walked through the streets. The entire village can be spanned in just a matter of hours. There's a temple there. Today, Little Sparrow is trading songs with the songstress who frequents the inn."

"Is it good to be back home?" he asked.

"It isn't home."

He led the mare to drink by the river and they sat to rest on the rocks by the shore.

He decided to try again. "How do you trade songs?"

She gave him a look as if surprised he wouldn't know. "You teach a girl one of your songs and she teaches you one of hers."

"How long does one take to learn?"

"A few hours, perhaps. You play the song until it sounds right."

"And then you're done? It's yours."

"Yes."

"What happens if you forget the notes?"

"Then the song changes little by little."

"Imagine if that happened with the writings of the classics."

"Your revered sages," she scoffed. "You think it doesn't happen?"

"My memory is very good," he boasted, earning him a skeptical look with eyebrows arched high. That look from Song Yi made everything worthwhile. "And all of the teachings are written down. Sometimes in stone."

"I should test your memory," she proposed.

"Tell me a story," he challenged. "One I couldn't have heard anywhere else. I'll tell it back, word for word."

"Do I get to strike you if you get it wrong?"

His chest warmed. He wouldn't mind. He wouldn't mind at all.

Li Chen thought she might take him up on his challenge and then he would learn more about her, but Song Yi wasn't in the mood for storytelling. Instead, she glanced overhead, to the cliffs that rose high over the river.

"Are you afraid of high places?" she asked him.

He wasn't.

"Will you go with me up there?" Song Yi glanced up again, the haunted look returning to her eyes.

"I'll go with you," he said.

He'd go with her anywhere.

SONG YI FOUND the path and began the climb. She'd done this in bare feet long ago. Or in sandals woven from hemp. The embroidered slippers she wore now weren't as serviceable, but the path up wasn't steep if you knew the way.

She looked behind her to see Li Chen following gamely. It was easy work for him with his longer stride. Her dangling sleeve caught against a tangle of brush and she had to stop to extract herself. What a peculiar sight they made, climbing over dirt and rock in flowing silk robes with sleeves that nearly dragged the earth.

"You've done this before," he said close behind her.

"With my father sometimes." She gathered up the hem of her robe to better find her footing over the sharp stones. "And my little brother."

"You have a brother?"

"Long ago, I did."

"He is still your brother," Chen reminded gently.

Her family didn't cease to exist even if they were lost to her. Sometimes that was hard to remember.

"Tell me more about your family," he implored.

"For your inquiry?"

"Because I want to know."

Song Yi turned away, quickening her step. "There's nothing to know. My family is gone from here. There's no trace of them anymore after the flood. I don't know whether they lived or died." It was easier to say aloud than she had thought. She trained her eyes on the ground beneath her feet.

"The girl I was before arriving in Changan doesn't exist anymore."

A hand closed over her wrist. She tried to continue, but Chen held on fast. Slowly, he turned her around to face him.

"I'll listen to all of it, but you only have to tell me what you want to tell."

His expression was so serious, so earnest. She realized she did want for him to know, just so someone besides her would understand that her family existed.

Song Yi told it like it was a story. There was a surveyor and his family and the challenge of measuring shadows in a place where fog blocked the sun so many days in the year.

The climb was longer than she remembered. And she was not as agile as she'd once been when she and her brother had trudged behind their father. Her brother had carried a roll of paper which he worked hard not to crumple. She carried Father's instruments and tools. Father had a heavy loop of knotted rope wrapped around each arm.

"My father would say that all land measurements are based on triangles," she explained. "A surveyor measures out different sizes of triangles and adds them together. This cliff is the side of one very large triangle."

The last part was rocky. By now she was breathing hard, her skin flushed from the exertion, but they were close now.

She stumbled near the top and Li Chen caught her, strong arms circling around her to set her right. It felt good to be held for a moment, but she slipped beneath his hold to keep going.

Li Chen had sought her out for the same reason he did in Changan. To unburden his mind. To listen to stories that were not his own. She might as well finish the one she had started.

Maybe she needed to unburden her mind too. She

glanced around the plateau, at the brush and rocks before the edge. Was this really the place?

She turned around. How did Chen appear so composed and unruffled, even after the long climb? His robe still looked impeccable, his hair pulled back in a careful knot. His gaze on her was the curiously thoughtful one she knew so well.

He was trying to make sense of her. Why this long climb? Why had her father made it?

"Will you hold onto my hand?" she asked him. "Don't let go."

All playfulness left his face. His look darkened as he took hold of her hand. Was this the first time they had done this? Held hands? A gesture so simple and affectionate, yet they'd simply bypassed it. Maybe they weren't two star-gazed lovers after all. Maybe they were something else.

Song Yi moved forward, slowing as she neared the edge. Li Chen's hand tightened over hers

"Song Yi," he began in a warning tone.

She had never gone up here or anywhere *after*. Little Jie had stared up at this cliff, unable to speak in his grief. Mother wouldn't even look at the mountains.

"I want to look down," she said softly, surprised at how steady her voice sounded. "I want to see how high it is."

She'd always been afraid to look down when she was little. When it was shrouded in fog, it was even worse. Then, the valley below would look like an endless chasm. One slip and she would fall forever.

The day was clear now. The morning fog had burned away and if she looked over the edge, she would be able to see the river down below.

She knew there wouldn't be any answers for her over the edge of the cliff. She would never have answers. The stories told in the tavern might speak of death and sorrow and scandal, but they were just stories. She could make them into whatever she wanted, but first she had to see for herself.

Song Yi couldn't find peace within the temple or the strangers in the village. Maybe she could find it here.

Chen was holding onto her with both hands now. One hand wrapped securely around her wrist while the fingers of the other hand were woven with hers. She inched closer to where rock disappeared into air and stared down.

Her stomach lurched into her throat. The river looked so far away. The current rushed by, but the strength and speed of it was diminished from up high. The thought of the plummet down into the churning water left her dizzy.

"My father fell from here," she said bluntly, unable to look away. "He would come up here to do measurements. He did them all along these cliffs. If you know the height and the distance from the foot of the mountain. And then you measure another cliff and another distance. And you keep on breaking up the shapes and adding them together. All along the river."

That was the tragedy that had befallen her family. A simple accident. Father had come up one day and never come down.

"Song Yi," Li Chen said again, gently this time. He was the one who drew her back from the edge.

"This is not an entirely tragic story," she assured.

He touched his fingers lightly to her hair, not saying anything, but looking like he didn't believe her, so she tried to explain.

"The story goes on to say that the surveyor's widow and his son lived in a house by the river. Several years later, the river flooded, carrying the house away."

"This is a great sadness for you."

Her eyes stung. "It isn't," she insisted as if her will alone could make it true. "Storytellers love twists of fate. If the surveyor's wife and son had died in that flood, if they had been swept away by the same river that had taken away the husband and father, the stories would have told that. Such tragic irony would be impossible to resist."

She pulled back so Chen could see her face. She wanted him to believe it, because it was a story she would only tell once, here.

"My family must have survived, but I won't ever know for certain. That is the sacrifice I made when I left them."

She'd seen the edge of the cliff and the river below. That was the end of the story.

Li Chen held out his hand again, but she moved past it to start down the mountain. She made it five steps before the shaking started.

It was first a breath she tried to take. Her chest seized and air wouldn't come. Then she started trembling. When she tried to hold still, it only got worse.

Li Chen caught her up in his arms just as her knees began to wobble. He pulled her close and said something in her ear she couldn't hear. She was shaking uncontrollably now, her teeth chattering as if winter had come early.

"Close your eyes," Chen was saying as he held her tight. "Just close your eyes."

She didn't know if that would help, but she did it. The darkness somehow made it better. She pressed her face into the crook of his neck to breathe in the familiar scent of his skin. He was warm and solid and she was rattling so hard she would fall apart.

He was telling her to breathe, but she tried and failed. Li Chen was telling her other things. Gently, soothingly. She just wanted him to keep talking and to hold her as hard as he could.

When the shaking finally subsided, shame rushed in to

replace the tremors. She tried to slip out of Chen's arms, but he refused to let go.

Moments passed before she dared to open her eyes again. Chen was watching her, the lines of his face sharp with concern. He traced his thumb tenderly along the line of her jaw.

"This is something I can do for you, Song Yi. If there is a record of your family somewhere, I can find it." He held onto her chin when she tried to turn away. "I can open inquiries. I can search records, have records searched. If some trace exists, I can try to find them for you."

A seed started to take root inside her. Li Chen wasn't the sort to make empty promises, but she didn't dare to hope.

"Can you stay?" she asked plaintively. "Until we return to the village?"

"I can stay."

They started down the mountain. Much slower, for some reason, than they had climbed up.

～

CHEN TRIED the door of the study that night and found that it wasn't locked. He'd just assumed it was all these years.

He brought his oil lamp inside and first swept the room in a slow, reverent arc. His father's room. All of his books. And where something unspeakable had happened.

But Song Yi wasn't afraid of ghosts. He shouldn't be afraid either.

He took a step farther inside and moved to the desk. His father used to sit there with his papers and ledgers. His stone chop still rested upon the desk next to the inkstone. There was not a speck of dust on anything.

Chen set the lamp carefully on the desk and turned to the shelf of books against the wall. His father's library contained copies of the Classics, the Analects, the Annals. All of the required texts to study for the keju examination, but they had been left untouched in this room after his death.

The rest of the books had been reports for many years past. Their family had administered the lands in the county seat and the surrounding towns. Li Chen had been listening while Song Yi recounted her story. He remembered every word of it, as he'd said he would.

His memory had always been good. As was his eye for detail.

His father had always kept his own records. He made official copies for the land office, but he always wrote down everything in his journals first. Chen was often set to task copying the final documents for his father. It always seemed like extra work, writing all these records down twice, but he never complained.

It was good practice. And he never questioned his elders.

His father would have had a record of the flood and how many homes had been damaged. There would certainly be record of tenants and perhaps even where they'd been relocated to.

Chen had always been good with books. He could at least do that for her.

He searched through the books, checking for dates by the lamplight. The records were meticulously kept and organized, but the ones from just before his father's passing were gone.

The flood and any associated reports would have been recorded in those books. Chen searched through twice to be certain. The last records that remained were from ten years before his father's passing. The ones from the years immediately prior to his death had been removed.

∾

THE THREE DAYS of his visit had gone by and Chen was ready to return to the capital. He told his mother she didn't need to see him off, but she insisted on waiting beside him for the ferry.

"The boat is usually here and ready," she remarked.

The ferryman had gone to fetch Song Yi and Sparrow from Longyin village upstream. Chen braced himself. This was going to potentially become awkward.

Even more awkward than he was about to make things.

"I went into Father's study last night," he began.

Mother's face remained blank as she looked over the water.

"I was looking for some records he would have kept. Remember the year of that big flood?"

She showed no sign of recollection.

He went on. "I figured it made sense that Father's administrative responsibilities would have been handed over to someone else and perhaps they wanted his journals. But when I checked with the county magistrate, his office is missing the records as well."

The clerks had been flustered when he'd come in to make his request. A magistrate from another, more prominent jurisdiction showing up to look into operations was a cause for alarm.

"All of those papers would be with Prefect Guan," his mother explained. "He sent his secretary to come collect them shortly after your father's passing."

He remembered the prefect helping to get his father's affairs in order. "Perhaps I can inquire with him when I return to Changan."

"Why do you need those old records..." His mother's voice faded away as the ferry approached the dock.

Song Yi and Sparrow stood at the prow with their robes fluttering in the breeze like two butterflies in flight. Little

Sparrow was in yellow silk while Song Yi was in her usual blue, the color of a clear sky.

"I was just curious," Chen replied, answering his mother's earlier question, but she was no longer listening.

"Who is she?"

Song Yi had caught his eye. She was practiced enough to keep her expression neutral, but his mother had made a discipline out of reading unreadable expressions.

"That's the head surveyor's daughter," he replied. "From when Father was...still with us."

Mother's shrewd gaze remained fixed on Song Yi. "Is that your ferry as well?"

"It is."

"They are traveling with you then." Mother's tone remained even.

"The ladies are *yiji* and registered in Changan. When I learned they were also coming to Yu prefecture, I offered to escort them."

"Courtesans. *Song girls,*" his mother remarked with a heavy sigh. "Chen. My son. Is this just one of those passing fancies?"

"Yes, Mother....one of those." He felt sick to his stomach as soon as he said it. It wasn't as if he was out all night carousing with women hanging over each arm, but Song Yi wasn't just a fancy. Neither was he in the habit of lying to anyone, let alone his mother.

The servants moved to load his belongings onto the boat along with the various gifts and delicacies Mother insisted on sending back with him. This left them enough privacy for Mother to be blunt.

"You are my only son."

"Yes, Mother."

"You are of the age to settle down," Mother told him.

"Yes."

"I would like to hold my grandchildren soon."

He said yes to everything, dutiful son that he was. With a bow, he bade her take care and that he would see her soon, but his mother wasn't finished.

"Be careful. Women in the capital are known to have clever tongues." She eyed Song Yi sharply. "The land surveyor didn't have a daughter. Only a son. Your father was very generous to the family after the tragedy that befell them."

CHAPTER 19

$\mathcal{L}$i Chen was impatient to get her clothes off as soon as they were alone together. Yu prefecture was behind them now.

"They say that distance produces beauty," she said between kisses.

"Nonsense," came his response, his voice rough with desire.

They undressed just enough to feel skin against heated skin. The dull ache inside her sharpened as he took her breast inside his mouth. His clever fingers reached between them, parting her intimately to stroke at the small knot of flesh that left her breathless.

As he positioned himself over her, something changed. Chen's gaze fixed onto her. His chest heaved with each deep breath, not from exhaustion, but from desire. Song Yi met his eyes, willing him to continue.

He reached for her hand just as he had over the edge of the cliff. An ache shot through her as their fingers intertwined. He bent to kiss her passionately before easing himself into her.

Song Yi squeezed her eyes shut. Suspended in darkness there was nothing to distract her from Li Chen. Li Chen throbbing and eager inside her.

They held on, still hand-in-hand, as his body moved with hers, sending her over a different edge.

Only after they had both reached their blissful release did Chen return to finish what he started. He ran his tongue lazily over her nipple while she lay, back arched and panting.

He hadn't forgotten her. She could never forget him.

They made love again, as if to make up for the days apart, before Chen finally rolled onto his back beside her.

"What if there's a child?" he asked, turning to look at her.

His tone was curious as he said it, almost conversational. How typical of a man. Li Chen had been spilling his seed into her with wild abandon, not stopping to think twice about it until this moment. At least he didn't sound regretful or suddenly afraid. She would grant him a little measure of grace for that. And also because he looked so wide-eyed and beautiful looking at her, lying a breath apart on the mat.

"There are herbs to prevent such occurrences," she informed him.

The remedies were well-known in the Pingkang li among courtesans and song girls. A brew taken to prevent pregnancy and another brew to take in case the first one failed. She had experience with both.

"Most don't even think to ask," she said. "These are women's matters that don't concern them."

A frown line sharpened over his brow. She could imagine the thoughts that must be eating at him.

"These matters do concern me," he said finally.

But she could tell he didn't want them to. Li Chen was just a man who couldn't overlook things. He worried about procedures and practicalities. Even so, they had carried on with their affair for a while before he had stopped to think. It was like the matter of patronage and monetary concerns. Easy to overlook in the heat of desire and something Li Chen could forget without consequence.

She didn't have that luxury.

"It's nothing you need to concern yourself with at the moment," she assured him, just so they could move along. "If you're fortunate, you may never need to concern yourself."

"No, Song Yi." He gathered her up in his arms. He met her gaze fervently. "It wouldn't have to be unfortunate, would it?"

Her heart squeezed painfully. This part was also typical. Scholars and their romantic notions. Love and desire could overcome all things—except for filial piety and indentures and class lines.

"Chen, you're the only son of a prominent family."

His arms remained around her, but his embrace loosened somewhat.

She hadn't meant to be cruel, but to let him go on like this was cruelty to her. She knew her place in this affair and she could accept it.

She was meant to be the wound that would never heal. The affair that Li Chen would look fondly back upon in his later years.

Scholars would write about those lost loves with such emotion and passion. Calling them winged birds or flowers or candles weeping in the night. They became symbols on which men could act out their fantasies and draw inspiration to immortalize in their poems.

She didn't want any of that from Li Chen.

"There are...other ways," he offered, thinking that he was being kind.

There was no measure he could think of that Song Yi didn't already know of. She had seen his mother, Li Furen, and felt the woman's cold-eyed stare on the dock. If Song Yi

195

were to bear him a son, the child might be accepted into the Li household, but she never would be. If she bore a girl, Chen was likely to disappear.

He would disappear anyway. To a new appointment, to a marriage his mother would finally arrange for him, or simply because they lost interest in one another. Such melancholy endings were woven throughout Pingkang. It was why all the songs sounded so mournful.

She didn't want to dwell on such sadness when things were still in the rose-colored sunrise of their affair. Before the initial glow started to fade. She didn't want to spoil it.

"Magistrate Li," she cooed, teasing him with his title but also liking the distance it provided. She ran her hands down along his spine, feeling the muscles start to loosen and relax. "I believe you still owe me a story in return for the one I told you. I want a happy one."

～

Do not trust *Magistrate Yang Yue.*

Li Chen stared at the letter he'd received at the relay station from Constable Gao. It was in the constable's hand which was easily discernible from his wife's flowing calligraphy. It was also, at last, finally evident what all the other cryptic messages were trying to convey.

He considered his options. It was possible Constable Gao's warning stemmed from some misunderstanding. Gao didn't particularly like deferring to authority or etiquette or any other rule. But Chen had hired the constable because he trusted his judgment. Especially in matters where he himself might be short-sighted.

They were still a week away from the capital. It would be faster if he traveled by horseback via the relay stations rather than continue by boat. Under emergency situations, a message could be dispatched through the system by passing from station to station where fresh horses and supplies could be taken up. Li Chen could be back in Changan within days.

Chen didn't have the exact authority to commandeer the horses. Messages were expedited through imperial command and stealing an imperial horse was a capital offense. But he was magistrate in the eastern section of the capital, a title he might be able to brandish effectively over the servants working the stations.

"Magistrate, you look as if you're a thousand li away," Song Yi remarked when he came to the tavern.

A thousand li was about what he'd need to travel.

"Something important has come up in Changan. I need to return immediately."

She frowned. "Is this about—"

He knew why she was curious, but he couldn't say for certain what was happening back at the capital. "It's...official business."

Her mouth clamped shut. "Of course. I understand."

The only reason Gao had to bring up Magistrate Yang was the murder inquiry at the House of Heavenly Peaches. Which meant whatever this urgent matter was, it involved Song Yi.

He'd tried to remove himself from the inquiry to stay away from any potential for bias or misjudgment, but handing over his authority on this case might have been his greatest misjudgment.

That was the heart of it. It wasn't about a single inquiry and Magistrate Yang's handling of it. If Li Chen had brought an untrustworthy agent into the inquiry, then he was the one responsible. It was his misconduct.

And Song Yi was tangled up in the inquiry as well. Her entire house was involved.

"I'll need to leave you early. The ferry should be able to take you and Miss Sparrow safely back to the capital."

He'd be there a few days ahead of them. Maybe that would be enough time to clear everything up. Maybe it was best if Song Yi wasn't seen returning to the capital with him.

He could see the questions in her eyes.

"It's nothing," he tried to assure her, touching his fingers to the back of her hand, even though they were in public where anyone could see. "Just bureaucratic matters."

Commandeering the horse was not as difficult as he feared. The station head barely resisted at all after he identified himself and made his demands. The entire time, he kept thinking of the legal code and lamenting silently that he was likely abusing his authority.

Perhaps it was just a minor abuse of power.

He rode out before sundown.

"MAGISTRATE YANG FALSIFIED RECORDS, REMOVED EVIDENCE," Lady Bai spoke rapidly as she counted out Yang's many perceived failings. "Declared injunctions on a whim. Exerted undue authority."

Chen had come directly to the constable's house to dig into the matter and he was learning just how fast Bai Wei-ling could talk. He stared at her, dumbfounded.

"He's hiding something," Gao said in his more succinct fashion.

"It's a very serious matter to make an accusation against an appointed official," Chen warned. "A false accusation is a punishable offense."

"Why do you think I was being metaphoric about it?" Lady Bai replied.

"This last letter was quite plain."

"But you're the only one who's seen it, right?" Gao interjected.

He conceded that point.

"So you would have to be the one to punish me for it." The constable appeared amused at the prospect. "I told her that."

Chen paused, pondering over the implications.

"This is beside the point," Lady Bai said impatiently. "I looked at the submitted reports, and it was clear there was information missing."

He held up a hand to stop her, trying very hard not to let his agitation show. None of this was beside the point, and he was not going to be trampled over by Gao's she-demon of a wife.

"How were you able to see the reports?" Chen asked slowly.

Lady Bai quieted suddenly. She cast a quick glance at Gao who tossed the look back to her.

"My brother was able to request the records on my behalf," she admitted.

"Lord Bai files and composes decrees in the imperial records office," Chen pointed out. "How would he have access to county records?"

Lady Bai fell even more silent, if that was possible. Chen waited. He was very good at waiting for answers, being a magistrate.

"My brother has certain connections given his position and resources—"

"Bribery," Gao interjected gleefully.

"It *wasn't* bribery," his wife snapped.

"Alright, to the point." Chen would have to sort out all the rest of this later. "What exactly did you mean when you said falsification? And removal of evidence...and..."

"Undue authority," Lady Bai offered.

"I'm afraid of you," he muttered, echoing the same words he'd used when they had come up with the plan to extract themselves from the unwanted betrothal. He was ready to listen.

"Yang Yue rewrote your original report. Your writing is completely removed, it's now in his hand. He removed your observations about the condition of the body when it was found in the alleyway. All mentions of the jade ring that Gao removed from the corpse."

"I know from the word on the street that Yang found the inn where the victim was staying. He went there with his own constables," Gao added.

"Also left out of the report," Lady Bai chimed in, eyes bright.

"Was the inn located in the eastern or western county?" he asked, earning him a look of supreme impatience from Bai Wei-ling. Gao merely grinned.

"The truth of the matter is Magistrate Yang has full authority in this case—"

Gao and his wife both opened their mouths to protest.

"—but the removal of evidence is troublesome."

The codes of conduct for a magistrate were more detailed and stricter than the rules that governed thieves. Yang was engaging in a cover-up, yet he wasn't being particularly clever about it. Chen didn't like what that implied. In Changan, that meant Yang Yue had someone even more powerful behind him.

Chen took a moment to gather his thoughts before looking up to Gao. "Constable, I'll need you to accompany me to the western magistrate's office."

Lady Bai followed them excitedly to the door but stopped at the threshold. "Tell me everything that happens," she said to Gao.

"I will," Gao replied with fondness.

Gao came to join him. Together, they walked out to the street.

"Will I need my knife, Magistrate?" Gao asked in what Chen hoped was an attempt at humor.

"You absolutely will not be needing your knife, Constable."

"One can never be certain."

CHAPTER 20

ang Yue was in his offices behind a desk piled high with petitions. Li Chen and Gao caught him with his cup of tea raised halfway. Yang set it down without drinking when he saw them.

"Magistrate Li," he greeted cordially.

"Magistrate Yang." Chen's greeting was not so cordial.

"I didn't realize you had returned. What brings you here so unexpectedly?"

"The inquiry into the courtesan house killing," Chen replied calmly. "It has come to my attention there are some irregularities with the report."

The other magistrate blinked at him before casting a glance in Gao's direction.

"Constable Gao, if you could please wait outside?" Chen asked.

Gao hesitated but left without further argument. When they were alone, Yang Yue immediately stood, stretching to his full height. He was dressed in the official forest green robe of office while Chen hadn't taken the time to don his uniform.

"It was my understanding that Magistrate Li did not wish to become involved with this inquiry."

"You changed details of the report," Chen accused bluntly. "Who are you protecting?"

The senior magistrate regarded him for a long time. "I am protecting someone," he conceded after a pause. "But not for the reasons you might think. We found the identity of the victim, but it was determined including such information would cause unnecessary speculation."

"It isn't within our power to make that decision."

"Magistrate Li." He seemed pained as he continued. "He was an administrator in Yu prefecture and apparently an associate of your father's."

Chen was certain he had misheard.

"The reputation I am trying to protect is yours, Magistrate."

Not only did Yang Yue not deny his actions, he brought out all of the evidence he had withheld. It was all written down and organized.

The victim's given name was Chu, family name of Zhou. Zhou was a lower level bureaucrat, recently promoted. He had traveled to the capital alone. His belongings had been discovered in an inn located in the Xingdao ward.

Chen stared at the deluge of information, trying to absorb it.

"I meant to discuss all of this with you privately, but you were away," Yang said gravely. "Out of courtesy. I even considered this was the reason you had come to me," the senior official went on. "That this matter was closer to you than originally represented and you required a certain…discretion."

How had this suddenly turned again? Chen felt his throat tightening. Now he was the one under suspicion.

"I don't recognize this man. His name isn't familiar to me. All of this is completely unexpected."

Li Chen wouldn't know all of his father's associates. He had been devoted to his studies. Other than copying out the reports, he was unaware of the details of his father's work.

"I did consider that the connection might be purely coincidental," Yang continued. "But you see my hesitation at coming to such a conclusion. An official from your prefecture, an associate of your father's. Killed at the courtesan house that you have been known to visit. As a magistrate, how would you see this?"

Chen stared at Yang, his pulse quickening. "I would find it highly suspicious as well," he admitted.

Yang was staring pointedly at him. Was the official watching his expressions? Searching for signs that might indicate he was lying or telling the truth?

"Magistrate Yang." Chen could barely breathe. "You don't suspect I did this?"

The elder magistrate didn't blink. "Of course not. I trust your word."

Did he? Was Yang truly intent on protecting a respected colleague? Or was there something else?

"Zhou asked for one of the courtesans at the Heavenly Peaches," Li Chen pointed out.

"Miss Song Yi," the magistrate affirmed. "Perhaps because of her connection to you. It's well-known, isn't it?"

Li Chen's blood ran cold. It wouldn't be the first time Song Yi had been threatened because of her connection to him, but it was more than that. This had to do with his father and the secret they had struggled to keep hidden for so long.

His father had hung himself in his study and left them with the empty house and a lifetime of questions. His mother had tried to shield him from that knowledge, but the stain of it was impossible to erase.

Chen had always known he would have to come to terms with his secret shame. Why would an upstanding, well-respected man with a good family and adequate means take his own life?

The only plausible answer was his father wasn't as upstanding as Li Chen had been led to believe.

Li Chen had pondered this question for half of his life now. For longer than his father had been alive to him. Now, finally coming face-to-face with the wrongs of the past left him cold.

A crime committed left indelible marks. Chen believed that. Some of those marks were physical wounds, evidence left behind. Those marks allowed him to track down the guilty and enact punishment. Wash away those wrongs.

But there were also wounds not of the physical world. Those marks lay deeper. On the soul. On those affected, who might suffer without knowing. Those marks were invisible, but the earth could see them. They were visible from the heavens.

Some people called those wounds in the rightness of the world, ghosts. Some called it karma or an imbalance of light and dark energy. The important thing to realize was that the wounds did not wash away with time. They did not disappear with neglect.

"In any case, this matter should be coming to its conclusion soon enough," Yang declared.

"Conclusion? A man was killed. We haven't arrested the offenders."

"*I* haven't arrested the offenders. Yet. You were correct in handing this case to my office, Magistrate Li. Any connection to you is tangential at best. The courtesan and the manservant are the obvious culprits. They strangled him and ran away. There are warrants out for their arrest now."

That wasn't the entire story. Yang Yue knew that.

"And the behavior of the courtesan house cannot be excused either," Magistrate Yang went on gravely. "Hiding evidence. Lying to officials. Such acts cannot go unpunished."

Chen wanted to point out that Magistrate Yang was guilty of the very same, if not worse acts of falsification, but a sickening realization came to him. In protecting him, Yang was protecting himself as well, and sacrificing the House of Heavenly Peaches to do so.

Because the scholar-gentry protected their own.

"I want this case transferred back to my office," Chen insisted.

"That is not a possibility."

"Pingkang li is under my jurisdiction."

"Magistrate Li." Yang Yue paused, then lowered his voice. "You know that would be unwise. You should also know that I have decided the House of Heavenly Peaches will be closed down permanently."

Chen stared at him, startled. "Is that a just decision?"

"More than just," the older magistrate declared.

He had to do something. Chen could petition imperial authorities, but to what end? His connection to the victim would put his motives into question.

"The killing occurred on the premises and they lied while the offenders escaped," Yang explained. "It is a suitable punishment for their involvement." The official met Chen's gaze squarely to head off any protest. "Those women are fortunate I don't have them arrested and beaten as a warning to all who might subvert the law."

THE MOMENT SONG Yi stepped out from the carriage, she knew something was wrong. The wooden signboard above the door of the House of Heavenly Peaches had been covered. The ugly yellow injunction paper was still pasted out front, but another order had been pasted over it. She swallowed, the blood draining from her as she read over the new proclamation, written in angry slashes over the paper.

Mother came out onto the steps and held out her arms. "Song Yi, Sparrow, come inside. Quickly."

A crowd was gathering behind them.

"When did this happen?" Song Yi asked.

She stared at the parlor as Mother hastily shut the front door behind them. The room had been stripped. The furniture had been removed. Even the curtains had been torn down.

"*Mother*," she demanded sharply when no answer came.

"They came and took everything."

"Is this what Magistrate Li left to do?" Sparrow wailed.

Song Yi stared at the girl in disbelief, then looked back to Mother.

"What is she saying?" Now it was Mother's turn to ask questions. Song Yi didn't have any answers.

Auntie shuffled out from the back room. For the first time Song Yi could remember, the old woman's shoulders were slumped over. She was always as straight as a sword, intent on wielding every last bit of her tiny stature.

"It was that other magistrate and his brutes," Mother said. "The house has been removed from the registry. We can no longer do business. They'll come to evict us next."

"That won't happen. You still own this place. They can't take it away." Song Yi didn't know if that was true, but she needed to remain calm.

Mother's fear bled over into Sparrow. "I'm going to be sold to a brothel!" the girl wailed.

"Sparrow!" Song Yi snapped.

The girl slumped onto the stairs, weeping. Auntie looked at Sparrow with sad, cold resignation and Song Yi would have done anything for a sharp reprimand from the old woman to set her straight.

Song Yi needed to think. Sparrow wasn't incorrect. She and Song Yi had value. Mother owned their papers, her indenture and Sparrow's, but Song Yi couldn't let them get to that. They had to have some other assets.

"Did the bastards really have to take all the furniture?" Song Yi said aloud, which seemed to revitalize Old Auntie.

"Turtle egg, dog-headed bastards!"

There was a time when Mother had been the one with influence in the city. When Mother had protected her. Now Song Yi was the one who needed to take care of all of them.

"You have to speak to Li Chen," Mother implored. "You have to tell him."

Li Chen who had left them abruptly three days ago, without explanation. Magistrate Li Chen who had been Mother's last gamble.

What was she supposed to tell Mother? Instead of ensnaring him, she'd been caught herself? If she hadn't spent the last month chasing a worthless affair with Li Chen—

An urgent pounding came from the door, making both Mother and Auntie jump. Their eyes darted back and forth like cornered alley cats. Two of the most fearsome and composed women she knew. She could see the desperation in their eyes. What else would be taken from them?

Song Yi took a deep breath, even as the pounding continued. She realized, with dismay, that it might not take much before she was reduced to where Mother and Auntie were now, but she wasn't there yet.

Steeling herself, she moved to the door.

It was Li Chen. Of course, it was. For a moment, the sight of his face bought with it a glimmer of hope. Her beloved noble gentleman, here to save them.

"Miss Song Yi," he began, and the glimmer of hope flickered. His expression was calm, resolved. He'd come here with a plan and a purpose. "May I come inside?"

Slowly her fingers curved around the jamb of the door. Instead of drawing it open, she formed a barrier with the slight form of her body. "Magistrate Li."

How alike they truly were, now that it had come to this. Li Chen was so adept at his rules and codes. At remaining composed as he submitted to the laws he was a servant to, whether or not it was what he wanted. But she was a master as well, of the unspoken rules. Of the small pockets and hidden ways someone small and helpless and vulnerable could still draw power.

The last thing she would do was to let Chen see what was behind this door. That they had nothing left, but to beg for mercy and throw themselves into the hands of fate. Which really meant the hands of men.

"I need to speak with you," he said. "Privately."

"Magistrate, you shouldn't be here," she advised. "There will be scandal."

There was already scandal. Curious faces peered at them from the street.

"I'm sorry for this, Song Yi."

He meant it. She could hear it in his voice. The only barrier she had left was this door. She certainly had no protective walls left to crawl inside.

They'd traded secrets with one another in the dark. He cherished her above all others, but he couldn't fight societal rules. Family bonds. Fate. She knew all the laments. Girls who meant everything to the men who, for all their powerful influence, could or would do nothing to save them. Alas. The tragic poems that ensued were spectacular. Meant for the ages.

Madame Shi tried to push past her, a sure sign that Mother wasn't thinking clearly.

"Magistrate Li," she pleaded. "You're an honest man. A just magistrate. We've done nothing wrong. You know us. You've enjoyed our hospitality. Surely you can help us?"

Song Yi watched his expression. She saw the small crack in his exterior, even though he tried to hold steady. Li Chen was a compassionate soul. That was why it was so easy to let herself fall. But he was also a man of the law and of duty. Impassioned pleas might tug at his heart, but his mind would always overrule his emotions.

"Mother," Song Yi said gently. Her gaze locked with Chen's even though she addressed her den mother. "It won't do any good to beg the magistrate for leniency. He's come to tell us that he has no control over this case. He relinquished control so he would wash his hands of responsibility."

So he could pursue her with a clear conscience. And do nothing now with just as clear of a conscience.

"You can't be seen showing favor," she finished for him. She'd heard him echo the words so often. "The legal code is a powerful thing in the hands of such a righteous magistrate. It keeps you from having to make any hard decisions."

CHAPTER 21

*C*hen flipped to the last panels of the folding book and inked out a rough triangular shape with the fine tip of his brush.

Porcelain shard. From broken plate. Blood stain along tip and edge.

He drew a ring next, swirling the brush to try to capture the design.

Ring. Yellow mutton fat jade. Interwoven carving.

"Li."

"Constable." Chen didn't look up from the record.

"What source of abuse and corruption are you uncovering today?"

"Apparently my own."

He finished recording his observation before turning his attention to Gao. The constable stood over him, looking curiously at the book he was writing in.

"What is that?"

"A record of everything I can remember from the case."

If Yang wouldn't allow him access to the case records and evidence, Chen would have to use his own account. He could see why his father would keep his own journals. His judgment was best when he was able to look over details on paper, re-reading as he pondered from different angles.

"Yang Yue was covering for me," Chen revealed.

Gao looked genuinely shocked. "You?"

He set down his ink brush slowly. "Magistrate Yang wants to close the inquiry and lay all the blame on the courtesans of the Heavenly Peaches. I have to solve this case if there's ever to be justice."

"You've re-written all of that from memory?" Gao asked as Chen flipped through the panels.

"I recovered an early copy that I had discarded when the ink had gotten smudged."

Gao gave him an odd look. "Interesting thing about that." The constable pulled out his own book and set it onto the desk. "From my wife."

"This couldn't be—"

Gao sat down in the seat opposite him. "That's not Yang's actual report. Wei-wei was only allowed to view it once, but she wrote down everything she could remember immediately afterward."

"Lady Bai is a remarkable woman," Chen murmured, eagerly sifting through her account.

"Women hold up half the sky, as they say," Gao intoned.

Chen looked up to see Gao was still giving him that strange look. Like a wolf deciding whether or not to pounce.

"I was just thinking that if you had been a little less honorable," Gao said. "Or myself a little more."

Li Chen didn't like the direction of the constable's thoughts. Lady Bai and he had never gotten betrothed. She would have found his attitude confining and he would have found her rebelliousness insufferable.

"Everything happened as it should," Chen said, hoping to calm the waters.

The predatory look disappeared, and Gao appeared to shrug the thought away.

Chen focused back on the two reports. Yang's report had been stripped of nearly all detail, just as Lady Bai had claimed. The changes were drastic.

"This can't all be just for me," he remarked.

"Hmm...?" Gao politely interjected.

"Magistrate Yang created an entirely new record. This level of falsification puts him highly at risk. There has to be more to this."

There were too many coincidences. What was the connection?

Zhou Chu. Yu prefecture. Director Guan.

The banquet.

"Zhou Chu had to have been at Guan's banquet that night," Li Chen concluded.

Gao frowned, confused.

Chen explained as quickly as he could. Guan He had served as prefect of the Yu region before coming to the capital. Guan was known for promoting and elevating people close to him. It stood to reason that Zhou would have been invited. It gave him a reason for being in the capital.

Song Yi had been at the banquet as well. Zhou could have seen her there and sought her out the next day.

Li Chen needed to figure out why.

Song Yi strode up the stairs of the drinking house. Li Chen stood waiting for her inside a private sitting room. The low table had been set behind him with two porcelain cups and a flask of wine.

"Is this a ploy to get me to come to you?" she asked.

The letter had come to what was left of the House of

Heavenly Peaches along with a small chest of silver—the same quantity of silver that had already been sent and refused once before.

Li Chen's eyes were fixed on to her. "Not a ploy," he said, his voice strained.

The sight of him was enough to send her heart racing. "I'm not going to humbly return your money. I'm going to spend all of it without a second thought to you because that's all you are to me now."

His jaw hardened, but he took the blow without flinching. "I want you to. I'd give more if I could."

To assuage his guilt. She had no problem taking his money. They needed every last coin.

"Will you sit?" he asked.

She remained standing. "Do you want me to play the tragic courtesan? Should I weep in your arms so you can comfort me and tell me you wished this wasn't so?"

"No," he said harshly. "Song Yi."

He spoke her name sharply as a reprimand. That was a first from him.

She couldn't maintain her composure. Their house was in ruins. Her family desolate and fearing they wouldn't survive the winter. Yet here she was, still wanting Li Chen to feel something for her when it would do nothing for any of them.

"You couldn't bear to leave things so cold between us," she prompted bitterly.

"*Stop*." Chen bent his head, rubbing a hand over his temples in agitation. "I couldn't, but—that's not why I asked you here."

"Why did you ask me to come?"

"The man who came looking for you was once an administrator in Yu prefecture. His name was Zhou Chu. Do you know him or why he would come looking for you?"

She closed her eyes, trying to remember. "My father passed away unexpectedly. I was told there were debts."

Chen frowned. "What sort of debts?"

"Debts." She had been so young, she couldn't remember more than that. The memories were buried so deep, they seemed to belong to someone else. "My father died in an accident and we were left with nothing. I went with the procurer so my family would have one less mouth to feed."

She sensed Chen moving close. When she opened her eyes, he was watching her. He reached for her hand gingerly.

She didn't expect the ache in her chest. "There are stories like mine throughout Pingkang."

"I know." His expression remained troubled. "But this is your story."

She knew he cared for her. It only made things harder.

"You went with the procurer so your family would have one less mouth to feed?" he repeated carefully. "Or was it because of your father's debts?"

Song Yi tried to remember. Her family had needed money. Did it matter what it was for?

"I went to the city." She could see an official building with wooden columns in her mind. She'd gone there for help finding her father. "Would this man Zhou have known the land surveyor?"

"It's possible."

They regarded one another, the space between them laden with promise. The last time they had been alone like this, they had still been lovers. If only it could have lasted longer. If only they could still play that game now.

"I meant what I said up on the cliff," he told her. "I want to find out what happened to your family."

"For the inquiry."

"For the inquiry, and for you. And for me. There is a

larger story here and I believe we can find it together, but you need to tell me everything, Song Yi."

She didn't like thinking of the past, but if it would save her family, her new family, she would do it. She would search through time and fog.

"My name," she began. "The name I was born with wasn't Song Yi."

CHAPTER 22

*I*t was a common occurrence for Li Chen to call on the director for tea. After his father's death, Guan He had seen to his education. He'd become a mentor, almost a second father.

Guan had also made the necessary recommendations for Chen to be appointed magistrate in the prominent eastern county of the capital.

If it wasn't for the dark and foreboding presence of Constable Gao beside him, this might have been any other visit. Having Gao there made things serious business. Chen had discovered that just Gao's presence unnerved people, which at times was a valuable trait.

The gated mansion was the largest on the street. Just inside, they were greeted in the front parlor by the young retainer Chen had seen at the banquet attending to Guan.

Li Chen remembered him because of the slight asymmetry in the shape of his jaw as well as his penchant for questions. He'd asked Chen something about taxes, which was odd in conversation, but the young man was studying for the imperial examinations. Chen had told him the examination typically didn't ask about taxation.

"Magistrate Li," Guan called out at the sight of him and grinned wide. The elder bureaucrat met him with clasped arms, his eyes darting momentarily to Gao who stood just behind Chen.

"How long has it been? A month?" Gao said as a maidservant poured tea for both of them.

Chen exchanged a few pleasantries, relayed his mother's well wishes along with the parcel of tea she sent as a gift. He thought he detected Gao stifling a yawn.

"This incident in Pingkang li, have you heard of it?" Chen asked finally.

The slight shift in the director's expression told him the answer even before Guan answered. "The man who was found dead there? Worrisome indeed."

"I typically wouldn't discuss an inquiry so openly, but the matter was passed over to a colleague, Magistrate Yang Yue. It has since become known that the victim was at one time an administrator in Yu prefecture."

Guan made a noise of acknowledgment. Drank more tea to hide his reaction.

"I wondered if you might know him."

The director made a good show of ignorance. There had been so many levels of bureaucracy when he'd been prefect. Perhaps Zhou was someone he'd crossed paths with here or there.

"Do you have a list of the guests who were at your banquet?" Chen asked.

"I'm certain we do," Guan said.

Guan called his retainer over, the same young man with a thoughtful look about him. As he approached, Chen detected a sudden twist in the retainer's expression, but it quickly disappeared.

"Lu Xian, retrieve the list of guests from the banquet last month for Magistrate Li."

The retainer bowed before disappearing into the depths of the mansion. As Chen started to conclude the visit, he finally revealed the real reason he'd come.

"Director Guan," he began. "I respect you greatly. You have been a presence in my life for as long as I can remember."

Guan was touched by his words. "Chen, my boy. I can proudly say you are like a son to me."

He remembered then that Guan had no sons of his own. Perhaps that was why he made a habit out of taking on young proteges and mentoring them.

"To the director's credit, he has always sought to support and protect those close to him. I am honored to be one of those few."

Guan was in the midst of humbly accepting the compliment when Chen delivered his final blow.

"Did the director intervene in the inquiry on my behalf?"

Once again, Guan's reaction told the answer before he ever said a word. The director actually looked proud to have been exposed.

"Value your good reputation like gold, my son," Guan counseled.

"The director asked Magistrate Yang to protect my reputation," Chen stated bluntly.

"At first, I thought not to interfere," Guan admitted. "But I couldn't let what was an unfortunate accident bring a promising young career to ruin."

It wasn't his association with Song Yi or the House of Heavenly Peaches that Director Guan wanted to scrub away. The problem was this case. The murder inquiry itself.

Magistrate Yang had made an extraordinary effort to clean the case record of any connection to Li Chen. Yang had rewritten the original report to remove details about the victim and erase any connection to Yu prefecture. Even the ring no longer existed. Perhaps Guan was trying to protect himself from any hint of scandal. It was well-known in Changan that Director Guan was Li Chen's sponsor.

So much offered protection without Chen ever lifting a finger. All it cost was the lives of Song Yi and Sparrow and the rest of the courtesan house. The Heavenly Peaches, already tarnished with scandal, provided a convenient place to lay the blame. A traveler had gone there unwittingly to meet a tragic end. The poor girl Pearl was still missing and couldn't defend herself when she was accused of murder.

Chen had to pull himself back. He couldn't let sympathy cloud his judgment. He needed a clear head for their sake as well as his.

He understood the reason for the concealment now. Director Guan wanted to ensure there would be no tie to Yuzhou and no scandal, but the question of the murder was unresolved.

It could have still been Pearl and the manservant. Yang was right, unfortunately. All other entanglements aside, they remained the most likely culprits.

Lu Xian came to them just as they were about to leave. "Magistrate, the guest list you requested."

The young man held out the paper. Chen paused, staring down at his extended hand, before reaching out to take the list. When he glanced up, Lu Xian was watching him carefully. The young man's jaw twitched.

"You were the one who asked about land taxes at the banquet," Chen recalled.

Lu Xian looked startled. "Yes, sir."

Something tickled at the edge of his mind. "My father used to administer land taxes. In a county at the heart of Yu prefecture."

~

LI CHEN OPENED the folding book and spread out the long sheet of paper over his desk so he could see all of his notes at one glance. He added in the guest list he'd just procured.

Zhou, the stranger who was no longer unknown, had indeed been at the banquet.

Yu prefecture was at the heart of it. Song Yi was at the heart of it.

Somehow Li Chen and his history were also a part of it.

His father had worked under Guan as a land tax administrator. He'd kept records on who owed what. Every few years, land would be reapportioned. The equal fields law required surveyors to map out the territory outside of the capital.

When his father had died, Guan's secretary came to take those records. Had that been Zhou, the man who'd been killed?

Constable Gao's arrival interrupted his thoughts.

"I left you here yesterday and here you still are," Gao taunted amiably.

"What is it, Constable Gao?" Chen asked, more terse than he typically was.

"I have a gift for you."

It was a bundle wrapped in paper. Chen started to open it, but then a sudden realization stopped him.

"It's not really a gift," Gao assured.

That wasn't the problem. Chen picked up the parcel and held it out to Gao. "Hand this to me again."

Gao complied, the corner of his mouth quirking upward.

"Now give it to me with your other hand."

They repeated the cycle. He returned the parcel to Gao, who switched it over to his left hand before giving it back.

Chen tapped his fingers over the parcel thoughtfully. "'Do you know of anyone who favors their left hand?"

Gao shrugged. "Maybe one or two."

"It's not something you see among scholars," Chen pointed out. "It's discouraged, which is to say, we are all trained to use our right hands regardless of what we might favor. Giving someone any item with your left hand, a cup of tea, for instance, would be considered utterly impolite."

Back in Guan's mansion, Lu Xian had handed him the guest list with his left hand, Chen realized. That was why the exchange felt so awkward. The young scholar's other hand had remained by his side, hidden by the drape of his sleeve. Why had he needed to conceal his right hand?

"There was a shard of porcelain found at the courtesan house." Song Yi had given it to him. Chen had drawn it into his record.

"The victim was stabbed with it," Gao concurred, beginning to understand.

To use the porcelain as a weapon, someone would have had to grip the shard firmly to stab the pointed end. The sharp edges would have cut into their palm.

"Constable, if someone were to cut themselves on something like that, how long would it take to heal?"

"You've found him, haven't you?"

"Possibly," was all Chen was willing to allow, but his pulse pounded as the pieces began to fit together.

There was a process to follow. Chen would need to authorize an arrest. Right under the roof of Director Guan, his very own benefactor.

"My discovery doesn't seem as impressive in comparison, but you should open that package," Gao said.

Chen looked down. He'd forgotten he was still holding the thing. With a tug, he loosened the string and opened the paper wrapping to reveal blue silk with silver embroidery.

The robe Song Yi had been wearing the night of the banquet. The same one Pearl had put on the night she disappeared.

"I found it in a pawn shop in Xingdao li," Gao reported.

"Xingdao is outside of our jurisdiction." The ward was in the western half of Changan.

"That's why it took so long to find. The robe was sold to the shop a week ago."

ourteen years ago...

The girl gathered her father's papers and letters, placing them carefully together before sliding the stack into her traveling pack. She couldn't read what was written on them and neither could her mother, but there were correspondences from the land bureau in there. Letters from the people in the city who'd employed her father and who might be able to help them.

Her mother was staring at the empty hearth when she left to make the long walk into town. There was no more wood for the fire.

It was her younger brother who tried to stop her. He ran out to grab onto her hand, tugging at it to pull her back inside. Little Jie had arms like sticks. She was older and stronger, twelve years to his five. She shook him off even as he tried to cling to her.

"Stay with Mother," she told him.

He didn't say anything in reply. Just pleaded with eyes that were round and wet. If he had called after her, she might have stayed, but she hadn't heard his voice in days. Not since their father had gone.

Even in the morning fog, she knew the way. Follow the river until it met the road. Follow the road into the city. Water lapped at the bank as she picked her way over the smooth stones. She missed the sound of the river when it was time to turn away.

The sun rose to burn away the fog as she walked. At midday, she ate a ball of rice that she had pressed together and kept walking. The sun was sinking again by the time she reached the city. She stood at the edge of it, staring at the winding streets and wooden structures.

All she had to go by were the letters. She pulled out the letters to show people she met in the street.

"Where do I go?" she asked and asked. They shook their heads and couldn't help.

In the drinking house, someone pointed her to a large building with red columns and a curved rooftop at the center of town. The land offices were in there, they told her. But the doors were closed for the day. She would have to wait until morning.

The innkeeper let her sleep on the floor in his common room. Another traveler there watched her for a long time before retiring. Then she was left alone to think about what she would say when those large wooden doors opened the next morning.

Everyone was certain by now that her father had drowned. Three days ago, he had climbed up into the surrounding cliffs but had not come back down. The villagers searched the surrounding hills, the river, the shore. Fallen from the cliffs and washed away, their neighbors proclaimed when nothing was found.

The girl wanted to keep on looking. The day before, she

had searched from sunup to sundown with Little Jie trailing sullenly at her heels. She and her brother were the only ones still looking. Two wayward children without more important work to do. Her mother seemed to have already given up.

The fog rolled in thick the next morning. She woke when the inn started stirring and went to draw water from the well to wash her face before going to the land office. The traveler from the night before was already there. He was broad featured, with a face that was both round and doughy. He lifted the bucket from the well for her, and she thought it strange a guest would take on such a menial chore.

"Pretty girl," he crooned looking over her face.

She hurried away into the fog.

At the land office, the doors were already open. Rather than leading inside, the doors opened into a courtyard that surrounded several different offices. She wandered from office to office, forced to repeat her story to every clerk and runner. Her father was a surveyor. He was gone. She needed help.

She was ready to weep when she stumbled into a room full of shelves of scrolls and papers. There was a boy seated at the far end of the room reading from a book. He looked up curiously at her.

"Who are you looking for, Miss?" he asked.

No one had ever spoken like that to her. She was only a child, her hair unpinned with wild strands slipping from the loops. Her clothes were frayed and rumpled. Her slippers were muddied from the road and the river.

The boy was older. His hair was pulled back neatly into a bun and set with a wooden pin. Everything about him seemed so clean and cultured. His clothes were fine and the way he spoke seemed so clear and resonant, as if it weren't even the same language, even though she understood the words.

Instead of answering, she turned around and ran back into the courtyard. This time there was a tall man with a pointed black beard standing there.

"You're the surveyor's daughter?" he asked.

She nodded meekly.

"Come inside, child."

Inside a dark and foreboding office, she explained the entire story once more. Her father had disappeared. They said he was dead. There was no money left for food, for firewood, for a funeral.

Her family wasn't like the others in the village who cast nets and set traps and gardened for food. Her father was paid by the land office. Her mother bought and bartered for the things they needed. But when she'd asked her mother what they would do now, Mother had kept on saying she didn't know, she didn't know, she didn't know.

The girl had been so lost until the tall official with the beard had found her. The official took her to the juncture where the rivers met. There was a ferryman there who sometimes pulled large fish from the river that had washed downstream.

As they neared the ferryman's hut, she realized the mass covered by large banyan leaves was not a fish at all.

"Two days ago," the ferryman said to the official.

"Do not look, child," the bearded official said to her.

But she had to look because her mother was at home staring into an empty hearth and her brother had lost his ability to speak.

The gray dead thing beneath the leaves did not look like her father, which only made it worse when she understood this was what Father had become.

The bearded official spoke quietly to her as he led her away. Her father must have fallen, he said, just like the villagers had told her. He'd hit his head on the rocks below.

She nodded, feeling numb. She'd seen where the skull had been crushed. The dark mass that had been there instead of her father's face.

The bearded official had heard her father was a good man. What a tragedy it was. Her father must have been up in the mountains taking measurements and lost his footing.

"Father couldn't have taken measurements," she murmured.

The official halted abruptly, and she stumbled to keep from running into him. She glanced up meekly to see him staring down at her.

"What was that, child?"

His tone had been quiet and soothing up until that moment. She didn't know why she'd chosen to contradict him. It was just something to say.

"N-nothing, sir."

"Tell me again what were you saying, child," he implored, trying to recapture the same calm and soothing tone he'd used on her before.

"There are r-ropes used for measurement."

The villagers hadn't found any when they had searched the cliffs. All of the ropes and instruments her father would use were still in his trunk at home.

The official tried to ask more questions. Who typically assisted her father? Where had they searched? But she could only shake her head at the questions. She didn't know, she didn't know.

He saw she was becoming flustered and kindly allowed her time to calm down. Then he told her he would help her family. The ferryman needed to be paid and handlers could be hired to transport her father's body home. And there was the matter of the tenant tax and her father's other debts.

"Debts?" she'd asked.

Her mother and father must not have told her, he

explained gently. Her family couldn't remain in their home unless they paid the tenant tax. And her father had a growing list of debts. Perhaps that was why...

Perhaps that was why...the official never finished that sentence.

Instead, he spoke of practical matters. He would try to help with the money for the funeral and the taxes and the debts. He would help their family sort things out as much as he could.

To her, the official had seemed so kind and generous. He hadn't known her father well, but he was willing to help. All she needed to do was go home and gather up all of her father's instruments and notes. Everything her father had written. If she brought all of those belongings to the land office, he would pay her.

And then she would have enough to have her father brought home.

She didn't understand everything the official had tried to tell her. Father hadn't said anything about debts, nor had her mother, but her father often didn't tell her things when she tried to ask about them. She was just a daughter.

Perhaps that was why...

Why had Father climbed up into the mountains alone? The villagers, after searching for only a single day, had stopped trying to help. Why did their neighbors speak in hushed whispers? Why did she hear talk of wandering ghosts and strange shadows that were following her father around?

She turned to take the long walk back home where she gathered up all of Father's belongings, as many as she could carry. She told her mother and Little Jie that she had found him.

Her brother cried and once again tried to hold onto her when she left this time, but she could only think of her father lying cold in the ferryman's hut. As a daughter, she had no greater duty than to bring him home.

She returned to the city on the second day. Her feet were sore from the road and her slippers worn thin. The bearded official allowed her into the land office even though the sun had gone down. He lit lanterns inside his study and looked over the papers she had brought.

"Very good," he murmured. He reached into a cabinet and took out a lacquered box. She watched as he reached inside and counted out the coins. Three in total. He reached over to drop the coins into her waiting palm.

"Such a dutiful daughter," he said with an air of approval.

She'd been so stupid then. She'd thought that was a lot of money. That her mule-like trudging back and forth from their village to the city had somehow solved all their problems.

The ferryman took one of the coins and the handler took another to prepare her father's body. It was ill-omen to handle the dead and no one did it without payment. The one coin left wasn't enough to hire a cart to transport her father home.

When she went back to the land office, the kind and generous official would no longer see her. She returned to the inn with aching feet and a hunger that gnawed at her insides, but the inn keeper's generosity was also spent.

Only the pale, doughy-faced traveler had any charity left to give. He brought a bowl of rice porridge to her and stood by while she spooned every bit of it into her mouth. She thanked him humbly, clutching onto the one coin she had left.

"Such a pretty girl need never go hungry," he said.

She straightened then, the hairs on the back of her neck rising in alarm. Her face was grimy from road dust and sweat. No one ever called her pretty.

"What do you want?" she asked, too exhausted to be polite.

He was looking for girls from good families, he told her. "Families who have fallen on hard times."

Her father had refused to teach her numbers and sums, but she performed her own calculations then and there. A calculation that incorporated her mother's despair, her brother's grief. The cold body of her father and his ghost awaiting its final rites. The cold hearth at home, the empty larder, one less mouth to feed, and the long, long walk that she could not bear to make again.

She made a better deal negotiating with the procurer than she had with the official at the land office. He gave her enough to pay for her father's body to be transported home. The remainder of the money she tucked inside the shroud wrapped around the corpse.

"If you steal it, his ghost will haunt you forever," she warned the handler who promised to deliver both her father's body and the stash of coins to her family.

She left the city with the procurer, knowing she had done her duty to her family the only way she could.

That was the day she learned to be wary of acts of kindness. That was the day she learned to leave her past behind. Those lessons were cut deep into her down to her very bones. The memories themselves she let fade away into the mist.

She barely remembered the face of the tall official with the beard. She had been a wretched and grieving child, too afraid to look a grown adult in the eye. Time and death could also change how a person looked, rendering them unrecognizable.

What she mostly remembered were those cursed three coins and the brief space of time when she had been lulled into thinking the world was kind. The official had closed his hand reassuringly over hers after handing the money to her. As if to say her fate was truly in her own hands now and everything would be taken care of.

She had stared at that hand as it closed around hers, but over the years, she'd forgotten that moment. Until now.

There had been a pale ring around the official's finger, carved in jade.

∿

SONG YI MOVED AS FAST as she could, but it was two thousand paces to the magistrate's yamen. She moved past gates and through dirt roads, weaving past wheelbarrows and oxcarts. It was impossible to get anywhere fast in Changan with its walls and streets and wards.

Would her memory make any difference? The man who had come to the Heavenly Peaches to see her had been some lower-level official in Yu prefecture. The same man who had been responsible in some part for sending her to Changan. What could he have wanted with her after all these years?

Song Yi hadn't recognized his body. She'd been so young, so frightened. Afraid to even lift her head as she'd begged for help. At the time, the official's actions had forced her down the path of desperation. Now, after everything that had happened since, he was nothing more than a moment from a time she wanted to forget. One more nameless, faceless man who'd dismissed her as worthless.

She hadn't thought of those three coins in a long time. Or the callous hand that had given them to her. Just enough money to recover her father's body from the ferryman's hut.

Bitterness filled her heart. Maybe this was karma. The combination of a stranger's casual cruelty and her own grief had taken her away from her family. Whatever forces his disregard set in motion had led in a winding road back to his death.

She couldn't be held responsible. Yet why did she feel so cold in the face of this knowledge? She didn't need another tragedy on her soul.

It was an hour before the yamen gates appeared. She was exhausted after spending the entire day on her feet. Just a little farther and she'd be able to tell the ending of the story to Li Chen. A tale of accident and misfortune that had followed her through all these years.

Maybe she could finally be absolved of the past. Maybe everything and everyone she touched would no longer have to suffer.

She started toward the gate, but a young scholar in blue and grey robes suddenly blocked her path. His jaw was square in shape, but slightly crooked. It caused a slight quirk of his lips when he spoke. Instead of moving aside, he fixed his eyes on her.

"Are you playing the same game I am?" he asked with a quiet fierceness that set her back.

Song Yi frowned. "Pardon me, sir?"

His directness startled her. There was something untoward about his manner, but they were out in public. He was a scholar and a gentleman. Etiquette demanded she treat him with civility, but the wildness in his eyes made her want to turn and run.

"They say that you're having an affair with the magistrate," he said through gritted teeth. "With the *honorable* Li Chen."

She took a step back. "I don't know you."

"Don't you?" he questioned.

Anger seethed from him, though his hands remained at his sides. One hand was wrapped in a bandage. When she looked back at his face, she remembered where she had seen this man before. It had been at Director Guan's banquet. He was the young scholar she'd seen speaking to Little Sparrow and then Pearl.

Pearl. The two of them had been in conversation briefly. Pearl had tilted her head toward him, flashing a half-smile.

Did Pearl have a lover after all? What was he doing here?

Song Yi braced herself as the man took another step toward her. He was taller than her. Slight of build, but still able to overtake her if he tried. His youthful face belied a steel-eyed intensity.

The magistrate's yamen was just behind him. If she shouted from out here, would anyone hear her?

"There are three men responsible for Father's death," he declared coldly. "Two of them are dead now, but one still draws breath. The one who is most responsible."

"I don't know what you're talking about," she protested, but a pit of dread formed in her stomach. The more she stared at the scholar's face, the more familiar it became. The shape of his eyes tapered toward the corners. Like her own eyes.

With a jolt, she realized she did know this face. He had the face of a man she had last seen fourteen years ago.

"Our father was murdered, Lihua."

Song Yi hadn't heard that name spoken to her in so long. She started shaking. It began in her knees and spread through her entire body until she couldn't stop it.

"Jie," she whispered, unable to draw a full breath. An image came to her of a scrap of a boy, all elbows and knees. "Little brother."

CHAPTER 24

*T*he problem wasn't that Li Chen didn't have the evidence.

The problem was that he didn't have the authority.

He spent the better part of the day reviewing the legal code while Gao paced by the door of his office, waiting for orders.

"If you knew how these things played out in the street, Li, you'd understand that we can sort this out later," the constable insisted.

Chen's eyes remained on the text. "Absolutely not."

The code of conduct for magistrates in legal matters stretched out longer than the Yellow River. There were rules.

Chen had instructed Gao to dispatch his constables to Xingdao ward, which was not only outside his jurisdiction, but there was also a warrant for Pearl's arrest issued by Magistrate Yang Yue. Li Chen had the authority to arrest the young scholar Lu Xian on suspicion alone, but Yang held all the official records and evidence from the investigation, not to mention the official authority over it.

Then there was the delicate matter of Director Guan

being Lu Xian's protector, as well as Li Chen's own complicated relationship with the director.

Finally, there was the even more delicate matter of his relationship with Song Yi and the House of Heavenly Peaches. They had been caught up in this through no fault of their own.

Any arrests should be handed over to Magistrate Yang. But Magistrate Yang had made clear he was under Director Guan's influence and ready to sacrifice the lowly courtesans.

All of that couldn't be covered in any text that existed in this world. Li Chen only knew two things. If he acted against Lu Xian, he'd be doing so without Guan's favor, something he had relied on to get where he was. The second thing he was certain of was that he needed to protect Song Yi and the other ladies of the Heavenly Peaches.

"Constable, can you please bring your wife here?"

"My wife?" Gao had that dangerous look in his eyes again.

"Yes, your wife," Chen said firmly.

Bai Wei-ling came into the office beside Constable Gao within the hour. Even in plainer clothing, her refinement was evident. There was an elegant quality in the tilt of her chin and the straightness of her spine. Her gaze moved longingly over the shelves of books in his office before settling onto him.

"Lady Bai," he began, running a hand tiredly over his face. "How does one go about wielding influence with your brother?"

Her eyes brightened.

Runners were dispatched. Chen made a trip himself to the imperial records office to see Bai Huang, the assistant collator of the left imperial records office. Despite the seemingly trivial administrative job, the young Lord Bai far outranked him.

In Changan, status roughly corresponded to how close

one was physically in relation to the Emperor. The records office was located in the gated section to the north called the Imperial City. It was the site of an ancient palace, but the complex had been converted to a maze of departmental and administrative offices.

Bai Huang was also notably disliked by Director Guan and his faction, so he was certainly not under Guan's influence.

The nobleman listened with a thoughtful expression on his square-jawed, well-formed face while Chen explained the situation. Chen had known the young Lord Bai from his academy days. It was often said that scholars who took the keju in the same cohort would form bonds. Those bonds would later prove useful as they rose through the ranks together.

That wasn't the case between himself and Bai Huang. Though Chen had managed to pass and earn his degree in one try, Lord Bai had failed that exam period and then went on to fail another before passing. As students, their paths had rarely crossed. If Chen had a reputation as a know-all *daoshi*, Bai Huang had a reputation for being what they called a flower prince with a pretty face. In his day, he'd enjoyed his wine, his women, and, rumor had it, he would have gambled away the family fortune if it wasn't so vast.

Their paths had crossed more than once over the last few years in Chen's time as magistrate. Then a year ago, their families had nearly come together in marriage. The young Lord Bai had surprisingly supported the arrangement, yet showed no enmity when the arrangement had dissolved.

"Corruption charges," Bai Huang repeated thoughtfully. He wore the dark robes of office and an imperial cap, presenting a much more serious figure than the notorious playboy he was reputed to be. "Against your benefactor."

"If it comes to that," Chen replied, feeling hollowed out. "If he tries to intervene."

Director Guan had supported Chen and his mother after his father's death, but the bureaucrat didn't own him.

"Magistrate Yang Yue is also your superior."

Chen nodded. Magistrate Yang's conduct needed to be challenged, even if it brought Chen into a bad light. "Can this be done quietly?"

"Of course," Bai Huang replied with a hint of humor. The corner of his mouth twisted. "No one likes corruption charges. Hopefully, your adversaries will quietly concede."

"Do you outrank Guan He?"

Huang shook his head. "Not officially." He seemed quite pleased to qualify that.

Bai Huang's noble family was entrenched in the capital and imperial politics. They had generations of influence and wealth behind them.

"This maneuvering doesn't suit you, do they, Li?"

Chen squared up across from Bai Huang. His head was pounding so hard the pain had to show in his eyes.

If he had married Bai Wei-ling as his mother had wished, he and Bai Huang would now be family. Chen's path into the upper ranks would have been assured.

A magistrate was the lowest of the imperial ranks. He worked directly with the people. A magistrate engaged with men like Gao, who were considered immoral and untouchable.

The legal code changed as it flowed upward. Words apparently had different meanings to the upper ranks.

"It doesn't suit me," Li Chen admitted, feeling a bit of the weight lifting from his shoulders.

Song Yi liked to tease him that he was a man of rules. It wasn't always an insult. He'd made it this far by navigating the rules. It wasn't an insult if she could accept him that way.

"Thank you for your assistance, Lord Bai."

They stood and bowed in farewell. He had a plan in place, and for the first time since he'd returned to Changan, he sensed that balance would be restored.

Until he discovered Song Yi was missing.

THEY WERE IN XINGDAO WARD. Constable Gao stood beside him while their assembled band of constables and runners searched the area.

"I should have protected her," Chen muttered.

He waited for Gao to at least politely assure him that he couldn't have known. That a magistrate couldn't protect everyone. That they were doing their best and would find Song Yi soon. But Gao offered no such courtesies.

The constable instead had a map in his hands. He was tracking progress as his runners scoured the streets. The two of them were situated outside the pawn shop where Pearl's silk robe had been sold. The search radiated outward from there. It was the best guess they had for a starting point.

Constable Gao had gone to arrest Lu Xian himself the night before to find the young scholar was also missing. That action had alerted Director Guan and Magistrate Yang of their activities. Li Chen remained out in the streets to avoid their summons.

"Scholar Zhao reported that Song Yi had come to him yesterday morning to ask for money," Chen said, his heart heavy. "He gave her twenty taels of silver. That was the last anyone saw of her."

The bureaucrat reported that their arrangement had been concluded. He had been her patron for a time, but there was no longer any association between them. It was like a contract. With perhaps some affection in the early days.

Duty was duty, but Chen would have rather walked through a nest of snakes.

"Constable Gao." He beckoned Gao over and handed him a set of paper. "I brought you these. Census information. The latest information about the residents of this ward. I thought it might assist us in our search."

Gao sifted through the papers skeptically. "Who lives in each house and how much they paid in taxes."

Each county housed hundreds of thousands. One needed to be methodical in approach.

Fortunately, Xingdao li itself only had five hundred households. Chen took the map and papers from Gao. "These buildings were vacant as of the last accounting. The courtesan Pearl and the scholar have been in hiding. Focus your search on those first."

"Constable Gao!" One of the runners came to them. "We found a possible witness."

The public notices had gone up in the evening with Pearl and Lu Xian's descriptions. An elderly woman was brought to them. The washer woman had been hanging laundry in her yard the day before.

"I saw a young man in scholar's robes going up the stairs next door," she reported. "There was a woman with him. I noticed her because she was so beautiful, Magistrate. She was crying, but she seemed to be following the young man willingly."

Crying. He prayed no one had been hurt.

"Let's go," he said to Gao.

The washer woman led them back to her hovel and pointed to the second-floor room next door. Gao took the lead up the stairs, and Chen insisted on following closely behind. A group of the runners gathered on the ground floor to provide support if needed.

Chen expected to see Gao kick down the door or something frightening like that, but instead, he simply knocked. When there was no answer, he knocked again, louder.

"Come out," Gao called. "We have you."

There was a long pause. The door finally opened to reveal Lu Xian with dark circles beneath his eyes. He had the appearance of having slept in his clothes.

"So it goes," the young scholar said quietly.

"Where is she?" Chen demanded, ascending the last few steps.

The scholar's eyes darted to him. A look of hatred twisted his smooth features. Without a word, Lu Xian spat at him. "The bastard son!"

Gao shoved a hand against the scholar's chest and pushed him back. There was movement from behind him in the room. The moment Chen saw Song Yi, he moved past Gao and the scholar to go to her. Before he could reach her, Song Yi froze and stepped back.

"Magistrate Li," she said, her voice thick. Her eyes were swollen. Immediately behind her was the missing Pearl, her eyes wide with confusion and fear.

A shout came from down below, including a commanding voice that ordered the runners to stand aside.

"The Great Yang Yue has arrived," Gao murmured, still holding the young scholar back.

Lu Xian's eyes burned into him. "You're not fit for her, Li Chen. Son of a murderer."

Chen stared at him, startled. What was the scholar talking about? He was a man of order and everything he knew had been thrown into disarray. From outside, he could hear footsteps charging up the stairs. Magistrate Yang's constables.

Song Yi finally reached him. She touched a hand to his arm.

"Have you been harmed?" he asked her, full of concern, but Song Yi wasn't listening.

"He's my brother," she said desperately. "It's Jie. My younger brother."

Chen looked back at the scholar who glared at him with the cold eyes of a cobra. The young man spat again at the ground by Chen's feet. "Son of a murderer. You're not fit to uphold the law."

CHAPTER 25

The prison rooms were located in the corner farthest away from the magistrate's residence. Li Chen strived to have them unoccupied, but that wasn't always possible.

The interrogation was to occur in one such prison cell. It had been stripped of everything but a mat of straw and a chamber pot. Lu Xian kneeled before him, his wrists in chains. His scholar robes had been removed and he was left in white underclothes, his hair untied. Even his shoes had been stripped away. Murderers weren't afforded such courtesies.

Li Chen might have considered being more lenient given this man was Song Yi's brother. He might have shown mercy given that their pasts were linked.

"This is not your case, Li Chen." Lu Xian stared straight ahead, refusing to look at him.

Magistrate Yang hadn't objected to Chen stepping in for this interrogation. It turned out Yang was truly in the same predicament Li Chen was in—trying to follow rules of conduct that had so many twists and turns.

243

"You can be punished merely for speaking before you are addressed," Chen began.

"I can be punished for any whim you might have," the youth retorted.

He was only nineteen. The same age Chen had been when he first came to the capital. Guan did like to recruit young talent to his side.

"Would you like water before we begin?"

Lu Xian sneered. Chen imagined he would have spat again if he hadn't been deprived of anything to drink. The other magistrate's methods were different from his own, but they were not out of bounds.

"Did you kill Zhou?"

"I did," he said without a trace of remorse.

"Did Pearl help you do it?"

At the sound of the girl's name, Lu Xian faltered for the first time. "She's innocent," he proclaimed. His tone lost its hard edge. "I forced her to come with me."

"Did you go to the House of Heavenly Peaches intending to kill Zhou?"

His face was a mask. "He was coming for my sister."

"For Miss Song Yi."

"That is not her name."

Chen paused. There was a resemblance between Song Yi and Lu Xian. It was in their eyes.

There was something else eerily familiar about Lu Xian, or Jie as Song Yi called him. When Li Chen had seen him attending to Director Guan, the youth had reminded him of himself. Fresh-faced with a look of concentration creasing his brow.

Even now, with Lu Xian stripped down and in chains, Chen still could not banish the association.

"You told your sister three men were responsible for your

father's death," Li Chen continued. "And that Zhou Chu was one of them."

"Your father was another," the prisoner spat.

Sharp pain stabbed through his chest. Chen would have to listen and endure the insult if he was to ever know the truth. He had long suspected his father was not entirely honorable due to the manner of his father's death, but Chen was still his father's son with a son's sense of duty.

"Your father was a surveyor assigned to Yu prefecture," Chen prompted, forcing his tone to remain steady. "His death was said to be an accident."

Lu Xian trembled. "It was no accident."

"What evidence do you have of this?"

His jaw turned to stone.

Chen repeated the question, but Lu Xian wouldn't answer. He could see the young man's mouth twitch and the look of anguish that crossed his face.

"Did you see something that led you to believe your father was murdered?"

Lu Xian stared straight ahead. Nothing.

Chen thought of the long climb up to the edge of the cliff. Song Yi had led the way with him trailing behind. She had told him a story that day about how her father would climb up the mountain with instruments. Sometimes she and her brother would come along.

At such a young age, a boy might see something he couldn't make sense of. Chen had been fifteen years old when he had seen the ligature marks on his father's neck. Lu Xian would have been five years old when his father passed away. What had he seen?

"If you tell me—" Chen started to say that he might be able to help, but that wasn't a promise he was free to make. "If you tell me, then someone besides yourself will finally know the truth."

Lu Xian swallowed. He forced the next words out through gritted teeth.

"A son cannot live under the same sky as his father's killer. I killed a man who deserved to die. That is my confession."

~

Song Yi embraced Pearl for a long time in the holding cell. They clung to each other. Her little sister seemed thinner and she trembled in Song Yi's arms.

They had been left alone. A runner had brought tea, which Song Yi hoped was a good sign. They were free of any manacles or chains. Also a good sign, but Pearl didn't see it that way.

"I'll be beaten," Pearl cried. "I'll be branded as a criminal."

She stroked Pearl's hair and tried to hush her. "You did nothing wrong," she soothed.

Pearl finally quieted by the time Li Chen came to them, but she grew tense once more in his presence.

Chen lowered himself onto a stool to meet Pearl's eyes. "Are you hurt, Miss Pearl?"

Pearl shook her head. He spoke quietly and evenly, telling her not to be afraid. Telling her she was safe now. Song Yi was grateful Li Chen was being so careful with Pearl.

He proceeded with questions about the fateful night. The gentleman had come late in the evening and Mother had sent Pearl in to pose as Song Yi.

"The moment we were alone, he knew immediately I wasn't you. He started demanding, where is she? Where is she?"

Zhou had grabbed onto Pearl and as she struggled to free herself, that was when Lu Xian, who Song Yi knew as Little

Jie, had appeared. But he was no longer the little boy she'd known.

"He dragged the man away from me and the two of them fought, knocking the table over." Pearl shook as she described how Lu Xian had grabbed onto a shard of porcelain and stabbed it into Zhou's arm. "But then he wouldn't stop," she said, horrified. "It was like he was possessed. He grabbed the old man by the throat. He wouldn't let go."

"Did you call out for help?" Li Chen asked dispassionately.

Song Yi shot him a look, but Chen ignored it as he waited for an answer.

Pearl stared at him, wide-eyed. "I don't know."

Only when it was done did Lu Xian look over to see that it was Pearl there and not his sister. By that time, both of them were frantic. Lu Xian had grabbed Pearl and dragged her out the back door.

"Did you go with him willingly?" Chen asked.

To that, Pearl couldn't answer. She had been in hiding with him for a month. She had been afraid of Lu Xian. She was both afraid to go with him and afraid to stay.

Pearl turned to Song Yi in the middle of her account. "Lu Xian told me he had seen you at the banquet, but he wasn't certain it was you."

Song Yi hadn't recognized her brother either. Now when she looked at him, she could see traces of her father. The shape of their eyes, however, was from their mother.

Pearl finished her account of the weeks that followed where she'd hidden in the room above the stairs. At first, she was afraid of being blamed for the murder. Then the arrest warrant was posted, and Pearl was certain she'd be thrown into chains if she escaped Lu Xian only to be caught by the constables.

Eventually, Li Chen had all of the information he needed and he allowed Pearl to go.

"I still have questions for you, Miss Song Yi," he said when she tried to leave as well.

Song Yi had watched Li Chen's face as he asked his questions, but he remained composed and unreadable.

Once they were alone, she assumed it was her turn to be interrogated, but Chen's demeanor changed. The grim magistrate slipped away and he was Li Chen again.

"That was the brother you spoke of," he said.

She nodded weakly.

He grew quiet. "And your mother?"

"Jie doesn't know where she is."

The flood washed their house away, but her mother and brother had survived. Desolate, they had left Yuzhou to seek help with family.

"One day, they took shelter with a couple who took pity on them. The couple had no son and the next morning when Jie woke up, Mother was gone and the strangers were telling him they would take care of him as their own. He never saw our mother again."

The last memory Jie had of her was immediately after waking up. He'd peered out the window to see a small figure disappearing down the road into the morning mist. He only realized later that it must have been their mother.

"Song Yi, I never knew," Chen said. "I never imagined."

It pained Song Yi to realize her mother had done the same thing she'd done. Song Yi had left, thinking the only way to take care of Jie was to sacrifice herself. Revenge was the only way for Jie to keep the memory of the family he once had alive.

"My brother says that your father and Zhou were involved in a corrupt land tax scheme," she said, her voice barely a whisper. "Is that true?"

"I don't know." Chen met her eyes. "That is the difficulty of all this. It is sometimes impossible to know for certain, but I owe you one thing. Something my family has kept hidden for many years."

Chen looked anguished. "My father changed in the last years of his life. Mother said he was generous to your family after your father's death. As if he was trying to make amends for something. After the flood came and your house was washed away, something broke in my father. Whatever ghosts haunted him, they finally took over. He hanged himself in his study."

He let out a long breath. "We don't speak of this in my family. I never knew why he did it. If what your brother claims is true, my father had done something unforgivable."

Silence fell between them.

"That does not absolve him," she said bitterly, forcing the words past the tightness in her throat.

"I know it doesn't."

All this time, there had been fate between the two of them after all. But not the sort of fate they had thought.

"My brother didn't intend to kill the man," Song Yi pleaded.

"Your brother's life wasn't in danger," Chen argued, looking troubled. "Nor was Pearl's. If he had thought he was defending her and had unintentionally caused a death, he could have come forward. A confession before the crime is discovered could warrant some leniency, but he hid for a month."

"He thought I was in danger."

Chen met her gaze directly. "I just spoke with your brother. I would say he was very clear that he meant to kill Zhou Chu. He might not have come to the Heavenly Peaches with murder on his mind, but once he encountered the man he claims was responsible for his father's death, your brother chose revenge."

She squeezed her eyes shut. "Please show my brother mercy. For my sake."

"I can't, Song Yi," Chen replied, which is what she'd known he would say.

Chen's father had been responsible for her father's death and now Chen would send her brother to his.

Karma was not a benevolent force. Karma did not resolve old wrongs. The cycle just repeated.

CHAPTER 26

*L*i Chen went to pray to his father's spirit at the shrine set up in his residence. He prayed for forgiveness for what he was about to do.

All of his life, Chen had fought to be a good son and uphold his family honor. Now he had no choice but to destroy it. He would have to be a better son in the next life.

He settled into his office and started writing. There was an order for the reversal of an injunction. A stay of execution. A petition for clemency.

A son cannot live under the same sky as his father's killer, he wrote in bold calligraphy.

Why spend so much time learning so many characters if he was not going to use them all?

"Corruption charges," Bai Huang proclaimed as he looked over the papers Chen had handed to him. "Two of these men are already dead and one is alive."

"My father died years ago. Zhou Chu was killed in the capital in an act of revenge. And Director Guan He is still very much alive."

"You don't need your father's name in here. The case can

251

be made without it," Bai Huang pointed out. "No one needs to know of that."

His stomach knotted. After finishing the report, he'd become physically ill.

"Heaven knows. Earth knows. You know. And I know," Chen quoted. "It's the truth. There's no weight to the argument if it doesn't tell the whole truth."

Three in number also had a certain fatal poetry to it, Chen realized.

It had taken him a month to search through the past. He was aided by Lu Xian, still in chains, but still alive. Lu Xian also still hated him but was willing to provide Chen with the information he had uncovered.

Song Yi's brother had spent his life building his case to avenge his father. Given time, he might have succeeded, but a twist of fate had put him in a position to strike out in anger.

Chen's father, Li Wan, was a land tax administrator like his family had been for generations in Yu prefecture. Zhou Chu was a financial officer and tax collector. It was easy for them to distribute land, collect taxes, and issue false reports on land holdings in order to send a lower amount to the imperial treasury. The difference was divided between them.

Both his father and Zhou had reported to Guan He at the time, who was prefect.

The final piece was given to him by Song Yi who agreed to see him only once during the month. They met in the parlor of the House of Heavenly Peaches, which had been reopened for business. He paid for an hour sitting. She poured him wine and he asked for her to tell the ending of the story she'd begun during their journey together.

She told him of the ring and the bearded official who she had thought, in her innocence, was acting out of kindness. Zhou Chu had asked for her father's papers and instruments in return for money to pay for his corpse. And then he'd left her to her own fate. A stray orphan was no threat to him.

"Your father was appointed to the region to provide accurate measurements of the land holdings," Chen explained. "He discovered the scheme and would have exposed them. When Zhou Chu received a warning fourteen years later about his past crimes, he was certain it was the surveyor's daughter who was threatening him."

She listened to the entire plot, her face drained of any emotion. "If I had only known what I held in my hands. I would ask my father about his work, but I was just a useless girl asking useless questions."

She could never be useless. He wanted to tell her that and so much more, but there were other things that needed to be resolved first.

"Father would explain things to my brother that he wouldn't tell me," she recalled. "Even though Jie was only a child. He would sometimes follow my father up into the hills. I think my brother saw something that day. Afterward, he kept on staring up at the cliffs, unable to speak. And my mother, she was beside herself."

Song Yi was the only one left to speak for her family. She'd tried to do the best she could, what she'd thought her family needed, just as he had done.

The hour was nearly up. He had one last thing to tell her.

"When you went to the land office, the morning was thick with fog. There was a young boy reading in the library. I would go to the land office with my father to study for the keju examination. One day, a young girl wandered in from the mist. I remembered her eyes. They were so expressive, and there was a depth of sorrow in them. I'm certain now that girl was you."

The girl's sadness had set something in motion for him. Her sudden and inexplicable appearance had pricked at his sense of rightness and order. He had known instinctively from that moment that something had been thrown askew, even if he didn't know what it was.

Song Yi looked away. Li Chen cursed himself for his stupidity. Falling for a tragic heroine with sad peach blossom eyes. What had been a schoolboy's fantasy for him was an unhappy memory for her.

He tried to apologize. He tried to touch her hand, but she pulled away.

"Where has the time gone?" she murmured, looking at the candle which had burned down over the hour.

When he tried to see Song Yi after that, his request was always politely deflected. It wasn't because she was otherwise engaged. The start of winter was upon them and business had slowed. He once called there to see Sparrow playing in an empty parlor.

He tried to send money to the courtesan house only to find it promptly returned. This time without any attempt to continue the conversation. No further words were needed. He understood the message well enough.

CHAPTER 27

*L*ight snow drifted down as Song Yi hurried along the street with the jug of wine she'd been sent to fetch cradled against her side. Last time, they'd sent Sparrow and the wine seller had overcharged. The girl's musical ability might be progressing, but she needed to practice her haggling skills.

A dark figure caught her eye as she neared the Heavenly Peaches. Her heart leapt. He was standing beneath the eaves of the teahouse and she knew who it was immediately, even through the thin curtain of snow, with those squared shoulders and arrow-straight spine.

Li Chen. He'd seen her as well. He caught up to her in the street.

"Magistrate." Her breath formed a cloud in the air.

"Miss Song Yi."

His voice. The sound of it sent a tendril of warmth down her spine. She had thought, she had hoped, it wouldn't do that anymore.

"I didn't want to leave things the way they were," he began, struggling for words.

"It's cold," she protested, her heart pounding. "Come inside."

This wasn't a conversation to be had out here.

Chen fell in beside her and they hurried toward the door together. A welcoming warmth enveloped her as soon as she was inside. Chen shut the door as she shook snow from her cloak. When he turned to her, there was a hint of pink in his cheeks.

"You weren't out there long, were you?" she scolded.

"Not long."

Silence fell between them. Li Chen stood there, taking her in with those dark and serious eyes.

"Magistrate, *a-chi*." It was Little Sparrow who came to save them. "Oh, there's the wine."

Sparrow retrieved the wine jug before flitting off toward the kitchen.

"Ancient Well Baijiu," Song Yi explained absently.

Li Chen made an effort to work with that. "Ancient Well? That must mean…"

"Our best customer has returned."

Lin Yijin, their notoriously hard-drinking, spendthrift patron had returned, and the House of Heavenly Peaches was flourishing again.

"Good news," Chen offered.

"Good news," she echoed.

A look of longing flashed in his eyes but then disappeared. She still felt it in the pit of her stomach. It was as if they were back in the early days of their association. They had been uncertain around one another, still finding their way.

She was a courtesan. This sort of navigation was supposed to be easy for her, but she was finding it was no longer true with Li Chen. Everything between them had too much weight.

"Will you have tea?" she invited.

He looked grateful for the opening. "Yes. Tea."

Old Auntie ducked her head out from the back of the house. Black eyes peered at them from her creased paper face.

"Auntie, could you bring us—"

"I heard. You go on."

Li Chen gave her a cordial nod as they passed by, which Auntie even returned without scowling.

Song Yi led him to the stairs and went to the upper floor, to the room in the corner. As he came inside, Chen was surprised to see they were inside her private room.

"I had to leave the room downstairs."

"Quite understandable," he replied.

They had converted her room downstairs into a parlor. She'd been unable to sleep there ever since the incident. On the other hand, Lin Yijin liked to hold gatherings there where fantastic ghost stories were told over expensive wine. Scandal was apparently good for some business.

Sparrow came with tea, which she set dutifully onto the low table before departing, and then Song Yi and Li Chen were finally alone.

He'd come in his magistrate's uniform and she tried to discern what that could mean. Her brother had been released unharmed from confinement a week earlier. Jie had come to the Heavenly Peaches and had immediately fallen asleep.

Song Yi had watched over her brother, marveling in the resemblance to their father, whose face she'd only dared to look at in sidelong glances. Pearl had come in once to check on them, leaving quickly before Jie woke.

"I see you're still magistrate," she remarked, indicating the forest green silk.

"Yes." He ran a hand absently over the front of the robe. "Surprising as it is."

257

The last month had been a series of battles for Li Chen. There was speculation he had made too many enemies and would be removed from his position. It would have been a loss for the city. Li Chen was undeniably suited to be magistrate. He put his heart and soul into finding answers and righting wrongs.

"Thank you," she said softly. "For my brother."

"I didn't do anything," he protested.

"I know you risked your reputation to defend him. Against high-ranking officials."

"Don't thank me. My petition failed. Guan He couldn't be touched. He denied any involvement," Chen said, frustrated. "He simply threw the blame onto the dead."

She knew this as well. Once Jie had recovered, her brother had said his farewell and left Changan. He couldn't bear to stay in the city knowing the man who was responsible for their father's death lived there enjoying both wealth and status.

Tentatively, she reached out to place a hand onto Li Chen's arm and his breathing deepened. His muscles tensed.

"You don't wish to hear all of this," he apologized.

"You can tell me anything."

They were sitting stiffly beside one another on the chaise. He ventured a breath closer, watching her closely.

When Chen bent to kiss her, there was hesitation. She returned the kiss gently. The feel of his mouth on hers was familiar, yet also unknown. They only dared the lightest of touches, uncertain with one another after all that had happened.

This wasn't them at all.

He pulled away. "I'm worried what your kindness right now must mean," he admitted. "Is this just...the illusion?"

It was what courtesans were trained to do. Put minds at

ease and make assurances of devotion. Were Li Chen's overtures just acts of familiarity?

Was she already a memory?

"This isn't out of kindness," Song Yi insisted, her fingers curling into the front of his robe to draw him closer. She had to know.

They kissed again, pressing further, daring more. It was different between them now. Each touch was more deliberate, less swept away. She could see the thoughts flickering across his face as he undressed her.

His eyes darkened as she loosened the tie of his sash and opened his robe. She ran her hands along the plane of his chest and the play of muscle along his shoulders. The memory of gripping those shoulders came to her. Of kissing his collarbone and running her fingers down his spine. She did those things now, retracing the steps they had taken together during all those nights.

For Chen's part, she knew immediately what parts of her he missed most. He captured her mouth as his hands cupped her breasts, then her hips to pull her to him.

Song Yi closed her eyes when his tongue traced the shape of her nipple and the dark pleasure of it tugged at her.

Their lovemaking had become fragments of old memories, new memories, and a slow heat burning beneath it. Unlike the flash of desire that had consumed them before.

Her body resisted at first, then clenched possessively around him as she took him inside. He made a sound deep in his throat. A sound indicating he was both lost and found.

"I don't want this to ever end," he whispered, moving inside her.

Their coupling lasted longer than it ever had before, as if they were willing it to go on. Fighting the end. Because it really would be an end, Song Yi realized, her heart seizing.

Chen was tender in a way he'd never been before. Sentimental. Drawing out each moment.

He must have sensed the change in her, in some unspoken way. He deepened his kiss, his tongue thrusting against hers, trying to pull her back to him. He reached his hand between them, willing her to accept, to forget that their time was and had always been hurtling toward its end.

She bit his neck as he started to thrust harder. She would leave her mark any way she could. His fingers moved in an endless cycle, teasing the delicate bud at her center.

They couldn't hold on even if they wanted to.

Desire demanded release. It broke over her in a wave, a flash of heat, all-consuming and then gone. Chen flooded her with his essence immediately after, while her inner muscles pulsed around him. Small tremors in the aftermath of the quake.

There was an inevitable sadness after. The emptiness of a fire extinguished.

He kissed her again before slipping out of her. He didn't want to leave things unsettled between them. She wondered as he lay over her, drained and satisfied, if things were any more settled between them now.

"I THOUGHT OF YOU EVERY DAY," he confessed.

She closed her eyes and let the words settle warmly over her like a blanket.

"I thought of you as well."

"I remember every moment we had together. Our journey down the river. Our time is like that for me. Endless."

Poetry. From Li Chen. Her heart squeezed so hard it hurt. The refuge of scholars trying to find pretty words to smooth out ugly emotions. This will end. It was ending now.

"A river," she said airily, drawing a curved line down his chest. "How imaginative. What will I be in your memories? The moon. A candle weeping in the night?"

She braced herself for the answer.

Li Chen failed to detect the change in her mood. "You would be a red blossom in the snow," he continued dreamily.

"That sounds so tragic."

"It's not," he insisted. "Plum blossoms symbolize resilience and endurance, despite the harshest of conditions. They blossom in the cold of winter. That's you, Song Yi," he said earnestly.

Resilience. I know you will forget me, the great poets would say, in parting.

"You're stronger than anyone I know," he continued, thinking it was a compliment. As if she had any other choice but to bend, to endure, to go on.

"I hear that Li Furen is returning to the city," she interjected.

He started, loose muscles suddenly going tense. She lay in the circle of his arms.

"My mother?" he said. "She spends time in the capital as well as back at the family mansion. Where would you have possibly heard that?"

Which meant it was true. His embrace became a touch less welcoming. She'd jolted him out of his haze of bliss.

Why was she trying to ruin the moment instead of cherishing it? Song Yi pulled his arms around her, almost in defiance.

"There were times over the last month I thought things were over between us," she admitted.

"I tried to come see you."

"I thought an order for Jie's execution would come down any day. And that might be a day where you had held my hand or I had permitted you to kiss me."

He held her tighter. "I only wanted for us to talk."

"But that would have been even worse." Their conversations were everything to her. Thoughts were the deepest things they shared.

"I've wronged you," he said.

"You haven't wronged me."

His family had. His father had. And her brother hadn't forgotten. Even though Jie, or Lu Xian, was a stranger to her, he was the only blood she had left. Those were the wounds that wouldn't heal between them.

But they could still close some wounds. They could end their passionate affair with grace.

"I just want you to know, when I think of you, Li Chen, I don't think of all that happened after. I think of the very first time you kissed me. Showing up at my door. Looking so lost. That's what I'll remember. When there was only hope and none of the pain."

"The pain is part of it."

She shook her head. She didn't want their family tragedies to be what tied them together.

Li Chen tried to turn her to face him, but Song Yi resisted, no longer able to hold back her tears. She didn't want him to see she was crying.

Eventually, she stopped fighting. Chen turned her around and kissed her hard.

"What will you remember?" she asked him when the kiss ended.

"I don't need memories," he said, his eyes never leaving her face. "You're right here."

"Your mother is returning to Changan, which means she'll be arranging a new match for you." Her voice caught. "You don't seem the sort to want to continue an affair with a wife at home."

He swallowed. "You're right about that."

"So?"

"So," he echoed and nothing else.

"So you'll be married soon and all I want is for you to give me a memory. It's a lover's game. Play along."

She was becoming agitated. Now he was ruining it.

"Song Yi, I'm not going to be married soon."

"If it's in a month, or a year, or two years, then it's soon," she retorted.

He sat up abruptly, pulling her with him. He cradled her face in his hands. The strong, serious lines of his face filled her vision.

"Song Yi, the only way I would be married soon is if it's to you."

She tried to pull free, but he wouldn't let her. "Don't joke about that."

"It's not a joke. It's not a romantic illusion. This is fate."

"Because your family has wronged mine?"

Song Yi reached for her robe. She had to tug it out inelegantly from beneath him before pulling it around her shoulders. Beside her, Chen shuffled around to retrieve his clothes.

She knotted her sash impatiently. "You can't say these things because they're not promises you're free to make, Chen. I thought you were honest and practical enough to remember that."

"I am being honest."

"I'm indentured to this house. I'm too expensive for you."

He rose to his feet, which forced her to do the same if she didn't want to be towered over. Chen had dressed hastily as had she. He was a mess, his hair loose and his uniform disheveled.

"I'll pay off your debt. That's practical enough, isn't it?"

There was a note of desperation in his arguments. He was trying so hard to make things fit in his mind.

"You're the only son from a prominent family. You have a bloodline to uphold."

"It seems like you're the one who isn't being practical," he argued, then stopped suddenly. "Is it because I'm the son of a—"

He couldn't say the words.

"That isn't why," she said, horrified.

She wanted to weep again but in frustration this time. If there was a way to ruin happy memories, this was surely it. Laying out to each other all the ways they were ill-suited for one another. All the ways they would never have worked.

Instead, they could have kissed and parted and not said these things out loud. If only Li Chen hadn't insisted on arguing that impossible things were possible.

"Nothing works with you," Chen railed. "You say you're practical, but you won't take my money. You want me to court you, but you won't accept my poetry."

He ran a hand over his face as if trying to scrub away the emotions. She'd only seen him lose his temper like this once before.

He stared at the ground, searching and desperate. "I love you, Song Yi," he said, stricken. He looked up at her. "I've loved you since the first moment I saw you."

Her stomach lurched. Her heart beat at her insides, prodded by hope.

"That can't be true," she said, her tone flat.

"It can be if you can let yourself believe it."

They were completely unhinged, both of them. Clothes askew. Hair undone. Anyone seeing them would think they were mad. She wanted to believe.

"Which time?" she asked, her voice trembling.

He was breathing hard. "What do you mean?"

It wasn't their first kiss that she remembered. She had lied about that. That kiss had been the easy part.

She remembered how Chen had held onto her as she looked over the cliff down into the river below. And how he'd held her afterward, refusing to let go even when she tried to slip away.

"Which first moment?" she demanded.

Chen looked at her long and hard with every bit of conviction he had.

"All of them," he answered.

"The will of heaven," his mother declared with an air of resignation when Li Chen told her about Song Yi. "The two of you have fate together. You will continue to be brought together in this life and the next until whatever debt you owe one another is resolved, for better or worse."

It wasn't the same sort of excitement his mother had shown as when he was to marry the daughter of the rich and influential Bai family, but Chen could accept that.

He wondered if his mother knew, in some part, what his father had done. Why else would she speak of debt? Father had tried to atone for his wrongs by being generous to the surveyor's widow and her remaining son, but it hadn't been enough. Then he'd tried to atone for his crimes by taking his own life, passing the blood debt on to those who remained behind.

Madame Shi was considerably more joyous when he went to the House of Heavenly Peaches to pay off Song Yi's indenture. It helped that their best patron had returned to host expensive banquets once more.

Shrewd business person that she was, Madame Shi quoted a higher amount than what was listed on the papers.

"Our girl has increased in value over the last fourteen years!" Mother insisted. "She is like a daughter to me, how can I cut out my heart for any less?"

"He's the county magistrate, Mother," Song Yi had reprimanded. "He knows that's not how the indenture works."

"It's only a hundred taels more."

Li Chen was prepared to pay until Song Yi pinched his hand beneath the table. "Fifty," she countered.

"Such a good girl," Madame Shi declared with tears shining in her eyes.

THEY MARRIED within the month when the plum blossoms were in full bloom and vibrant against the fallen snow. Surprisingly, it was Li Chen's mother who was the force behind the decision for them to be wed so quickly. The astrologer had found an auspicious date. They should begin their lives together before the start of the new year.

Song Yi's younger brother, Lu Xian, managed to bury the past enough to come to the wedding. He attended in his scholar's robes and kept to himself, quiet.

Director Guan sent along a gift of silk, with a letter proclaiming how happy he was for Magistrate Li Chen, who he had always and continued to think of as a son.

"I would have thought you made an enemy when you brought corruption charges against him," she remarked.

Lord Bai had brought corruption charges against Guan before the Emperor, but with two of his alleged co-conspirators dead, Director Guan had easily blamed his two subordinates for the scheme. He managed to keep his position in the Ministry with hardly a scratch to his reputation.

Li Chen glanced at the letter from his former mentor before throwing it into the fire. "I have made an enemy."

Song Yi would have thrown the bolt of silk into the fire as well, but Pearl and Sparrow snatched it up.

"She must be wealthy now," Pearl glowered. "Throwing away quality silk like that."

Pearl was big sister now with Little Sparrow trailing along to learn from her.

After the wedding, Song Yi took up residence in the magistrate's quarters in the yamen. Pingkang li and her courtesan sisters were only two thousand paces away.

In the cold winter months, activity in the markets of the capital was more subdued. There were fewer skirmishes and disputes. Even thieves and scoundrels seemed more intent on staying sheltered and warm than committing petty crimes.

Whether true or not, the petitions to the yamen slowed as the days became shorter. Chen made the walk along snow-covered paths to the offices every day but was quick to come home to Song Yi.

They lost themselves and found themselves in each other's arms.

She would play gentle melodies on the pipa for him in the evenings. He would read to her from his books.

Occasionally, Li Furen would visit for dinner. "I want grandchildren," she'd say to them, quite succinctly.

Once they retired to their bedchamber, they would happily oblige. Li Chen would kiss Song Yi passionately while he worked the ties of her robe loose with clever fingers.

"I told you it wouldn't be so unfortunate," he'd say softly to her afterward while they were entangled together. "If there was a child."

Song Yi would lay in his arms, watching the snow fall

through the lantern-shaped viewing window. She could imagine it. A dark-eyed little boy. A little girl full of questions. Li Chen would answer each of them, patiently.

Their daughters would not be raised lowly and docile, unworthy of knowledge. Song Yi would never allow it and Chen was incapable of withholding any part of himself from the people he loved.

Which is why she loved him.

"This is what I will always remember," she told him, her head resting against his chest. His heart beat a steady rhythm, unfaltering. The moment included the hope as well as the pain. It held the memory of everything that had come before, as well as the promise of all that would come after.

AUTHOR'S NOTE

This story was forming in the background of *The Hidden Moon* where the beginnings of Li Chen and Song Yi's relationship could already be seen. At the time, I had no idea how the two could ever be together. When Li Chen says, "That isn't possible"—he absolutely believed it and so did I.

In the first books of the series, *The Lotus Palace* and *The Jade Temptress*, I wanted to explore the dual nature of agency and subservience that the courtesans of the Pingkang li experienced because I feel that that duality encompasses much of what it means to find agency as women throughout history and in the contemporary world as well. The other thing I wanted to do in the *Lotus Palace* series was avoid the trope of "virtuous girl manages to escape becoming a sex worker" through luck and cleverness.

That twist of somehow keeping the seductress pure was prevalent in many of the old historical romances I loved. It even reared its head in an early novel of mine, *The Dragon in the Pearl*.

In Song Yi's case, I wanted her to undoubtedly be a sex worker. I wanted her to have had previous patrons, to have learned from them, to even have past lovers who broke her heart.

But I didn't want her to be broken because of her experiences. This was her life, her livelihood, and it reflects the life of many women. Her life as an entertainer and a courtesan in the capital would be part of her rise, not her fall.

I can say that each story I write has some part of me and my family history within it, even though my family is from Vietnam and this series takes place in Tang Dynasty China.

My grandmother was arranged to be married to a man that she didn't want, so she ran away from home temporarily only to find herself unable to return. By the time she did make it back to her village, decades had passed. Everyone she knew—her mother, her brother, the cousin who ended up marrying the man she didn't want, were all gone.

Song Yi took on that piece of my family history as the girl who was brave enough to make a move, but not experienced or wise enough to know what to do next.

Instead of fighting against the constraints of her courtesan house, Song Yi embraced her new family and her place within it. Through *Red Blossom*, I wanted to explore the positive and supportive relationships that must have formed between the women of the quarter.

The madams in Pingkang were referred to as Mother and this led to the exploration of Song Yi's relationship to Madame Shi, a woman she genuinely loved and cared for after being rejected by her own mother.

Unlike Song Yi, Li Chen has a long history in the series.

He was first introduced in *The Lotus Palace* as "there's a new magistrate in town". In *The Jade Temptress*, Li Chen saves Constable Wu Kaifeng when he's being tortured, securing Wu's release by filing many petitions. *The Hidden Moon* sees Li Chen emerge as a potential suitor for Wei-wei and prepares him to have his own book.

As Li Chen's career spans the series, it stands to reason that his office has earned a reputation for handling many complicated cases.

Every time I write another Lotus Palace book, I research deeper into the Tang Dynasty. This book required more research than any other. I already had my foundational research into the courtesans of the Pingkang li, also referred to as the North Quarter. Add onto that more detailed research into the Tang Code of law as well as research into death rituals and customs.

All this was required because Li Chen is a rule follower. That doesn't mean that the rules he set out for himself have to follow every known law and regulation, but I certainly needed an understanding of what was considered acceptable legally and culturally. From that foundation, I could define Li Chen's character based on how he interprets such things.

From the research, I derived Li Chen's opinions on filial piety, duty toward the empire, but also larger duty toward a higher morality based on Daoist and Confucian ideals.

This actually played into the romance plot as well. There are specific periods of abstinence prescribed around mourning and death memorials which I felt needed to be mentioned since this was a story that revolved around how the deaths of Li Chen and Song Yi's fathers in the past continued to affect their present lives.

Because Magistrate Li Chen is a man of rules, I wanted to know what the Code might say about getting involved with a potential witness in a case. Surprisingly, the Tang Code had very specific provisions dictating that an official was not allowed to have "illicit sexual intercourse" with bondsmen, retainers, or slaves within their area of supervision were to be punished by resignation.

There is also a provision that dictates an official who

commits "illicit sexual intercourse" within their jurisdiction would be disenrolled.

"SUBCOMMENTARY: Illicit sexual intercourse within the area of jurisdiction refers to illicit sexual intercourse by officials with commoners."

This left me with a dilemma—was Li Chen breaking the law by pursuing Song Yi while he was magistrate of the county?

Status-wise, Song Yi was less than a commoner because of her indentured status. But that left me wondering whether the act would be illegal because she was within his jurisdiction or was it not illegal because she was too lowly, which doesn't make Li Chen out to be that great of a guy, would it?

Then I wondered about the term "illicit". There was a provision that specified that sexual intercourse with a retainer, bondsman, or slave would be considered illicit regardless of whether the act was consensual or not. Now, that's pretty progressive if you think of it—the statute is saying that an official is abusing power by having sex with his servant, even if they consented to the act.

But bondsmen, retainers, and slaves are very specific statuses of which Song Yi is not.

At the end of the day, the Tang Dynasty of the *Lotus Palace* mysteries is a constructed reality—just like the Tang Dynasty in many a C-drama is a constructed reality. It's a fantasy told with a healthy dose of dramatic license.

In Mythbuster style, I would say that after careful research, I deemed the romantic scenario in *Red Blossom* plausible, though certainly on the edge of the forbidden....which makes the romance a little more saucy, does it not?

CUT SCENE #1

This scene actually takes place during the event of *The Hidden Moon.* Li Chen puts the city on lockdown after his head constable, then Constable Ma, is found dead. This is the last time Li Chen and Song Yi speak before the prolonged absence that leads up to the beginning of *Red Blossom in Snow.*

My original intention was to write a flash fiction to include in my newsletter and/or blog as a teaser for when the book came out.

All these cut scenes are unedited, so please excuse any errors!

The city drums beat out a steady rhythm that thudded through the streets. Song Yi could feel the answering thud of her pulse. As a resident of Changan's pleasure quarter for more than a decade, she knew the sound of the drums. They beat every morning near sunrise and again as the daylight faded into night to signal the closing of the wards.

This was different. The insistent pounding had come about suddenly and it was hours before sundown. She knew it in her heart, her body tensing with awareness. Her fellow residents of the Pingkang li knew it. They all looked at one another with questioning expressions, wondering what was happening even before the rider came galloping through the streets on horseback to warn the citizens to, "Get inside! Clear the streets!"

Lady Bai, who she'd been with only moments earlier, had

ordered her driver to get to the gates and swiftly disappeared. Song Yi wondered if the noblewoman even remembered the promise she'd just made to help.

Song Yi was left alone, staring at the surrounding streets at a loss. There wasn't panic, just a restless confusion.

"Song Yi!" Little Sparrow was calling her from the door of The House of Heavenly Peaches, a lofty name for a humble pleasure house. "Come back. Something's happening."

Something. Something, indeed. She started back toward the steps when a dark figure came sweeping toward her through the streets.

"Magistrate Li."

"Song Yi."

He'd forgotten to address her with his formal "Lady" or only slightly less formal "Miss" in his haste. The drums beat louder from the distant towers.

They both spoke at once.

"What's happening—"

"You need to be inside—"

The look on his face was one of distress, though he tried to mask it. "Everything will be fine," he assured, circling an arm around her to usher her to the door.

The unexpected touch made her heart race even faster. Li Chen was one for propriety. The urgent press of his hand against the small of her back was out of character and made her even more alarmed.

All around, people were hurrying off the street. Though inside, they remained with doors open to peer outside.

"We need to secure the streets. It's only temporary," the magistrate assured. From the catch of his breath, he'd been running.

He stayed beside her the few steps it took to reach the door where Little Sparrow was waiting, eyes wide. Song Yi shot her little "sister" a look which Sparrow dutifully caught. The young girl disappeared inside in a flutter of curtains.

Song Yi turned to Chen. "Is there trouble?"

His eyebrows raised at that. He didn't know about what she'd found in her chamber that morning. She'd feared it to be a threat or a warning and now, with the city in turmoil around them, she couldn't help but think her instincts had been right.

"I found him—" He stopped himself. His dark eyes held onto hers, desperate to reveal something. That was what she was there for, wasn't it? So he could unburden himself, say the things he couldn't say out loud, to anyone else.

"Are you in danger?" She asked voice lowered. Chen had told her his latest investigation was like a tree with roots deep and tangled.

She thought of warning him. He should know that someone was trying to send him a warning, but he looked as if he already knew.

"Stay inside," he said fervently. "There's danger out in the streets. I couldn't bear it if something happened to you."

He held her gaze for a moment longer before turning away and tearing down the street, as fast as he'd come. A dark-robed and solitary official set out to expense his duty at all costs. Assigned to administer the sprawl of a city that no one person could contain.

CUT SCENE #2

One of the hardest parts for me to write is the beginning of the story. It's not unusual for me to write several beginning and scrap them as I'm trying to figure out how to begin.

This scene was originally supposed to follow the opening scene. There was going to be a scene in Song Yi's point-of-view followed by a scene in Li Chen's point-of-view.

In the scene that follows, we see much more interaction with Guan He and also a hint of interaction with a person that will turn out to be Jie. When I read this over during revision, it just seemed like a lot of time spent for setup and I figured readers would be more interested in seeing the sparks fly between Li Chen and Song Yi than, you know, all this boring cocktail conversation.

So, as interesting and full of clues as this was, I made the decision to cut it and jump into the romance quicker.

~

Li Chen entered the banquet to the sound of music and the sight of her. Song Yi. He hadn't known she would be there and now couldn't forget that she was.

She was dressed in layers of silk and gauze. The deepening blue of an evening sky, of twilight fading into dusk. Song Yi's presence was quieter than those around her. She carried herself with an almost stately presence. Dark and richer colors compared to the butterfly-bright robes of the pleasure quarter.

Not vying for attention created the opposite effect for her. One couldn't help but notice Song Yi. He'd never noticed anyone else.

Her wrist curved elegantly over the pipa. Her fingers touched over the strings with skill, and her gaze was distant, transported by the music. The curve of her bare neck as she bent over the instrument was enough to take his breath.

Their last parting had been abrupt, without farewells. He'd been in danger and uncertain whether his presence would put her in danger. There was conspiracy and murder and threats on the life of public officials. Chen had duties to fulfill, publicly as magistrate, and privately as well.

At the time, it had seemed best to remove himself, but he couldn't remember why now that Song Yi was before him. He started toward the circle of musicians, forgetting that this wasn't the pleasure quarter.

It was the venerable host who intercepted him.

"Magistrate Li," greeted the elder official.

"Director Guan."

"So formal!" Guan said with a chuckle, clasping Chen's shoulder fondly. "Your office has been busy."

"Not so much," Chen replied off-hand, even if it wasn't entirely true. He didn't want to be seen as complaining. Guan had been influential in recommending him for the position in the first place.

The man was like an uncle to him. Guan had served for a time as prefect in Chen's home province. Life in the capital suited him. Since coming here, Guan had gone round about the middle and there was a healthy glow to his countenance.

"Congratulations on your promotion, Director," Chen said.

"This is good for all of us, my son."

Chen shifted uncomfortably at the remark. The practice of imperial appointments was undeniably a political one, but Chen wanted to think that his success relied on how well he dispensed his duties, not on a favor from bureaucrats on high.

Guan led him to a seat and gestured for wine to be poured. The music stopped as the song ended and Li Chen couldn't resist stealing a quick glance toward Song Yi. She hadn't seen him. A new song started. A lively one that brought Song Yi's fingers dancing over the strings.

Perhaps he could find some way to speak to her later.

It was time to share wine. Politely, Li Chen offered a toast on Guan's new position within the Ministry of Personnel. Guan had people he wanted Chen to meet. He drank with Guan and his associates and kept hoping for a chance to meet Song Yi's eyes, but the two of them couldn't seem to align.

Perhaps she was focused on her musician duties.

"—brought on a young fellow as an assistant," Guan was saying. "Very bright. Reminds me of you, Chen."

Li Chen struggled to catch onto the thread of the last conversation. When he followed Guan's gaze, it lead him to a young man dressed in nondescript gray robes who was engaged in conversation with two ladies Chen recognized. They were both attendants at the House of Heavenly Peaches —the same courtesan house Song Yi hailed from.

Before too long, the wine was finished. Guan moved on to speak to other guests. The songs had changed and changed again. Li Chen stood to search the hall for a flash of blue silk. Luminous eyes.

He moved from the table to try to find Song Yi only to be stopped once more. Another group of bureaucrats. They were interested in the Incident at the Yanxi Gate. It had all the makings of good gossip. Bloodshed, conspiracy, war.

"Such matters are of the official record. I do my best not to speak of them lightly," Chen replied, extracting himself.

He wasn't going to add to the gossip. It was more rampant in the city than rats.

Song Yi passed by so close if he stretched out his arm he could have touched her, but then she was gone and Chen was obligated to carry a conversation with the promising young clerk that Director Guan had decided was worth his attention.

The young functionary was saying something to him about land taxes.

"The examination questions are not so practical as that," Li Chen said craning his neck to track where Song Yi was going.

She slipped out of the front doors. Was she leaving? Chen started to follow, only to be intercepted by Guan again.

"How is your mother?" he asked.

"She is well."

The gathering was thinning in the late hour. The elder statesman took the opportunity to speak in more familial tones. "I hear that Li Furen retreated to Yuzhou early this year."

If it were anyone else asking such probing questions, Li Chen would have considered it rudeness.

"Yes, she—" Li Chen paused, searching for a way to avoid the subject and finding none. "There were some matters at home she wished to tend to."

The truth was his mother had left the capital out of frustration earlier that year.

Guan nodded gravely. "The Bai clan are fine enough people," he said, without conviction. "It is understandable your mother would consider marriage to that family advantageous, but, in the end, it is probably best for you not to become entangled with them. They have a tendency to fall in and out of favor with the season."

Chen assumed the statesman was referring to inner rivalries within the capital, something he managed to avoid. A magistrate typically dealt with the concerns and disputes of common people rather than the power plays of the elite.

Guan went on about the Bai family installing their allies within the administration. How they were able to use their name to push up people who were talentless and unworthy. Chen listened, nodding, while he stole glances toward the door.

"The eldest son," Guan ranted. "Is it any wonder how he was able to suddenly pass the exams? And then to immediately be given an imperial appointment!"

By the time he managed to agree enough and take his leave, Chen hurried out to the front entrance. The street outside was empty. Song Yi was gone.

The sudden hollow feeling in his chest had no place there. He could have come to the Pingkang ward to find Song Yi at any time. He had held back and talked himself out of going to her until it had just become easier to stay away.

CUT SCENE #3

Song Yi and Li Chen start their affair as they travel along the river and we get to see many scenes back-to-back of them together as their relationship builds. As much as I enjoyed writing those "sexy times", it was a challenge to create scenes that didn't sound like more of the same, over and over.

Sometimes a passage like this is necessary for me to write in order to hash things out and see how they look on the page. The same way you might see actors improvise a scene to figure out character motivation. Bits and pieces of this scene did make the final cut even though this particular one of them reading together does not. In my head, they still had this moment together, even if we never see it happen in the book.

This scene was cut and replaced with the "crickets chirping by the river" exchange which brought a different tone and setting.

They separated to see to personal matters. He called for the attendant to bring a basin of water and Song Yi moved to the corner to wash. Chen took the opportunity to look over the message.

It was signed by Constable Gao. He might assume it was Gao's message, to begin with, but what was the meaning? Was Gao, once again reminding him to be wary of courtesans' games?

Chen glanced to where Song Yi was tending to herself. There was a light robe draped over her made of gauze that was thinner than a morning mist. She ran the was cloth down her leg and Chen quickly averted his eyes.

The humble act, a simple bath, was more open than anything they'd engaged in with one another. The intimacy of it stole his breath.

Maybe Song Yi had wanted to seduce him. Maybe he's wanted to be seduced, but they'd become more than that. He felt it in the pit of his stomach. He felt it as sure as his heart was beating.

"Here are the infamous books," she purred as she returned to him.

Chen was seated on the sleeping mat and trying, very hard, to focus on his copy of the teachings of the sage Mengzi. Song Yi had tied an outer robe around her, but he didn't need the sight of her skin to entice him. He was not without imagination.

"So many." Her hand rested lightly on the nape of his neck as she inspected the stack of books. There was a proprietary air about her touch which he didn't mind.

He'd declared she was the only lover he'd ever had. Li Chen was smitten. Besotted. Overcome.

"I care for you," he began. "I want you to be taken care of—"

She kissed him to stop his words, but he wasn't so easily diverted. He sat up straight and turned to face her.

"I'll make it right with Madame Shi."

She kissed him again, harder this time.

"Song Yi, you don't need to—"

"Please stop talking," she pleaded. "I just want you to know that this...I didn't come with you, thinking—" She had to correct herself. "I didn't come with you *only* thinking—"

"It's alright."

"If I could choose, if it could be anyone—"

"I know." At least, he hoped he knew.

"I wish things were different."

"I don't," he said fervently.

Song Yi was here with him. These last few days have been some of the happiest, the most carefree days he'd ever known. And their days together were far from over.

Certainly, there would be an end someday. He'd be reassigned outside the capital. Maybe they'd tire of one another eventually, but Chen hoped that wouldn't be for a long, long time.

When they returned to Changan, he would send his gift back to the courtesan house. Madame Shi would accept it this time, he was certain. The insinuation that it was now rightful and earned didn't sit quite right with him, but it was the way of things. Song Yi wasn't his wife and she wasn't his servant. The courtesans of the House of Heavenly Peaches needed to feed themselves the same as anyone else.

They didn't make love again. Maybe all the practicalities had gotten between them.

Instead, they lay beside one another with Song Yi's head against his shoulder as he read.

"What are you reading?" she asked after a while.

"The writings of Yangzi." He lifted the book she could see the words by the light, but Song Yi shook her head, her hair tickling against his shoulder.

"I'm unable to read the characters."

"Really? I was certain you could."

Given the number of poems and essays she was able to quote, he'd assumed she was well-versed with the writings required in the keju. She chuckled at his confusion.

"How would I ever find the time?" she posed to him. "Everything I know is from memory."

It made sense. He'd studied for hours a day, year after

year, since he was ten years of age. What courtesan had such time or luxury?

"Read it to me," she urged.

"From his?"

She nodded, snuggling in closer to his side. He did just that, reading the famous scholar's words aloud.

"We don't hear as much about Yangzi," she murmured after the first few passages.

He was surprised she was still awake. "As a sage, he's not as favored as Kongzi. Did you know he was raised almost entirely by his mother? His father died when he was young."

Chen's voice caught as he recounted the tale. Yangzi's mother was thought to have made great sacrifices for Yangzi to develop and thrive. His own mother had been in the same position, even if no one celebrated her. It was agreed between him and his mother that they did not mention personal matters. Certainly not to outsiders.

"I've always felt the canon was better read aloud," he went on in an attempt to cover his moment of weakness. If Song Yi had noticed it, she didn't say anything. "There's a certain rhythm to Kongzi's writing. Yangzi's as well. It's why poetry is such an important study for statesmen."

"I thought your talents didn't tend toward the poetic," she teased, echoing his own words.

"Not in terms of birds and candles and the moon," he concurred. "But one can appreciate the knowledge of poetry that went into the writing of the Classics. Skillful language creates a convincing argument. It's true for other writings as well. Legal codes and case records."

She looked up at him, smiling. "One doesn't rank seventh without being aware of such things," she said wisely.

"Song Yi, there's something I should tell you." Thinking of his mother and their family circumstances had brought on a mood. "This arrangement between us…my family might find it…umm…unusual."

"I'll be disembarking before Yuzhou, to go to my village, remember?" she said lightly, glancing away. "There won't be any need for explanations or any unpleasantness with your family."

That wasn't what he'd meant exactly. Or was it?

"Right," he concurred.

"The date of your father's remembrance must be approaching as well," she continued, matter-of-fact. "And you'll be observing the purity codes, proper gentleman that you are. So it would be best to maintain a proper distance between us."

He'd forgotten about *jìchén* and the period of observed abstinence from drinking, eating meat, and other pleasures. He should be grateful that Song Yi hadn't forgotten. Yet she'd removed herself from him, shifting to another spot on the pallet as if to find a more comfortable position.

"Don't be upset," he said when she closed her eyes without another word to him.

Her eyes flickered open. Long lashes cast delicate shadows over her cheekbones. "I'm not upset," she declared. "Why would I be upset?"

She closed her eyes once more. Clever language made a convincing argument, but sometimes blunt and simple language spoke even louder.

Li Chen blew out the oil lamp and cast the chamber into darkness. At least she didn't remove her hand when he reached out for it in the darkness.

ACKNOWLEDGMENTS

Special thanks to the pandemic writing crew who has helped me through these last few years with encouragement, laughter, and even a little writing once in a while. Shawntelle Madison, Sela Carsen (Silke Campion), and Amanda Berry—you're the best!

Also a huge thank you to Dayna Hart and Megan Kelley for helping me fix all the problems in the book before anyone else got to see them.

Finally to my readers. You keep these stories coming even through the darkest of times. I am so very grateful for your continued support.

THE LOTUS PALACE MYSTERY SERIES

The Lotus Palace - Book 1

The Jade Temptress - Book 2

The Liar's Dice - novella - Book 3

The Hidden Moon - Book 4

Red Blossom in Snow - Book 5

THE GUNPOWDER CHRONICLES SERIES

Gunpowder Alchemy - Book 1

Clockwork Samurai - Book 2

Tales from the Gunpowder Chronicles - Book 3

The Rebellion Engines - Book 4

Steampunk short stories:

The Warlord and the Nightingale

Sign-up for Jeannie's mailing list (www.jeannielin.com) to receive updates on new releases, appearances, and special giveaways.